Gus and Lillie Fiske
Ed and Frank
ca. 1912

PRAISE FOR "DANCING ON HIS GRAVE"

Ms. Richard has a powerful and difficult story to tell, and she does so with integrity, and with great vividness and feeling.

Robin Desser, Vice President, Senior Editor, Alfred A. Knopf

A brutal and compelling story--.

Elizabeth Stein, Editor, Simon and Schuster

Dancing on His Grave by Barbara Richard is mesmerizing, heartbreaking, vivid and utterly terrifying stuff.

Aimee Taub, Editor, Penguin Group

You have found such a skillful writer in Ms. Richard. It's amazing to witness her disadvantaged and nightmarish childhood, knowing that she grew up to become a talented writer--.

Johanna Bowman, Editor, Random House

I read the story, and let me tell you, it made me call up my dad and tell him how grateful I am to have him in my life.

Julia Pastore, Senior Editor, Harmony Books

Very, very moving and well done. The images of Barbara's family will be with me the next time I drive across rural Montana--.

Carolyn Carlson, Editor, Penguin Group

I read the manuscript–avidly, compulsively, because it was impossible not to finish once I started.

Beth Rashbaum, Editor, Random House

I've finished reading Barbara Richard's memoir. She's a wonderful writer, graceful and clean and powerful, and this book is just full of memorable scenes--

Sarah McGrath, Editor, Simon and Schuster

I found Richard's voice authentic and appealing and her portrayal of her family's struggles powerful.

Charles Conrad, Editor, Random House

There is something raw and appealing here–Barbara Richard's story is an incredible one.

Megan Lynch, Editor, Penguin Group

I have to tell you that I have never read a book so emotionally draining NOR as emotionally uplifting as yours. I've shared the book with several of my students, and they, too, are amazed at the power of the human will to overcome and survive. Thank you for being so courageous to share this story with others.

Carole Bettenhausen, High School English teacher

Chasing Ghosts

Prequel To "Dancing on His Grave"

A WORK OF HISTORICAL FICTION

BASED ON TRUE EVENTS

AND REAL PEOPLE

by

BARBARA RICHARD

www.trafford.com

Order this book online at www.trafford.com/08-1379
or email orders@trafford.com

Most Trafford titles are also available at major online book retailers.

For information or to order copies, contact the author by e-mail at MtBarb@yahoo.com,
by mail at 150 Elizabeth Lane, Sequim, WA. 98382,
or find the book at the Trafford website: On the web at: www.dancingonhisgrave.com

First EditionCover, layout & design by Russell Van Lieshout

Note for Librarians: A cataloguing record for this book is available from Library and Archives Canada at www.collectionscanada.ca/amicus/index-e.html

ISBN: 978-1-4251-8904-4

We at Trafford believe that it is the responsibility of us all, as both individuals and corporations, to make choices that are environmentally and socially sound. You, in turn, are supporting this responsible conduct each time you purchase a Trafford book, or make use of our publishing services. To find out how you are helping, please visit www.trafford.com/responsiblepublishing.html

Our mission is to efficiently provide the world's finest, most comprehensive book publishing service, enabling every author to experience success. To find out how to publish your book, your way, and have it available worldwide, visit us online at www.trafford.com/10510

www.trafford.com

North America & international
toll-free: 1 888 232 4444 (USA & Canada)
phone: 250 383 6864 • fax: 250 383 6804
email: info@trafford.com

The United Kingdom & Europe
phone: +44 (0)1865 487 395 • local rate: 0845 230 9601
facsimile: +44 (0)1865 481 507 • email: info.uk@trafford.com

10 9 8 7 6 5 4 3 2 1

For Kathleen and Frances — detectives,
genealogists and historians extraordinaire.

Chasing Ghosts

Railroads circa 1880 - 93,267 miles of track

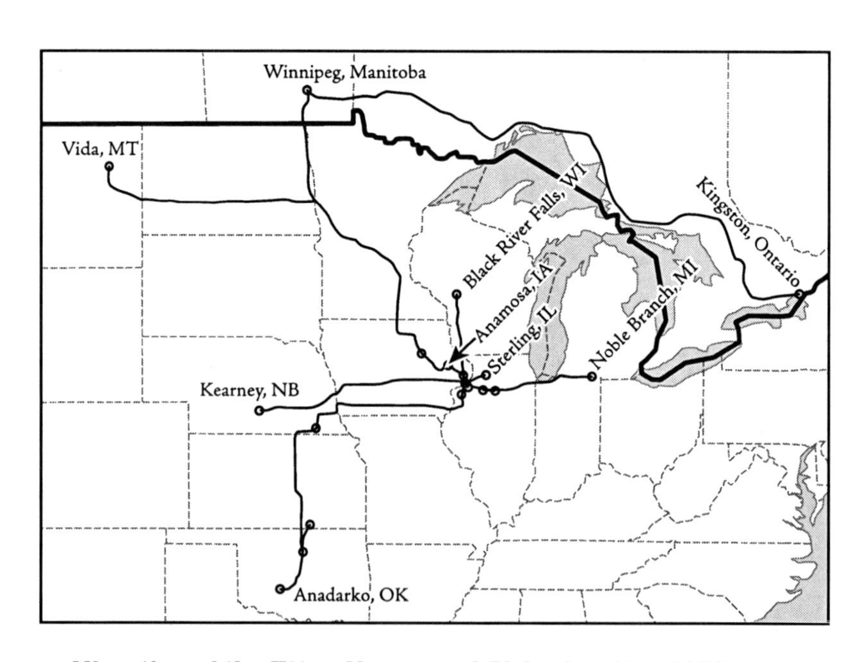

Migration of the Utter, Mecum and Fiske families: 1879 - 1912

Contents

AUTHOR'S NOTE

I spent five years producing two books, one called "Dancing on his Grave" and its sequel, "Walking Wounded." These books tell the story of my family from the time my parents married until after they both died. My father, Ed Fiske, has been labeled by a reviewer as "the most heinous character in the history of western literature." He married my mother, a teenager, when he was thirty, and for the next thirty-three years inflicted sadistic brutality on her and his five daughters, who arrived on a nearly annual basis. He isolated the family on a remote farm in eastern Montana to avoid detection while he tortured and murdered animals and beat us, his wife and children nearly to death time after time, demonstrating his dominance and assuring us that he had complete control and could do with us as he pleased. My mother spent her time in denial and teaching her children complete obedience.

After eight years and six children, my father had a vasectomy, according to him forced into it by my mother and her doctor. Five years later, safe from impregnating her, he raped his oldest daughter, thirteen years old. He used her as a concubine for the following five years, while my mother ignored all the signs and in her denial, deliberately misinterpreted his new interest in his daughter as "fatherly love." The physical abuse of my sisters and me continued and intensified. The second book describes the ordeal the daughters and my mother endured escaping from him, and the difficulty we had adjusting to the outside world, a journey still not finished.

The completion of "Walking Wounded" didn't finish the story. In the minds of my readers I left huge questions unanswered. "What was in his background that produced such a monster?" they asked me. "Was he beaten as a child? What was his relationship with his parents?"

Loathing the possibility that I might provide him with an excuse for the choices he made, I initially resisted spending any time delving into his childhood and ancestry. But as I developed the first two books, several of my sisters proved to be highly effective genealogists. In his background they found evidence of a family completely outside the boundaries of acceptable behavior, a family that exploited and flaunted the law and social norms. My grandmother and her brothers and sisters were illiterate, and eight had prison or arrest records.

My own research brought me to the conclusion that my father was a narcissistic sociopath, born without a conscience, genetically lacking the part of the human brain that produces empathy compassion and remorse–"that caring thing," to quote the Green River Killer, Gary Ridgeway. Professionals dealing with crime and psychosis do not consider this mental illness, but a personality disorder that cannot be treated. These people have no conscience. A professional estimate indicates that between four and eight percent of the population have this defect. A metaphor I heard recently stated that the development of a practicing sociopath has three stages: Genetics produce the weapon, environment loads the bullets, and life experience pulls the trigger. The metaphor defines the story of my father's life. It leads me to believe that his parentage and childhood environment did affect his adult choices and behavior, but in no way relieves him from responsibility for the consequences of his actions. Thousands of people in similar environments do not make the choices he did, nor do they deliberately flaunt the rules of decency that normal people use to guide their lives.

My father's relationship with his father was shown to be clear cut. Gus Fiske used the typical approach employed in the era–"Spare the Rod and Spoil the Child." He had no problem laying a buggy whip, leather belt, or razor strop on his two sons for any transgression. This was the environment that "loaded the bullets" in my father's evolution as a sociopath. If Gus's role was obvious, his mother Lillie's was not. One of the greatest mysteries of the story is my father's relationship with his mother. Evidence and facts about that relationship are shrouded in lies, innuendo, and secrecy. My father mentioned his mother only rarely, and when he did, he was likely to sprout tears, speaking of her as if she had been some kind of saint. Our family accepted the story he gave about the day she died with a kind of reverential reserve, unquestioning, with no thought that there may have been a lot more to his story. As he told it, he came in from the field to find her dead on the floor with a lump on her head from hitting the cast iron stove when she fell after having a heart attack. Experiencing his violence in subsequent years gave fuel to the suspicion that much about that scene remained untold. He was secretive about her with our mother. One time he said to Mom, "You'd like to know about her, wouldn't you? Well, I know, and I'm not gonna tell ya–about what I found in her stuff when she died." A few other clues revisited when we girls were adults helped us start forming an opinion about what his family secrets really were.

My research has convinced me that he was responsible for his mother's death. He had spent many of his adult years coming to the conclusion that *he* was the best man for her, and she should have no one else in her life. It is a near certainty that some kind of incest was involved, whether covert or full blown. If covert, it begs the question of whether it existed only in his head, with her as the innocent object of his hidden obsession. I suspect it was a classic case of the Oedipus complex. When his mother thwarted his possessive will and chose his father over him, his rage could not be contained. He had wielded his fists on dozens of male opponents since he was a child, but on a cold November day in 1930 she became the first female target of his unbridled, explosive temper, and she didn't survive.

This, then, is the story of my father's ancestors, particularly his mother's family, the Mecums, a strong-willed, lawless, renegade group that batted around fact and truth like a birdie in a game of badminton. The penchant of the entire Mecum family for telling blatant lies and allowing them to go down in family history as fact confounded my ability to develop a fully documented story, hence the assignment of the genre "Historical Fiction" to this leg of the family story. The people, the situations and the events are real, but details and dialogue have been added to round out the scenes and the stories.

Sifting through the mass of legend, story and fact was like working a huge jigsaw puzzle where many of the pieces have been lost, changed or duplicated over and over with slightly different twists. Extensive research of history books describing the living conditions and social norms of the era, when added to newspaper accounts, time lines and government records, helped me to establish, in many situations, that 1 + 2 + 3 decidedly must equal 6. Thus the story unfolded, and the jigsaw pieces fell together.

Lore passed down through the generations contains prevarication, misinformation and half-truths, along with the apparent conviction among the characters that a truth can be established by repeating a story often enough. It took many years of sleuth work and genealogical research on the part of my two oldest sisters to ferret out details that help establish the real stories. A good deal of intuitive discernment on their part went into identifying errors and flaws in the information and developing the underlying true stories. They relied on written records, most importantly archived newspapers reaching back nearly 150 years, census information, prison records, court documents, and later in their research, the remarkable resources available through the Internet. Their search extended to more than a dozen states and across the border to Manitoba and Ontario, Canada. Carefully catalogued and digitally archived, the stories they uncovered could fill many volumes. I've chosen some of the most outrageous characters on the family tree, and tried to bring them to life in this volume. Apparently the only one of the nine Mecum brothers and sisters who did not have an arrest or prison record was my grandmother, Lillie.

Also included in this volume is a brief description of my mother's family, the Vests, in order to allow the reader to examine the conditions of her upbringing and childhood grooming that made her the perfect victim of the sociopath she married at age nineteen, my father. Her family, along with the Mecums, included felons and alcoholics, violence and dysfunction, which she escaped by retreating into books.

When we were children, our dad regaled us with stories, especially around the table at meal time, and we accepted these stories as the unquestioned truth. The one that was the most prevalent and a blatant lie was that he, and consequently we, were part Native American from his mother's side of the family. He told it repeatedly, making up details about his various aunts and uncles, describing "Indian features, dark skin, little Indian feet," and impressing upon us that it was something of which to be extremely proud. It didn't occur to us that he, with his light Anglo skin, sandy hair, red beard and blue eyes, and his auburn-haired brother, had absolutely no Indian characteristics. He also claimed that his maternal grandfather, Joe Mecum, was French, another total falsehood. The only possible connection with the French was one of my great-aunts' second husband, and evidence that he spoke French was only by family tradition, not record.

My bigoted father used to sneer, "Hell, I'm lucky that old Frenchman didn't meet a nigger wench; I'd be part nigger. Them French don't draw no color lines." Although no evidence was found to reinforce the family story that there was Indian blood, his grandmother Etta Belle and virtually all her offspring had black hair, dark eyes and skin, and a relatively small stature. His mother Lillie, my grandmother, may have had the lightest complexion among the siblings, and even then, she was quite dark. Some research indicates that at least one branch of the family may have Irish origins. Along the Irish coast live enclaves of dark skinned, dark eyed, black haired Irish. Historians believe that some of their ancestors may have been Moors from northern Africa, who made sailing forays up and down the coasts of Europe in the middle ages, and settled or at least dwelt for a time in the Irish countryside. This would account for the swarthy complexions of apparently full-blood Irish. They became known as "Black Irish." These characteristics played into the Mecum family's scheme when they began to invent their stories of Native American bloodlines. Another brief anecdote–probably fictitious–quoted one of my great-aunts saying, as she prepared to run off with a Mississippi riverboat gambler, "Look at this Indian face. I'll always be throwed off on. I can't be too choosy."

The one branch of the family that probably did have Indian blood was my Grandmother Lillie's niece, Lola, the product of her mother Florence's ill-advised marriage to a forty-four year old man of French-Canadian ancestry named Hugh Warren. The 1910 Oklahoma census lists Warren's parents as "Indian and Canadian French," but he himself as

"White." From 1907 to 1910, Lillie's mother Etta Belle had a relationship with a man described by a local newspaper as a "half-breed Indian and a Frenchman." The affair produced no offspring, so there would have been no Indian blood introduced into the family bloodline from that sector.

Another blatant lie that has been passed down through family annals as gospel fact is the story that my great-grandfather Joe traded his daughter Florence, Lillie's sister, "to an Indian, out on the reservation, for two horses." This story, although partially true, is a massive injustice against Joe. Irrefutable evidence shows that it was Florence's mother, Etta Belle, who disposed of her by marrying her off to Hugh Warren at the age of fifteen. Joe was several hundred miles away in Wisconsin. It is highly likely that the ruthless Etta Belle did receive horses to seal the deal.

One of the most difficult aspects of telling this story was developing believable scenes of interaction among far-flung siblings who were illiterate and most of whom led a gypsy lifestyle. Research shows that Etta Belle's parents, Isaac and Mary Ann Utter, had solid roots in Branch County, Michigan, until Isaac's alcoholism caused the family to fall on hard times when Etta Belle, the oldest Utter child, was about fifteen. She and probably some of her siblings attended school for several years and knew how to read and write. But when it came to her own children, Etta Belle never bothered with schooling. Census records show that each of her nine children was born in a different town, indicating a nomadic life that made it easy to ignore such fripperies as literacy. Thus, family history was relegated to the oral type, subject to the whims of the story teller, and to newspaper accounts of the Utters' and Mecums' outrageous behavior. The exceptions to illiteracy were the two youngest children in the Mecum family who learned to read and write in a Kansas orphanage and subsequent foster homes, and Florence, who may have been taught the rudiments by her first husband, Hugh Warren. He, according to the census data, could read and write.

This has been a fascinating journey, and I hope the reader finds the stories about this wild, undisciplined group motivating to the point of launching their own search for family history. *B.R.*

FISKE | BRAWNER | MECUM | UTTER

Peleg Fiske
⇓
Phillip Fiske
⇓
Albert Henry Fiske (b. 1834) m. Mary Jane Brawner (b. 1833)

John Brawner
⇓
John S. Brawner
⇓
Mary Jane Brawner (b. 1833)

Daniel Mecum
⇓
Joseph Mecum
⇓
Joseph Wesley Mecum (b. 1853) m. Etta Belle Utter (b. 1862)

John Utter
⇓
Isaac Utter
⇓
Etta Belle Utter (b. 1862)

Children of Albert Henry Fiske and Mary Jane Brawner:
Edward
Harry m. Sarah Trollope
Anna m. Dr. Clay McCabe
Charles George (Gus) m. Lillie Frances

Children of Joseph Wesley Mecum and Etta Belle Utter:
Lillie Frances
Sophia J.
Joseph Wesley (Jay)
Florence Bell ⇓ Lola Warren ⇒ ⇒ ⇒ ⇒ ⇒ Common-Law Marriage 7 Children
Daniel (Ester)
Charles (Charley) ⇓ Common-Law Marriage 7 Children
Albert (Bert)
Elnora (Bertha)
Clarence Clifford

Children of Charles George (Gus) and Lillie Frances:
Edward m. Lona Belle Vest
Frank

Children of Edward and Lona Belle Vest:
Kathleen
Frances
Patricia
Edward Alger (Died at Birth)
Barbara
Norma

Dad's Family Tree

PART I

ISAAC AND MARY ANN UTTER

Isaac Utter
ca. 1882

CHAPTER 1

Michigan - April, 1864

"No, Ike, no! You don't need to go." The specter of her husband dressed in a Union Army uniform terrified Mary Ann Utter. Barely twenty and petite, her long dark hair twisted and snugged into a lace cap on the back of her head, she held her squirming eighteen-month-old daughter Etta Belle on her lap.

Isaac Utter had finally made the decision to step up and do his duty. He stunned his young wife with the news that he intended to enlist in the Union Army. Isaac was nearly forty, and all reports indicated that the Union was well on the way to winning the war. For three years Isaac's dray line business had boomed, as the burgeoning war industry called for more and more equipment and supplies. As a drayman, Isaac met trains with a horse and wagon and transported freight to businesses around his Michigan home town, Noble Branch. But in those three years, his conscience had begun to haunt him.

"Annie, can't you imagine how I feel, seein' all the able bodied men going off to fight, and me staying here and making money off the war," Isaac said. "I've made up my mind. I'm going to join the Indiana Volunteers next week. Six of us men are going. And Ma will see to it that you and the baby are okay while I'm gone. "

Mary Ann's voice elevated as tears welled in her dark eyes, "Babies, you mean! I'm gonna have another one. I was saving the news for a surprise."

Isaac's face registered his momentary shock. He said quietly, "I'm sorry, Annie honey, but in my mind, I can't back out and still feel like a man. I have to go. Ma and Pa will look after you."

They had been married on New Years Day, 1862, nine months into the Civil War in Branch County, Michigan. Isaac was nearly twenty years older than Mary Ann, thirty-eight to her nineteen. The Utters traditionally had very large families. Isaac, a twin, was the youngest son of nine children born to John and Anna Utter, a family that included two sets of twins.

In April 1864, when the war had been raging for three years, Isaac crossed the state line into Indiana and joined the Union Army. He had arrived in the thick of gory and ferocious battles in Tennessee and northern Alabama when his second daughter Evaline was born on Etta Belle's second birthday, September 20, 1864.

Isaac's service lasted just eighteen months, but his unit was involved in some of the bloodiest battles of the war, in Tennessee, Alabama and Mississippi. He served in C Troop, 12th Indiana Cavalry (Union Army) from May, 1864 to November 10, 1865, entering at the rank of Private, a designation that didn't change during his service. After only a month of training, the Indiana volunteers mounted boxcars and flat cars and traveled by train with their horses and equipment west and then south across Indiana and Kentucky to a staging area at the confluence of the Mississippi and Ohio Rivers near Cairo, Illinois. After a short trip downriver on barges, they headed east and crossed the Tennessee River, arriving in Nashville, Tennessee in June. Three weeks later, after several skirmishes with Confederate troops, the volunteers moved 100 miles further south to Huntsville, Alabama, where they were headquartered until October. During that summer they roamed an area up and down the Tennessee River, from Huntsville to Muscle Shoals, protecting the railroads in northern Alabama from destruction by the Confederate armies. The South was becoming aware that it was losing the war and wanted to prevent the northern armies from using the railroads to transport troops. On September 30, 1864, Isaac's company "C" took part in a two day battle repulsing Confederate General Buford's attack on Huntsville. They also fought successfully in a fierce battle undertaken to keep Confederate General Hood from crossing the Tennessee River and moving north to join the Confederate Army of Tennessee at Nashville. During the next six months the regiment took part in a number of bloody sieges and battles, several times severely outnumbered by Confederate troops. They moved north and south between Murfreesboro and Nashville, Tennessee, and Huntsville, Alabama, and east and west from Leighton to Decatur, Alabama.

In February, with the Confederates in retreat, Isaac's entire regiment moved to Vicksburg, Mississippi, then to New Orleans and east through Mississippi to Mobile Bay, Alabama. There on the Gulf Coast they took part in conquering Spanish Fort and Fort Blakely, with a two week siege that resulted in the surrender of the garrison on the same day as the surrender of Lee's Army of Northern Virginia at Appomattox Courthouse.

Lee's surrender did not immediately end the war in the rest of the south. Isaac's Indiana Volunteers, under the command of General Grierson, conducted wide ranging raids, battles and mop up operations for several months, in Georgia, Alabama and Mississippi.

Finally, the Indiana Cavalry mustered out at Vicksburg, Mississippi on November 10, 1865. Isaac traveled home via the Mississippi River to Davenport, Iowa and then east by rail back to Branch County, Michigan.

Isaac came home to his young wife and two daughters a damaged man. His ailment was called shell shock during World War I, battle fatigue in World War II, and in the current era, post-traumatic stress disorder. He had also suffered battle wounds. More than four years passed after his mustering out of the military before their next children, twins named for Mary Ann's parents, were born on April 16, 1869. The baby girl of the pair, Nancy, died at birth. The boy, John, was blind. Two years later, Mary Ann again gave birth to twins. This time the boy died at birth. Mary Ann gave birth to two more children, a boy and a girl, in Michigan. Isaac and Mary Ann would eventually produce thirteen children, including three sets of twins, with nine surviving.

The Utters stayed in Michigan for more than ten years after the war ended. The postwar industrial boom in the Midwest had begun, and Isaac returned to his prewar job as a drayman. In that era, when automobiles were still experimental, railroad builders saw rail as the wave of the future, for both freight and passenger service, and they built railroads at breakneck speed. Freight arriving at myriad train stations created a lucrative opportunity for draymen, who met trains and delivered freight as often as three or four times a day. Drayage required more brawn than brains, and Isaac's increasing taste for alcohol did not yet interfere with his ability to earn a living.

His delayed reaction to the stress of war manifested itself in alcoholism that became worse as the years went by. The lack of understanding and the intolerance by the general population of any psychological disorder only made the problem worse. In the late 1800s and early 1900s, each town seemed to have its drunkard, village idiot, and less-favored individuals. Some left town, urged by city officials, but others stayed and endured the stigma of poverty, alcoholism or mental handicaps. In towns where everybody knew everybody, avoiding the stigma was impossible. Society had a sense of worthy and unworthy poor. Widows were assisted and pitied. People with disability, misfortune or joblessness were deemed undeserving of help, and mental illness was an affliction hidden as a shameful secret. Isaac's alcoholism received no pity.

In 1877, Mary Ann made the decision to move her family west, from the home and county where they had spent their entire lives, to Illinois. Desperate, she hoped that a new start might help Isaac conquer the demon of the demi-john. When the family finally made the break with Michigan, he was fifty-three years old and had lost everything he had owned; even the horse and wagon that he needed to make a living for his family.

CHAPTER 2

Illinois - 1878

The Utters arrived in Illinois by rail, with six children and little else. Mary Ann was pregnant with yet another set of twins. Illinois had changed significantly after the Civil War. Mary Ann remembered stories her mother had told about what she had seen of Illinois, when as a young girl, she had traveled to Chicago via stagecoach to visit an aunt who had moved to the frontier city with her new husband.

"It was beautiful, Annie," her mother told her. "The prairies were just a sea of tall grass that could hide a horse and its rider."

The Grand Prairie, which began south of Chicago, covered the upper and eastern half of Illinois with big blue stem and switch grass as tall as ten to twelve feet. Even though the tall grass was named "blue-stem," it turned red as it matured, waving in the wind like a vast copper sea.

Early settlers at first thought the soil inadequate for farming because of the lack of trees. In truth, for thousands of years, prairie fires, lightning, or Indians–trying to increase forage for their horses–set fires that burned for days in the tall grasses and destroyed any fledgling timber growth. The first farmsteads, townsites and army bases were built on areas that were mown with horse drawn mowers and surrounded with rail fences. Parents cautioned their children never to stray beyond the fences, because "there are things in the grass" that could carry them away or they could be lost and never found. On these prairies, besides the tall grasses grew over a hundred varieties of wild flowers and wild strawberries so thick in season that horses hooves were stained red when they walked through the grass. Other fruits and berries thrived as well.

To Mary Ann's disappointment, the natural features that her mother had described seeing thirty years before had been all but obliterated. After John Deere invented the steel plow in the 1840s, the tall grasses were burned and plowed under to make way for corn and other grains. All around them were the signs of robust growth and settlement. Mary Ann chose to locate her family in a small community in central Illinois called Neponset, about 120 miles southwest of Chicago. She hoped that the location of the town, on the Chicago, Bloomington and Quincy (CB&Q) railroad, would afford Isaac an opportunity to resurrect his dray business.

The Utters settled into a rented house in Neponset, Mary Ann to await another birth, and Isaac to seek out fellow Civil War veterans at the closest saloon. Isaac's alcoholism had advanced to the point of rendering him nearly incapable of earning money to support the family. Mary Ann's only option was taking in other people's laundry, using a tub and washboard and hanging the clothes outdoors to dry. It was grinding, back-breaking work for a woman pregnant with twins, and as her pregnancy advanced, she depended more and more on handouts from the Salvation Army and local churches.

Mary Ann's fertility, producing a baby nearly every year and virtually every second birth being twins, would have been common and even welcomed on a farm, where having a big family produced the force needed for the labor intensive chores. But living in town, there was not much to occupy the children and little to feed them, so they were barely out of adolescence when they started getting into trouble.

"Etty Belle, you little tramp! Git back here!" Mary Ann's screech followed her daughter down the street.

"Ma, I'm going to the dance at Bauschbach's. You said I could!" Etta Belle yelled over her shoulder.

"Well I changed my mind. I need you to help with this washing," Mary Ann shouted. "Anyhow, you're just tryin' to see that worthless Joe Mecum, ain't you? He ain't nothin' but a no-good thief, and ten years older 'n you at that."

Etta Belle came to a halt and turned toward her mother. "You sure got room to talk, Ma. Daddy's almost twenty years older 'n you! He's only good for knockin' you up every year and drinkin' up all the money."

"Don't you talk about your Pa like that!" Mary Ann replied angrily. "You got no idea what he went through in the war. You just get back here right now!"

"Momma, Etta Belle took my new shoes! She's wearin' them." Fourteen-year-old Evaline came dashing out the front door of the ramshackle house.

"Quit your whinin', you brat!" Etta Belle glowered at her sister. "I can't wear those worn-out things of mine to a dance. I been wearing 'em a year, and the buttons are half gone." She turned and ran, with skirts and petticoats flying, down the street away from her scowling mother.

It was February 8th, 1879. The Utters, Etta Belle's ma and pa and their kids, now totaling eight with the new set of twins, had arrived in DePue, Illinois, from Neponset, thirty miles to the west, just weeks before. When the family moved over three hundred miles west to north-central Illinois the year before, Mary Ann had high hopes for a new beginning, but at age fifteen, Etta Belle resented leaving the home where she had lived her entire life. In Michigan, she and two of her sisters and brothers had attended school and enjoyed friendships, but her pa's drinking had gotten so bad that they began to be treated like beggars. Full of shame, her ma had told her pa that they were moving west, rather than face their friends and relatives any longer. Etta Belle, the oldest, spent most of her days tending to her sisters and brothers and hanging up laundry, while her mother stood over a wash tub and her dad lay in a drunken stupor on a pallet in the corner. He usually sat up all night in the saloon with other veterans talking about the war, playing cards or checkers and drinking rot-gut whiskey. Etta Belle resented their nomadic lifestyle, moving from town to town at the request of local officials, who asked them leave when gifts from the Salvation Army and local churches ran out, and Isaac's drunken presence on the streets became a nuisance. The moves had become easier and easier, as Mary Ann had sold or traded for food all the furniture and household goods. By the time they arrived in DePue, all the family's belongings fit easily into a couple of trunks. The baby twins were only nine months old.

"Well, things is gonna change, at least for me." Etta Belle thought, and she hurried toward the dance hall where Joe would be waiting.

A handsome man, twenty-six year old Joe Mecum was a slender five feet, seven or eight inches, about average for the day. With a medium to dark complexion, deep-set brown eyes topped by bushy brows and dark curly hair, he looked younger than his age and presented an appealing demeanor. Where most of the young men of the era wore flat, snap brim caps–also called golf caps–he affected the appearance of a riverboat or yachting captain, wearing a leather nautical "midshipman's" cap on the back of his head. His most distinctive feature was the shape of his mouth, a prominent point on the upper lip that extended over the bottom, which came to be known in family lore as the "Mecum Lip." Several of his offspring would bear the same characteristic.

Joe was born in Steubenville, Ohio, in 1853, the oldest son, third in a family of eight children born to Joe, Sr., and Lucinda Mecum. Shortly after his birth the family moved to the town of DePue in Bureau County, Illinois. Composed of respectable, upstanding citizens, the Mecum family considered Joe a bit of a black sheep, although only petty crimes show up on his record. He was nineteen in 1873, when, after spending three months in jail for not posting a $600 bail bond for petty theft, he was found guilty of stealing $90 in cash. He was sentenced to one year in prison, but the sentence was suspended for time served–still a harsh punishment for a man who apparently had no prior record and whose crime was simply pilfering a small amount of money.

Joe behaved himself for the next four years and trained to become a mason, but he had a problem with self-control when he'd been pulling on a jug of whiskey. In 1877, at age 24, he pled guilty to stealing "two pails of fine cut tobacco," valued at ten dollars each, from a rail car. He again received a suspended sentence because of the low value of the pilfered items. Two years after the second incident of thievery, he met Etta Belle at Bauschbach's dance hall.

Petite and pretty, Etta Belle had deep-set dark brown eyes, nearly black hair and creamy olive-tinted skin, but her thin-lipped mouth gave her an expression of sternness beyond her years. She kept the ankle length dresses in her scant wardrobe clean and mended, and tried to present a respectable appearance. At age sixteen, she had decided that the only way she would escape her miserable home life was by finding a man who would take her away.

She loved dancing and music. In those days before gramophones or radio, music was heard in open air concerts in summer, or in church, bars, dance halls and playhouses, so people had to "turn out" to hear it. Lucky was the family who had a parlor organist or pianist who could conduct sing-alongs. The Utters were not one of these families, so Etta Belle went to the "ballroom" as often as she could sneak away from her mother and her duties at home. She loved the waltzes, polkas and other folk music brought from Europe by new immigrants, but also the popular songs of the day, like "Grandfather's Clock," "The Man on the Flying Trapeze," and "Little Brown Jug." Stephen Foster's songs were the newest dance music, along with minstrel tunes like "Oh, Dem Golden Slippers."

A strict code of conduct was demanded from all in attendance at the ballroom. Alcohol or drunkenness was not allowed in any shape or form, and bad language, smoking or chewing tobacco could cause eviction from the hall. Girls went to the "ball" in groups of two or larger, never alone, although Etta Belle, new in town and virtually friendless, managed to circumvent that unspoken rule by tagging onto a group of girls at the door. The young men paid a nickel to enter, but girls were not charged. Inside, the girls joined other women seated in rows along one side of the hall, while the men stood and milled across the dance floor from the girls. Each girl picked up a dance card at the door upon arriving. During the social before the music started, unmarried men made the rounds of the seated girls and wrote their names on the dance cards of their chosen partners. It was a challenge for a man to remember whose dance card he had signed for each dance, and a shame and embarrassment for girls whose dance card was not filled. Each dance, numbered one to twelve, was composed of three different songs. During a "promenade" between tunes, the couples circled the floor two or four abreast, chatting with their partners until the music started again and they resumed dancing. This charming custom gave the dancing couples plenty of time to get well acquainted. A short break at midnight for consuming sack suppers or other refreshments also allowed socializing. Joe and Etta Belle had indeed gotten to know each other in the previous few weeks, since his name appeared on her dance card four or more times during the evenings, few enough to avoid a scandal, but more than enough to engage in serious planning. She made sure that they also shared the midnight suppers. In her determination to escape her dysfunctional home, Etta Belle had "set her cap" for Joe, and within three weeks of arriving in DePue and meeting him at the ballroom, she had convinced him they should marry.

Marriage laws in the nineteenth century were lax and heavily favored men. With a few lies and little explanation Joe could walk into a courthouse and buy a license to marry a girl who was not present, with no permission from her parents. Etta Belle knew that once the marriage was performed and consummated, there would be no reversal, so she was all for the intrigue.

In DePue, Joe ran into difficulty trying to purchase a license. The clerk knew him and his family, residents of the town for nearly twenty years, and suspected that there might be a bit of skullduggery going on. He insisted that Etta Belle be present and sign for the license. Afraid that Mary Ann might hear about their plans and interfere, Joe chose to ride the train ten miles across the county line to the town of Peru to buy the license. He hurried back to DePue and met Etta Belle at the ballroom.

"Did you get the license?" Etta Belle said.

Joe replied, "Yeah, I got it."

"Well, come on. Let's go see Reverend Averill." Unnoticed, the pair slipped out the side door of the dance hall.

The minister read the license carefully, and then took a long look at the couple. "How old are you, Etta Belle?"

"I turned eighteen last September," she responded, her chin held defiantly high, her stubborn mouth set in a firm line.

The minister gave her another searching look. "I don't believe you're telling me the truth," he said. "Besides, I can't marry you if I did believe you. This is Bureau County, and this license is for LaSalle."

"That's not fair!" Etta Belle stormed. "You're just like my ma, tryin' to tell me what to do. Come on, Joe. We're goin' to Peru." She snatched the license from the minister's hand and stormed out the door with Joe following meekly, worrying that he might be in trouble for lying about her age when he bought the license. They stopped one more time, at the office of the local Justice of the Peace, who, after searching the local statutes, also refused to marry them. They finally boarded the evening train for Peru.

Five days later, the local newspaper–the Bureau County Republican–published its version of the elopement, a flowery sentimental tale told, with tongue in cheek, by a romantic-minded reporter. Her age was actually sixteen years, four months.

By-line: Joshua Snooks

Last Friday, DePue had a real sensation–a runaway match. The parties, Joe Mecum and Etta Belle Utter, a fifteen-year-old girl, who recently came here with her parents from Neponset, concluded, as young folks will, to slip on the noose, notwithstanding the determined opposition of the girls' parents, on account of her extreme youth.

By some means, Joe procured a marriage license in Peru, and on Friday took the girl, who left home on the plea of going to a ball at Bauschbach's, and repaired to the Reverend Averill, who refused to marry them because the license had been obtained in another county. Squire Tinsely was next sought [by the pair], but he, with characteristic deliberation, began to turn over the pages of the statutes, until he found the right place where the exasperating, heart crushing, hope defeating information was given, that he had no discretion in the matter.

But the parties had started to get married, and undaunted by these adverse decisions given by unfeeling men, they rushed to the depot and boarded the first train for Peru where the twain were made one flesh. On the Sabbath, the happy pair called at the bride's house, when a scene ensued which we will not describe. Suffice to say that [Joe's new] mother-in-law was arrayed in war paint, and went for the young "family" in a way that was "childlike and bland." The guardian of the peace, G. Hophier, was asked in, but like a wise man, remained at home. Both parties can derive consolation from the reflection that a hundred years from now, the whole affair will have slipped from their memories.

The familiar use of given names in the newspaper indicates that, typical in a small town, Joe, if not Etta Belle, was well known locally. If only Mr. Snooks had been given a crystal ball, and could have seen the misery this match would inflict on their offspring and people who came in contact with them. The affair would not "slip from memory," not even a hundred years hence.

Mary Ann was livid. "You stupid young 'un," she stormed at her daughter. "Ain't you learned nothin'? Don't you know that the first thing is the babies start comin', and the babies start dyin', an' your man keeps drinkin' and pretty soon you ain't got nothin' facin' you but shame and heartache."

Etta Belle tossed her head. "Ma, Joe and me's going to Nebraska and you can't stop us. Joe's a good bricklayer, and there's lots of work out west. Kearny is going to be a big city, and we're goin'."

"Etty Belle, Kearny's out there in Nebrasky Injun country. Injuns goin' on the rampage and killin' white folks. And what people ain't Injuns, they's foreigners. I've seen 'em, them homesteaders, goin' through on the train, hunerds of them. Anyway, I need you to help with all these kids. The twins ain't even a year old yet, and little Bell is sickly."

"That ain't my problem no more, Ma," Etta Belle shot back with a triumphant smirk.

Evaline never saw her shoes again.

CHAPTER 3

NEBRASKA - 1879

Etta Belle and Joe left for Kearny by train from DePue on May 1, 1879, three months after their elopement. Etta Belle had become pregnant within a month of her marriage, and the swaying, jolting ride intensified her morning sickness.

The railway passenger cars in the 1880s and 90s varied in comfort and opulence that changed little in the years before 1920. On warm days, windows were the only means of ventilation, and opening them invited the smoke and cinders into the car. Passengers had to wear long canvas coats to protect their clothes from damage by the hot cinders. If the day was cold, closing the windows created suffocating conditions from the pot-bellied wood stoves located in the center of each car. Those seated nearest the stove roasted, and those at each end of the car received very little benefit from the fire. Lucky for Joe and Etta Belle, the May weather was warm enough for comfort without the stove.

In most cars, the bench seats all faced forward, except for two areas in the back where men could play cards and smoke cigars. Padding and fabric softened the hard seats, but only two people could sit comfortably on the narrow benches. Expectorating on the floor was a disgusting feature freely practiced, and it forced passengers to hold their reticules and carry-on bags on their laps. With no facilities for meals on the trains, one railway station telegraphed ahead to the next so that hot meals could be ready for passengers when the train arrived. They could de-train for about twenty minutes to purchase and gobble the meal while the train was being refueled and loaded with water for the boilers. Except for the relative speed, people did not enjoy rail travel.

After a one-day trip, Joe and Etta Belle crossed the Mississippi River from Moline, Illinois, into Davenport, Iowa, on the Chicago, Rock Island

and Pacific, the oldest rail line in the United States. The coming trip across Iowa, the longest leg of the journey, comprised nearly half the total distance from DePue to Fort Kearny.

Like Illinois, the tall grass prairies in Iowa had been wiped out by the time Joe and Etta Belle headed to Kearny, although the mixed short and tall grass prairies farther west had yet to fall under the plow. By the 1890s, barbed wire would eliminate the open range in the Midwest, but in 1879, Etta Belle saw a wide-open unfenced landscape dotted with homesteads.

Railroad planning placed the lines no more than twenty miles apart, putting a railroad within one day's travel by horse and wagon. The railroad companies built towns ten miles apart–again a one day round-trip for a horse and wagon–and virtually identical. Horse-drawn delivery wagons–hacks for transporting train passengers and drays for freight–made rounds twice a day from the train station, along dirt streets and lanes fouled by horse manure and urine. Watering troughs and hitching posts and rails prevailed, with livery stables located at the each end of Main Street. Most residents had small horse and buggy barns at the rear of their lots, adding to the litter, filth and cacophony. Some of the main streets boasted short spans of boardwalk, but shoes and the hems of the ladies' long dresses were quickly ruined when the boardwalk ran out.

Halfway across the flat, treeless Iowa plains, Etta Belle grew bored. She was familiar with train travel, but except for the move from Michigan a year ago, all her train trips had been short, ten miles or so, as it had been the evening three months ago when she and Joe eloped. The view of Iowa out the side windows as the train moved along at thirty miles per hour, changed little as they crossed the state. Etta Belle looked curiously around the coach. Seated near the back were a group of four men who were obviously foreigners, dressed in coarse woolen clothing and heavy boots. The murmur of their conversation was unintelligible, and to her ears, didn't sound like English. Trying not to appear obvious, she covertly turned her head and glanced at a nattily dressed man seated just behind them. He was clean shaven, wore a nicely cut woolen suit, a vest spanned by a watch chain, and bowler hat. He appeared to be some kind of businessman, about Joe's age. His wire rim eyeglasses sat on a sharply pointed nose. To her embarrassment, he caught her glance. "You folks going far?" he asked.

Joe turned at the sound of his voice, and gave him a cautious look without replying. "Sorry," the stranger said sheepishly. "An old newsman's habit–asking people questions."

"You a newspaperman?" Joe said

"Yes. I'm heading for Butte, up in Montana territory," the man said.

Joe reached over the seat, his hand extended. "Joe Mecum," he said. "This here's my wife, Etta Belle."

"Glad to meet you. Name's Smithson. James Smithson."

"Montana's a long way, ain't it?" Joe said. "What's goin' on up there?"

"It's about eighteen hundred river miles north of Omaha to Fort Benton," Smithson told him. "I've been as far as Fort Benton before, but not to Butte. We heard back in Davenport that an Irishman named Marcus Daly is building a big copper smelter there, and my paper, the Davenport Times-Herald, sent me to cover the story."

All Joe knew about Montana was what he'd heard three years before when an army general named Custer had his entire regiment wiped out by Indians. He said, "Ain't you concerned about the Injuns up there?"

"To my way of thinking, that so-called Indian problem is way overblown," said the newsman. "There are a few pockets of hostiles, but the army has posts all over Montana, and people are safe as long as they mind their business. Custer was a fool, from all I've heard."

"How you goin' to keep from crossin' paths with these 'hostiles?'" Joe asked.

"I'm going upriver to Fort Benton on the Red Cloud, and then cross country by stage to Helena and then to Butte. There are soldiers everywhere along the way, so I've been told," the man told him. "See those four men sitting at the back? They're from Cornwall, clear over in England, some of the best miners in the world. They told me they're going to Butte too–to mine copper. There are thousands of them coming to work for Marcus Daly."

"What's the Red Cloud?" Etta Belle joined the conversation and changed the subject.

"The Red Cloud is the best ship to ever navigate the Missouri, in my opinion. She's a sternwheeler. You should be able to see her when we pull into Omaha," Smithson told her. "I'm going to write a story for the Times-Herald about the owners of the Red Cloud, the I.G. Baker Company out of St Louis and Fort Benton. We heard that they made a lot of money hauling freight and passengers last year, mostly because of the Red Cloud. They paid taxes on $2.5 million in profits. They're the biggest taxpayer in Montana Territory."

The conversation was beginning to bore Etta Belle. She didn't understand nor was she interested in what the men were talking about–taxes, profits, freight. She turned back into her seat and feigned a nap, thinking about "hostiles," soldiers and what might be waiting in Kearny.

When their train pulled into Council Bluffs, a long, enclosed wagon-like car waited. The train passengers boarded the car, and a small locomotive pulled it slowly across the mile-long bridge over the Missouri River to the city of Omaha, the beginning of the Union Pacific railroad. Mr. Smithson told them that the bridge needed to be reinforced substantially before an entire train could pass over safely. Council Bluffs had been connected to Chicago by rail in 1867, and up until seven years ago when the trestle bridge was built, train passengers had disembarked at Council Bluffs, crossed the river on a ferry and boarded the Union Pacific at Omaha. The service aboard the Union Pacific was much different from the Illinois Central. Accommodations and services for the passengers would grow increasingly Spartan as they traveled west.

Etta Belle had seen steamships on the Mississippi when they crossed at Davenport, Iowa, on the train, but the number of them tied up at the Council Bluffs and Omaha docks amazed her. Steamboats had been coming up the Missouri to Omaha since 1848, Smithson told them. Hundreds of ships per year traveled up the river through dangerous, shifting channels. With the rapidly developing agriculture in Iowa and eastern Nebraska, the steamboats carried harvested crops to eastern markets. But, he said, railroads were being built at such a rate that the steamboats might not last long as the best way to move freight.

As they crossed the Missouri, Etta Belle thrilled at the sight of more than a dozen of the big ships moored at Omaha, heading both up and down the river. She caught sight of an enormous stern-wheeler tied up at the dock. It was painted glistening white, with scarlet trim and two towering black smokestacks. It looked taller than any building she had ever seen, but it seemed to sit on the surface of the river as lightly as a dragonfly.

"Is that your ship, Mr. Smithson? Is that the Red Cloud?" Etta Belle couldn't conceal her excitement.

"That's her!" the newsman said. "She's come all the way from St. Louis, and she's heading for Fort Benton. It'll take her nigh onto two more months, and she's already three weeks out of St Louie. The whole trip is 2400 miles."

"It's so huge," Etta Belle marveled. "I ain't never seen anything like it."

"She's 225 feet long and can haul over 350 tons of cargo and 400 passengers at the same time, and she only draws a couple feet of water," said Smithson, trying to impress the young bride. Etta Belle wasn't sure what "drawing water" meant, but she couldn't take her eyes off the big ship. "Folks call her a floating palace," the man continued. "The finest ride for passengers on the whole Missouri River."

"Look at all those red coats. What are those men, soldiers?" she asked the newsman. "I ain't never seen uniforms that color." More than 200 men in brilliant scarlet coats stood on the riverbank watching the crew or helping load passengers and animals on the deck.

"Those are new recruits for the Royal Canadian Mounted Police," Smithson replied. "Most all their replacements from the U.S., and their horses, too, take the steamboats up to Fort Benton and then follow the Whoop-up trail up to the forts in Alberta."

Smithson told them what he knew about the Red Cloud. "The Baker Company bought her two years ago," he said. "The first thing they did was make her fifty feet longer and widen her hull. That makes her float higher so she can make it all the way to Fort Benton even when the water goes down in the summer."

The Missouri was rife with hazards, from huge chunks of ice in the spring to rapids, submerged whole trees, snags, rocks and sandbars hidden in the current all summer. Hundreds of the wooden steamships sank on the upper Missouri during the heyday of the steamship, from 1860 to 1890. Frequent windstorms stopped the ships dead in the water. But in spite of these hazards, steamboats were still, in 1879, the fastest and most efficient way to move freight and passengers. Forty seven ships reached Fort Benton that year. The year before, with the great bison herds approaching extinction, 75,000 buffalo hides were shipped aboard the Red Cloud to eastern markets.

What Mr. Smithson didn't know and couldn't have foreseen, was that after only five years of service, on July 11, 1882, the Red Cloud, the ship that had dazzled youthful Etta Belle, with a full contingent of freight and passengers, hit a snag in the Missouri fifteen miles above old Fort Peck and sank on a sand bar up to the main deck in five feet of water. All passengers and deck cargo were rescued, but tons of flour and other freight in the hold was ruined and the ship was abandoned. Impossible to salvage, it took only one year for crushing ice and rushing water to break it apart. It disappeared into the shifting channels of the river and along with dozens of other wooden steamers like her, became part of the lakebed of Fort Peck Lake over fifty years later. During her five years of service, the Red Cloud brought more than 6000 tons of freight to the Fort Benton levee, along with more than 3000 passengers.

When Joe and Etta Belle took leave of the newsman in Omaha, she insisted that they accompany him to the levee to get a closer look at the Red Cloud. She gazed starry-eyed up at the towering ship and looked dreamily at the passengers milling about on the main deck of the ship as it prepared to pull away from the levee. "Joe, someday you 'n me are going to get on that ship and float all the way down to St. Louie."

Twenty years later, her daughter Sophie would keep the promise, on a different ship and a different river.

When Joe and Etta Belle arrived in Omaha the spring of 1879, the city had almost no paved streets, even in the business district. Stinking garbage, animal carcasses and horse manure glutted the streets, along with ashes from heating and cooking stoves. Gas lights, introduced in

Omaha earlier in the 1870s, were confined to the business district, and the general population made do with kerosene lamps. The city waterworks was a small and recent development, so most water came from private wells dug near the backyard privies. A sewage system was still far in the future. Disease from contaminated water was common, as was quackery in the medical field.

The Nebraska Territory, ancestral home of the Sioux and Pawnee, had been opened for settlement by the government in 1854, and became a state just twelve years before Joe and Etta Belle's arrival. Mary Ann Utter's worry for her daughter's safety from wild Indians in Nebraska was for the most part unfounded. White man's diseases had killed off half of the Indians by 1840. Small pox had wiped out all the Mandans, who lived farther north along the Missouri, and half the Pawnees. With the near total destruction of their food supply, the American bison, the few remaining bands of Pawnee were starving and diseased, and camped in their teepees near forts and Indian Agencies hoping that the government would honor its treaty commitments. Instead, they suffered crooked Indian Agents who stole the Indians' allotments and allowed them to starve. The skirmishes during the construction of the transcontinental railroad had ceased and homesteaders dotted the Nebraska prairies with little fear of Indians.

The Union Pacific and Central Pacific transcontinental railroad had been built by corrupt companies under a mandate of speedy construction by the U.S. government, and by 1879 it was falling apart and being rebuilt. The green wood used for railroad ties had warped and the rail bed had settled, making the ride slow, jolting and extremely uncomfortable. The short rail sections, requiring joints every twenty feet, added to the problem, and frequent derailments sometimes proved disastrous, in addition to consuming huge amounts of time getting the cars and engines back on the tracks.

Joe and Etta Belle rode through the vast countryside of Nebraska, more than 175 miles from Omaha to Fort Kearny, on an immigrant train moving at a top speed of 35 miles per hour, which was equipped little better than cattle cars. At Omaha masses of immigrants, newly arrived from the east coast or Europe, had crowded onto the train, as many as four people sitting on hard wooden benches built for two, children piled on the laps of their parents. Many others stood in the aisles and around the sides of the car. The smell of unwashed bodies, garlic and tobacco, and the babble of alien languages added to the clamor and confusion, and Etta Belle's stomach, already queasy with morning sickness, heaved and rode high in her throat.

Several hundred thousand people had already traveled up the flat Platte River Valley, America's first great highway to the west heading for California, Oregon, and in the case of the Mormons, to Utah. To the south the view from the train was level plains that seemed to go on forever. To the north, they could see higher ground, dissected by eroded gullies, utterly treeless. The tall grasses soon gave way to a mixture of short and tall grass and finally became flat, semi-desert grasslands.

It was hard to gauge the time of day as they traveled, but time really didn't matter to Joe and Etta Belle. National time zones were still four years in the future, so local time was a hit-or-miss system set by cities, counties or states, and required frequent adjustment of timepieces. Clock time mattered only to the railroads and telegraphs, since the general population measured its days from dawn to dark.

It took Joe and Etta Belle nearly a week to cover the 600 miles from DePue, Illinois, to Kearny. Nebraska. Train cars provided no way to lie down. George Pullman had invented the "sleeper coach" in 1864, but a compartment in a Pullman car cost five times the price of a seat in a regular rail car, limiting their use to wealthy Easterners. Some communities along the tracks had "emigrant houses" where people traveling west to settle Nebraska could stay free for a limited time. The houses provided meals, beds and laundry facilities, ready made for people like Joe and Etta Belle. In the evenings they left the train to find room in an emigrant house. Sometimes they succeeded, and sometimes they had to continue on to the next town. Once they stayed an extra day at the emigrant house, resting, washing their meager clothing and taking advantage of the free meals. The next day they arose at dawn and caught the first morning train heading west.

Ft. Kearny, named for Colonel Stephen Watts Kearny, an explorer of 1845, was established in 1848 to protect wagon trains heading for Oregon and California. The town of Kearny sprang up along the railroad, just across the Platte River from the fort. When they finally arrived in Kearny, Joe and Etta Belle knew nobody, and nearly out of money, they stayed in the emigrant house again. The Indian teepees pitched around the fort gave Michigan born and bred Etta Belle an anxious night, remembering her mother's warning, until she saw the occupants up close a few days later. The starving, lice-ridden and ragged Indians were clearly no threat.

The Mecums set about finding housing. With virtually no money, they needed luck and a friend. Joe talked to the owner of the general store who told him about a few empty houses and steered Joe to the bank down the street. The bank had been saddled with foreclosed buildings abandoned by settlers who had become disillusioned with the "West" and headed back east. The men shook hands on a deal that allowed Joe and Etta Belle move into a vacant house on the promise of cash rent to be paid within a month.

Etta Belle stood at the door and surveyed the interior of the house–more a shack–that Joe had chosen. A rickety table, two chairs and a bunk built along one wall comprised the entire stock of furniture. A pine board shelf nailed to the wall behind a huge cast-iron cookstove and another above the bunk, with nails for clothes hooks, were their storage facilities. More nails on the back of the door provided coat and hat hangers. The well in the yard and the toilet out back completed their accommodations. From the trunk partially filled with their paltry collection of household goods, Etta Belle lifted a stew pot, a wooden stirring spoon, a skillet and a teakettle, two sturdy earthenware mugs and a dinner plate with a knife, fork and spoon for each of them, and placed them on the shelf above the stove. She situated the kerosene lamp in the middle of the rough table, spread the two quilts given them by Joe's parents over a pile of clean straw Joe had brought in and placed on the bunk, and hung their few clothes on the nails above. She would have to wait until Joe got his first paycheck to buy ticking to make a straw mattress, and since they couldn't afford one of Singer's sewing machines, it would have to be stitched up by hand. Maybe she could raise some chickens and use their feathers to fill a couple of pillows. Folks that were better off topped their straw ticks with feather beds, but for now, she and Joe would have to make do with straw. She went out to survey the yard for a spot near the well to grow a vegetable garden.

They needed to find work for Joe. They soon learned that most construction taking place in and around Kearny still featured lumber, brought in on the trains. Bricks and mortar were scarce in this frontier town, with very little work for a mason. Joe found work as a day laborer, and occasionally with a section crew on Union Pacific Railroad, which, even though just ten years old, already needed extensive repair to keep trains running. His work earned enough for food and rent on the one room house.

After they settled in, Etta Belle had little to do besides tending her garden and cooking their Spartan meals. She loved to browse through the general store, although she had no money to buy anything beyond the basics. Open barrels of crackers, pickles, rice and beans allowed customers to dip up their own purchases. Patent medicines, china and household items lined the shelves, but she had to shop very carefully. She looked longingly at the bolts of yard goods in linen, cotton and wool, all measuring twenty-nine inches wide, which were stacked on tables. Her two dresses were getting tight around the waist. She'd had to rip out the side seams and cover the gaps with an apron, but fabric for new dresses was out of the question. She smoothed the bolts of flannel printed with tiny rosebuds, chicks and ducks. She needed flannel or Birdseye cotton to make diapers and clothes for the baby. She began reserving a penny or two of the money Joe gave her for food. Five pennies bought one yard of twenty-four-inch wide plain white flannel. Two yards made three diapers. With a needle and thread, she hemmed the flannel and secreted the finished diapers, one by one, in a wooden apple box under the bed. She splurged on enough of the rose-bud print flannel for a little jacket and bonnet, even though the fabric cost an extra penny per yard.

Etta Belle kept in touch with her mother back in Illinois that summer. By 1879, the railroads carried mail all over the Midwest at the reasonable rate of three cents an ounce. But at that time and for many more years most rural citizens had to travel to the nearest post office to collect their mail and weekly newspapers. Door to door mail delivery service within a few cities started in 1863, but it would be over forty years later, in the early 1900s, before RFD–Rural Free Delivery–was implemented, partly because of the lack of suitable roads during the ensuing years. Joe and Etta Belle's received their mail through "General Delivery" in Kearny, requiring a trip to the post office.

Etta Belle, now approaching the age of seventeen, grew fearful as pregnancy bloated her body. The only doctor in Kearny was an army man attached to the fort. She didn't feel good about having a man–accustomed to doctoring men and soldiers at that– serve as her obstetrician. She began to hatch the idea of having her mother with her when her baby was born, and scheme to make that happen. She started polishing her skills at prevarication, writing glowing reports of booming growth around Fort Kearny, and stories of the hundreds of people pouring into and beyond the area. She bragged about money Joe was making, but it was a product of her imagination. They were barely getting by.

In August, when they had been in Kearny four months, a perfect opportunity presented itself.

Dear Etty Belle,

Here's hoping this finds you well. It sounds like you and Joe are doing okay. Yore little sister Bell died last week. It's probly a blessing since she's always been sickly. Little Del is sure heartbroke. Yore pa's little problem ain't getting any better. Things is sure tough here. I could sure use yore help. Please rite back.

Love, Ma

Etta Belle was by now six months pregnant. She immediately stepped up her campaign to convince her parents to move to Kearny.

Dear Ma,

I was real sorry to hear about Bell. I think you and Pa should come to Kearny. They's plenty going on here. The railroad hires a lot of men, and the town is growing fast, what with all the homesteaders around here. They's lots of trains going threw, and Pa could get plenty of work if he had a dray line. Did I tell you about the immigrant houses you can stay in? They's places in towns along the track where you can get free food and beds for the whole family. It makes the trip out here a whole lot easier.

It would sure be nice to have you here when the baby comes. It don't seem fitten to have a man doctor, especially an army man. It'd be nice if you could help with yore first grand young'un.

Love, Etta Belle

In her determination, Etta Belle ignored the fact that Isaac's alcoholism had progressed to the point where it was doubtful that he could hold any job when the family arrived in Kearny. She also didn't address the problem that unlike the freedom she and Joe had enjoyed making the trip from Illinois, the Utters had six children who needed food, shelter and diapers, and who would need train tickets, requiring cash money even in the immigrant cars.

Mary Ann missed Etta Belle, the first of her large brood to leave the nest, in spite of the problems the headstrong girl had caused. Being present for the birth of her first grandchild appealed to Mary Ann, and she once again convinced herself that a fresh start would get Isaac off the booze. Relocation hadn't worked a year earlier when they left Michigan for Illinois, but Mary Ann was determined to respond to her daughter's crusade. She overruled any protests Isaac might have had, and he did not resist his wife when she declared that the family would make the journey to Kearny.

Ahead of them loomed the grim specter of the entire Utter family enduring the same ordeal that Joe and Etta Belle had gone through to get to Kearny. Their six surviving children ranged in age from Evaline, nearly fifteen, ten-year-old John who had been born blind, and the other four even younger, down to the surviving twin, Del. Isaac's presence had again become a local nuisance in DePue. When Mary Ann reported that her daughter and son-in-law were settled and prospering in Kearny, and had offered help, it wasn't hard for her to convince the Salvation Army to team with a local church and provide train tickets for the family.

They arrived in Kearny early in October with two trunks holding the same meager supply of household goods and clothing they'd owned when Etta Belle left five months before. A month later, on November 16, attended by her mother as mid-wife, Etta Belle gave birth to her first son. They named him Joseph for his father and grandfather, and called him Jay.

Isaac and Mary Ann found another vacant bank-owned house to rent, and with help from the Salvation Army, equipped it for their family of eight. They had arrived too late in the year to put up a store of food, so Etta Belle proudly shared produce from her own garden with her parents and brothers and sisters. Joe was by now making good money working on a section gang repairing the railroad, and for the next few months Isaac was sober often enough to provide for his family by working for an established dray company. Joe began joining Isaac in his off-time visits to the local saloons, although he didn't develop the need for liquor on Isaac's level.

The winter – 1879 to '80 – was mild, and trains from the east got through regularly. The settlers in the Midwest were completely dependent on the railroads to bring in all their supplies and foodstuffs from November through March, so keeping the rails clear of snow was imperative. During that winter, the problem was easily handled by the snowplows attached to the front of the locomotives. Kerosene for light, coal for heat and firewood from western Colorado were brought in by rail. The winter passed without undue hardship on the Mecum-Utter families. The Salvation Army provided warm coats and other winter gear, and brought coal when they ran out.

When they had left Branch County, Michigan, school attendance for the Utter children had ceased. Mandatory schooling for Americans was still forty years in the future, and arranging schooling for her growing brood became too much trouble for Mary Ann. They had been forced to move frequently, and the children fell farther and farther behind. Finally, the older children became so embarrassed at being the offspring of the town drunk that they refused to go. School for Mary Ann's younger children seemed to be a lost dream. Thus, she established a pattern of illiteracy that would follow the Utters and the Mecums for the next forty years. Since John was blind, Etta Belle and her sisters Evaline and Agnes were the only Utter offspring who had learned to read and write. In Kearny, Mary Ann never got around to even thinking about school. The younger Utters helped with the garden and the laundry that she and Etta Belle took in, and the rest of the time found ways to get into trouble, usually by petty thievery and fighting. Joe and Isaac spent their free time playing checkers at the general store or cards in the saloon. Isaac found an abundance of veterans with whom to swap war stories, and the more he revealed about his army service, the more liquor he needed.

During the summer of 1880, Mary Ann and Etta Belle both raised big gardens. They had to irrigate their vegetables with the hand pumps on their water wells, but several of the children were big enough to take turns on the pump handle. They had no money for canning supplies, so fresh produce had to be consumed quickly. Unable to buy a milk cow, they raised a few chickens and traded fresh vegetables for butter and milk. They stored winter vegetables–rutabagas, turnips, squash, potatoes and carrots, even an occasional head of cabbage–in a root cellar beneath the house where Isaac and Mary Ann lived, but for the eleven people in the extended family, the stores looked pretty sparse. By October 1st, the supply of food in the cellar had shrunk measurably.

Until the middle of October, the weather remained mild. Early in the month a soft, misty three-day rain, followed by a hard freeze, put an end to the gardens. Etta Belle and her mother stripped the remaining green fruit from the limp, black plants–tomatoes, squash, corn and pumpkins–and stored it in the root cellar.

One chilly October morning, Joe told Etta Belle, "There was some soldiers from the Fort in the saloon last night. They was sayin' that the

Injuns are comin' in beggin' the Agent for extra food. They're saying there's a real hard winter comin', maybe six or seven months."

"You believe Injuns?" Etta Belle scoffed. "How would they know such a thing?"

Joe looked thoughtful. "Have you seen the coat of fur the horses and cows are growin'? And the soldiers say there's no game anywhere – not even jackrabbits. Didja notice there's no geese or ducks on the ponds? They was goin' south a month ago. I say they and them Injuns know somethin' we don't. Maybe we should put in some extra beans and flour."

"We ain't got money for that, Joe," Etta Belle replied, her voice dripping acid, "what with you and Pa having your fun down at the saloon. We barely get by between pay days."

The supply clerks at Fort Kearny had begun putting in their winter supply of food, kerosene, coal and supplies by the middle of September. The commandant, a wily old career army man, had been around Indians long enough to know that sometimes they displayed an innate instinct when it came to nature and the weather. He quietly ordered an extra boxcar of items needed to supply the post. He sent out details of soldiers with teams and wagons in every direction to harvest "brushwood," composed of sagebrush, chokecherry and other brush that grew along waterways and drainages. He also ordered the hiring of local farmers to begin cutting extra prairie and slough hay and hauling it to the fort. The lure of the cash money paid by the army for each load of hay caused the farmers to delay putting up their own hay, a decision that would add to their peril during the coming winter.

The Indians' warning proved to be only too accurate. The first blizzard hit just ten days after the hard freeze, three days of howling hurricane winds that scoured the prairie bare and subzero temperatures that scattered the frozen bodies of cattle and wild animals like cordwood across the prairies. A few unlucky homesteaders joined the animals in death, newcomers to the prairie who had never seen a Midwestern blizzard, caught in the open far from shelter when the storm struck without warning. Some who died that winter were only a few feet from safety, but could not see their way in the blinding snow.

October 15th was extremely early for such a devastating storm. Many homesteaders were stunned by that first blizzard, with hay still in the fields and on the prairie, corn and other grain yet to be harvested and vegetable gardens full of produce. Shocks of corn, oats and wheat that stood waiting for their turn with the traveling threshing crews were carried away by the gale force winds or completely covered by deep snow. Those settlers who were fortunate enough to have threshed and sacked their grain, but didn't have the foresight to grind a supply of flour after the blizzard, would not be able to make it to the flour mill in town during the coming winter.

The storm filled in all the deeper cuts along the railroad with snow. Joe and Isaac picked up a dollar a day riding hand cars with a work gang to shovel out the tracks for the trains to pass. That blizzard would be followed by six more two and three-day storms before January first, including one that began on Christmas day. By January 1, snow in Kearny reached the second story of store buildings and hotels. Conditions worsened, and all through January the weather became one continuous blizzard with breaks of one day or less. Fierce, unrelenting wind, snow and subzero cold, sweeping always out of the northwest, assaulted the homesteaders shivering in their claim shanties and sod huts, the starving Pawnee Indians cowering in the lee of the fort, and the fear-filled townspeople. Then in February, a four-day blizzard with hurricane strength winds again scoured the prairies and streets clean and dumped the snow into sloughs and water courses. In the spring, these enormous deposits of snow and ice would melt and flood the countryside. The huge drifts in town, up to forty feet deep, were soon replaced as each new storm swept through. An estimated eleven feet of snow fell on the embattled Midwest during the seven months the winter lasted.

Kearny residents were fortunate to be living on the mainline of the transcontinental railroad, since that line received the highest priority from the rail companies in the task of clearing the tracks and keeping the trains running. In spite of these efforts, during December only one train per week made it to Kearny from the east, and none from the west. During the whole month of January, two trains made it through, one of those a work train carrying only enough supplies for the crew shoveling snow. The work trains carried huge snowplows, but as the brutal winds packed the snow into harder and harder drifts, the crews resorted to dynamite followed by swarms of men with shovels. The banks of snow on either side of the rails grew higher and higher, allowing more and more snow to cover the rails with each new storm, until finally, in some of the cuts, the drifts were over 100 feet deep.

By January, the town was completely out of drinking liquor, so Joe and Isaac were able to earn their dollar a day shoveling snow without interference from hangovers. The money they earned became more and more important, as the stores of food, coal, firewood and kerosene in the town dwindled and prices spiraled upward. The four day blizzard that began on February 2nd finally packed the railroad cuts solid and deep, beyond the reach of any human efforts to clear the rails. The railroads sent word by telegraph to towns up and down the tracks that the trains would be shut down until spring.

The eleven people in the Mecum/Utter extended family were out of food by the first of January. Joe and Isaac, along with many other Kearny residents, began a weekly trek, crossing the thickening ice on the Platte River to Fort Kearny on the south bank, to beg food and supplies from the dispensary. Little Jay, who had turned a year old in November, and Del, the surviving Utter twin who would be three in May, generated extra sympathy from the supply clerk and the post commandant, and Joe was not above loading his wife, mother-in-law and the two babies into a borrowed sleigh in the frigid winter air and taking them along. The post provided canned milk for the babies, kerosene, coal, sacks of beans, flour and every other item it could spare, but to Isaac's and Joe's dismay, no liquor.

Out on the homesteads, shanties and sod houses were completely covered with snow by the first of December. Occupants had to shovel out their chimneys and stovepipes to avoid asphyxiation, and dug tunnels to their barns and livestock. The positive aspect was that the snow insulated the humble dwellings and kept them warmer. The downside was that the windows were blocked to light, and kerosene for lamps was gone by mid-January. Traveling to the fort for handouts was not an option for the homesteaders as it was for the townspeople. The sod houses and shanties took on a similarity to the dens of animals. Even disposing of their own body waste became a serious problem to trapped settlers. With no light, they couldn't read or play games, but some of the families had a story-teller, and many had someone who could sing memorized songs. These were the only forms of entertainment and distraction, hour after hour, day after day, week after week. Many an immigrant baby was born in the dark hovels, the birthing mothers attended only by their husbands or older children.

By the middle of February, out of firewood and coal, homesteaders were burning twists of hay from the small supply they had salvaged from the October storm for their animals. Then they began to eat the animals. Breaks in the weather lasted only a few hours at a time–at the most, one short winter day–not long enough for the settlers to risk travel to Fort Kearny or the small towns along the railroad for any supplies that might remain there. In March, the settlers started eating their seed grain. It was a final defeat–they had been relying on the seed for next year's crop. They tried to find innovative ways to cook the grain, grinding wheat a cupful at a time in coffee mills, enough for one loaf of flat bread a day–even though there was no shortening or leavening–or cooking the kernels into a kind of mush, to be eaten without sugar, milk or salt.

Five hundred miles to the north, at DeSmet, South Dakota, a fourteen-year-old girl named Laura Ingalls lived through that same winter, on a branch railroad where all the trains were stopped by snow-drifts on December 1st and didn't re-start until May. This was the "Snow Winter" of 1880 to 1881, and later, as Laura Ingalls Wilder, she wrote about it in a book she called, "The Long Winter."

In mid-April, the population of the Plains woke to a warm Chinook wind. Within two days water was running in every hollow. Rivers were suddenly engorged with runoff and huge mountains of breaking ice that created dams, flooding vast areas of the watersheds and lowlands. At Saint Joseph, Missouri and Omaha, Nebraska, the Missouri River was over twenty miles wide well into May–and the Platte even wider across the eastern half of Nebraska. Fort Kearny and the town of Kearny across the river were perched on islands, with water up to five feet deep all around them for nearly a month. Other communities, especially those along the Upper Missouri including Vermillion and Yankton, South Dakota, were wiped out by floodwater. The rushing snowmelt washed out train tracks all across the Midwest, further isolating the small towns. Horse and wagon travel was also impossible, since the prairies had soaked up water like a sponge. Wagons sank to the axles and horses to the knees, and mud stopped all the farmers' efforts to get to town.

By the first of June the waters were receding, and the railroad companies hired vast crews of men to begin rebuilding the tracks. On June 15th' the winter weary, starvation-weakened citizens of Kearny came running to the depot when the first train whistle in more than five months echoed through the valley. It was only a work train, but they were assured the freights were just behind. The next day, boxcars unloaded food and new merchandise for the stores, and winter was over.

As for the Mecums and Utters, they'd had enough. Etta Belle's grand Wild West adventure had turned to near disaster. During the spring and summer of 1881, Joe and Isaac worked as day laborers on the railroad until they had accumulated enough money for train tickets, and the eleven members of the Mecum/Utter family boarded the train back to Illinois.

CHAPTER 4

Illinois - 1881 to 1902

In the fall of 1881, the Mecum and Utter families settled close together in northern Illinois at Sterling, ten miles from Dixon, the birthplace of Ronald Reagan, and near Abraham Lincoln's hometown. Etta Belle and her mother both gave birth in 1882. It would be the final birth for Mary Ann, age thirty nine, a daughter she named Sufronia, born May 1, who would die in 1901 at the age of eighteen. Etta Belle's second child was born in October in Sterling, a daughter she named Sophie.

The Utters' wandering ceased, and they spent the next four years in and around the Dixon area. Drink had finally consumed Isaac, and he lived for nothing beyond his jug of cheap liquor. In September 1885, only seven months before his death at age sixty-two, he was finally awarded a meager Civil War pension, with the designation of invalid. This only exacerbated his problem by giving him more money for whiskey. To feed her family Mary Ann was again reduced to begging and handouts from the Salvation Army and taking in laundry, except when Isaac, frantic for booze, sold everything they had, even her washtubs and scrub boards. Finally, in the spring of 1886, Isaac was killed in a horrific accident that made the newspapers in Dixon and Sterling, Illinois. The family, now with just six of Mary Ann and Isaac's nine children, had been living in a slum area of Dixon called Dement Town. The two newspapers carried the story, written by reporters with widely differing opinions of Isaac Utter.

The Evening Telegraph
Dixon, Illinois
April 8, 1886

UNDER THE WHEELS - A TERRIBLE ACCIDENT

A Dispatch from Sterling informs the Telegraph that Isaac Utter, of Dixon, had both legs crushed off by the cars last night while attempting to board a moving freight train, about nine o'clock. He fell under the wheels and the cars passed over his limbs.

The accident occurred at an unfrequented place, west of the water tank, and therefore the poor man was not discovered until another train passed over him. He was taken to a hotel where his legs were amputated, one below and one above the knee.

Our dispatch states that the man is doing well, has a good pulse, and the attending physician believes that he will recover. It is a wonder that he was alive when found, being so long without assistance after such terrible wounds. If it is true, as stated, that the accident resulted from intoxication, then we may imagine that the same stimulant that caused him to fall under the train also kept him alive until assistance came. The victim had been a resident of this city during the past year, coming here from Sterling, we believe. Last winter he joined the Salvation Army, but did not remain with the evangelists very long, his habit of drinking being too strong for him. Still we believe that he is a hard working and generally speaking an industrious man. He lives in Dement Town, where he has a wife and six children, three boys and three girls. It is certainly a very sad case.

From the Sterling Gazette
Sterling, Illinois
April 8, 1886

Isaac Utter, a good-for-nothing, worthless specimen of humanity, who has been known in this city for a number of years, and who has given the authorities a great deal of trouble at different times, managed to get under the wheels of a freight train last evening about nine o'clock, and lost both legs, one being severed above and one below the knee. He was intoxicated at the time, and therefore can give no intelligent account of how the accident happened. It is supposed, however, that he attempted to board the 8:05 freight going east, which was about an hour late, and missing

> his footing, fell to the track. Another freight passing over the same road about twenty minutes later, having twenty-three cars, passed over Utter also. The engineer on the second train saw the body lying near the track, but not soon enough to slacken the train before reaching Utter. The almost lifeless body was picked up and carried to the Boynton House, where both legs were amputated by Dr. A. P. Anthony, about ten o'clock. It is also thought by the physician that the man's skull is also fractured. At first it was thought that the poor wretch could live but a few hours, but this morning at seven o'clock he was much stronger, and all the symptoms for his recovery was favorable. The man's family lives in Dixon, and it is supposed that he intended to steal a ride to that place on the freight. He and his family have been sent from this city several times, but he has always managed in some way to find his way back. Had the wheels of the car passed over his neck instead of his legs, it would have been better for him and the community.

There was no sympathy from the Sterling reporter for the Civil War veteran who carried the emotional and psychological wounds from the stress of his service in the bloodiest war in American history. Fifteen days after the accident, on April 24, the following brief announcement appeared in the Sterling Gazette.

> The Sterling Gazette
> April 24, 1886
>
> DIED
>
> The man Utter, who was run over by a CNW train some time since, and who has been lying at the Boynton house in this city, his legs having been amputated, died yesterday afternoon. His remains were interred this afternoon at Prairieville. The Reverend Norris conducted the services.

Almost exactly one year later, Mary Ann married a man named George Wilson and moved to Davenport Iowa. She gave birth to no more babies. Much pity was taken upon widows and orphans in that era, and by marrying a widow nearly forty years old with six children, Mr. Wilson would have been seen as a hero. As soon as the family had settled in Davenport, Mary Ann enrolled her remaining children in school. Education widened the gulf between the opportunities for the children in the Mecum and Utter families. The mandatory school law wasn't enacted for another forty years, and Etta Belle's children would receive no education, even the most rudimentary, while under her roof.

Mary Ann was widowed again by 1902 and died in February, 1905, at age 62, at the home of her daughter Agnes. At that time Etta Belle, with her brood of children, was living in Wilton Junction, Iowa, thirty miles west of Davenport.

PART II

JOE AND ETTA BELLE MECUM

Etta Belle
ca. 1905

Joe Mecum
ca. 1905

CHAPTER 5

Iowa - 1903

"Sophie, girl, you been raised decent. Don't you go shamin' the family like this." Etta Belle stormed at her daughter, as Sophie tossed clothes and possessions into a trunk.

"You're dreamin', Ma. This family ain't so decent! Just keep out of my way. I'm goin'."

Joe and Etta Belle's oldest daughter had just dropped a bomb. After only a year of marriage, Sophie was leaving her husband to elope with a dashing twenty-three-year-old Irishman. James O'Dea made his living as a gambler on the paddle-wheeled steamboats that traveled the Mississippi River. Sophie, born a year after the family had returned to Illinois from Kearny, was nearly twenty one years old. Frank Crawford, the man she had married in January, 1902, was a decent man with a good job as a teamster (formerly called drayman.) He was four years older than Sophie. He treated her well, but Sophie quickly became bored with him, and the minute she saw O'Dea, with his suave manner, fashionable clothes and abundant cash, her marriage was over. Sophie was small and the darkest of Etta Belle's children, with black hair, a swarthy complexion and dark brown eyes. All of her life she had been accused of having Native American blood, and was discriminated against accordingly. With no education, she had grown up feeling unworthy and unattractive, and of value only for taking care of the babies her mother produced every other year. O'Dea made her feel beautiful.

Ignoring her mother's outrage, the same way Etta Belle had ignored Mary Ann more than twenty years before, Sophie loaded the trunk into a hired hack, drove to the pier and boarded a paddle-wheeler for St. Louis beside the gambler. She was as headstrong as her mother and had no thought for consequences. Before she had even left Iowa, her husband filed for a divorce. A sympathetic judge, not wanting to ruin Sophie's "good name," granted the divorce to Sophie, along with the restoration of her maiden name, Mecum. Five weeks later, ignoring the mandatory six month waiting period, she married James O'Dea.

After returning to Illinois from Kearny, Nebraska, the Mecum family's lives had been tumultuous and nomadic. During the waning years of the nineteenth century, they relocated repeatedly. The same restlessness that had resulted in the ill-advised two years in Nebraska kept Etta Belle seeing greener pastures over every fence. After her son Jay was born in Nebraska, she gave birth to eight more children at eight different locations in four states. Because of the transient nature of their lives, the Mecum family was missed in the 1890 census. In 1900, after twenty years of marriage, the census found them in Clinton County, Iowa, about thirty miles north of Davenport, with seven children. Jay, the oldest son born in Kearny, had married and moved out, and the ninth child, called Clifford, would be born the next year in Clinton. A family tale tells the story of the sixth child, a daughter named Florence, being born on a "shanty-boat" on the Mississippi River, and her siblings threatening to "drown her, because they were tired of taking care of all the new babies." Whether or not the tale was true, the practice of fable and fabrication was already well-established in the family by 1900.

By 1902 they were settled for the short term in Davenport. The family, in addition to Jay and Sophie, now included Lillie, Charley, Bert, Florence, Daniel Ester–called Es–and Elnora and Clifford. Davenport, located on the Mississippi River just across from Moline, Illinois, was a bustling town of about 35,000 people in 1902. The quad-cities area–Davenport, Iowa, along with Moline, Bettendorf and Rock Island, Illinois–was the most populous part of the state. Within ten years Iowa would have more telephones per capita than any other state and was rapidly becoming the state with more automobiles per capita than any other. But, like other Midwestern towns, it was a dismal place by modern standards. The main source of transportation in the early 1900s, other than the railroad, was horses. An early estimate indicated that there was at least one horse for every four people in Iowa towns, pulling hacks, delivery wagons and drays. Those nine thousand horses in Davenport deposited tons of dung and hundreds of gallons of urine every day in the muddy, littered streets. Typhoid fever, cholera and other diseases brought on by contaminated water were a frequent occurrence. The stench, cacophony of animals, shouting draymen and train whistles produced chaos and confusion in the commercial areas of town. Frequent thunderstorms in summer and fierce blizzards in the winter made survival a daunting task, but still the city grew.

Joe had a good work ethic and the potential of earning an adequate living as a mason, but Etta Belle's perpetual dissatisfaction crippled his ability to hold down a steady job. The pair's marital wars that began in Nebraska gained intensity as the years passed. Joe's response to the constant carping by his wife generally consisted of flight–leaving the house until her temper cooled down–and the increased use of whiskey. Etta Belle had no constraints against attacking him physically when enraged, and he, emboldened by booze, sometimes chose to physically defend himself.

Joe and Etta Belle were so caught up in their own violent battles that they ignored their children. The older Mecum boys learned young that they were on their own. With no school to bother with, they were free to make their own decisions on how to spend their days. Jay was caught stealing horses and sent to a reformatory for eighteen months. Charley, his dad's favorite, managed to stay out of trouble through his early teens, but Bert was running away from home, stealing and getting caught by the time he was an adolescent. In a later arrest statement, he said he had "Left home to fend for himself "at age ten.

The two older girls, Sophie and Lillie, two years apart in age, were close friends but different in temperament. Sophie tended toward rebellion and single-mindedness in getting what she wanted, where Lillie was satisfied to get along and wait for adulthood. Sophie left home when she married Frank Crawford, and Lillie, despising the violence and chaos in her parents' home, moved into a little apartment on Rockingham Road, to support herself as a domestic servant and seamstress. She had a health problem that was beginning to manifest itself in a "goiter," or enlarged thyroid. The condition caused no handicap, and she was able to control it with small doses of iodine, but the swollen gland on her throat made her self-conscious.

A year after their youngest son Clifford was born, soon after the move to Davenport, the battle between Joe and Etta Belle reached a crescendo. An explosive event again involving physical violence resulted in her demanding that he move out of their current rented house. The four youngest children stayed with Etta Belle, while Charley and Joe moved in with Lillie.

Jay Mecum was released from prison, and at age twenty-three, decided to try horse trading. He met Gus Fiske, twenty seven years old and already a successful horse trader, and brought him to Joe and Lillie's apartment occasionally for the next year. Gus and Lillie became acquainted. The visits grew more frequent, on Gus's trips through Davenport along his horse trading route from Minnesota to Oklahoma and Arkansas, and romance began to flourish between Gus and seventeen-year-old Lillie. Then the scandal of Sophie's elopement descended upon the family.

Lillie's dreams of a better life were severely shaken that day. She had listened to the screaming battles between her parents all her life, and now her brothers and sisters were beginning to scatter. She began to realize that she would have to take charge of her own life, if she was to have any chance to rise above her ancestry. The day Sophie married her Irishman 150 miles from Davenport in Henry County, Iowa, Lillie made the decision to cast her lot with Gus. A week later, on July 21, 1903, in Vinton, Iowa, two months shy of her eighteenth birthday, Lillie married Gus and adopted his itinerant lifestyle.

Eight months after Sophie and Lillie had both married and gone, on February 14, 1904, Etta Belle filed for divorce from Joe, the first of three times she would initiate the action. By then, she had been living apart from Joe for more than two years, supporting her four youngest children as a washer-woman. As she had watched the scandal that Sophie created unfold, a new possibility opened up. Divorce had never occurred to her. In that era, when only five marriages in a thousand ended in divorce, prostitutes and divorced women shared the same social status. Made brave and resolute by the relative ease with which divorce had freed Sophie, Etta Belle consulted an attorney and started divorce action against Joe. Her family had disintegrated rapidly. Bert was in an Iowa reform school, and at age eighteen Jay had married a much older woman just before being arrested for horse stealing. Now Lillie and Sophie were gone. At forty two, she was beginning to feel her age. She was ready for a major life change.

In her divorce complaint, Etta Belle asked for custody of the six youngest children, including Charley, even though he was nearly sixteen and had been living away from her for some time, first with his dad and Lillie, and then, when Lillie left with Gus, with his uncle John Utter. Thirteen-year-old Bert would be in reform school until he was sixteen. In truth, only the four youngest children, Clifford, age three, Elnora, who had just turned six, Es, age nine, and Florence, eleven, were left with Etta Belle. Her divorce action caused a stir in Davenport. Divorce was a rarity to the point that the event made the newspaper.

> The Davenport Democrat and Leader
> February 19, 1904
>
> ETTA BELLE MECUM ASKS COURT
> TO GRANT HER A DIVORCE
> Married a Quarter of a Century and
> Now Drink Must Float the Loves of Two Away
>
> Joe Mecum and his wife Etta Belle are in serious difficulty. They were married early in 1879 and lived together until February 11 of this year.
>
> Now Mrs. Mecum wants to be divorced after twenty three years of married life, alleging to her husband had always been brutal to her, compelling her to support him in idleness while she hung over the washtub. Liquor, however, has been responsible for it all. The custody of six out of nine children who are minors is asked for.

In the complaint filed in Scott County, Etta Belle cited her grievances against Joe: "Cruel and inhuman treatment so as to endanger her life, has frequently struck, choked and beat her, called her vile and vicious names, and frequently and without cause, accused her of committing adultery. He has become a habitual drunkard, and she is compelled to support her children by washing and other hard labor." The complaint also stated that the pair had lived together until three days before the complaint was filed, another deliberate falsehood.

The divorce action was the wake-up call Joe had needed. He had developed the habit of taking his family for granted and boozing his way through life to escape Etta Belle's fiery temper and nagging. Now he realized she was no longer bluffing. In twenty-three years of marriage and all the battles, it hadn't occurred to him that she would actually file for divorce. The sheriff showing up on Joe's doorstep to deliver the divorce complaint shocked him into sobriety.

Three months after the action was filed, halfway through the required six month waiting period, Gus and Lillie's horse-trading circuit brought them back to Davenport from Oklahoma. Lillie located her parents and heard the story of the pending divorce. For the next few days, she and Gus used all the influence they could muster to convince Joe and Etta Belle to reconcile. Unleashing his considerable power of persuasion, Gus filled Joe's head with stories of the opportunities that could be awaiting him in the Wisconsin woods. He convinced Joe and Etta Belle that they could get a fresh start there, and invited them to load up a wagon and join him and Lillie for the rest of the horse-trading trip to Wisconsin. Lillie was expecting their first grandchild in November, and Gus reminded Etta Belle that Lillie could use her help in camp. In a blitz of attention and supplication, Joe persuaded her to drop the divorce when he assured her that he had turned over a new leaf and would quit drinking. The divorce action was never completed.

CHAPTER 6

Wisconsin - 1904

The extended family, including Gus and Lillie Fiske and Joe and Etta Belle Mecum with their four youngest children, trekked north across Iowa and Minnesota. They crossed the Mississippi at La Crosse, Wisconsin, in early August. During the trip, Etta Belle became enthralled with Gus's expert horse trading abilities. Gus made it look easy; a great way to make a buck and have fun at the same time. The traveling caravan satisfied her life-long wanderlust, and having her daughter near and about to give birth provided her with a sense of family and roots. When they reached Wisconsin, she was reluctant to have the adventure end.

Gus had told Joe that the little town of Black River Falls, about forty miles northeast of La Crosse, would be a great place to settle. There were lumber mills and logging camps where Joe could find well-paying work. The area around Black River Falls was heavily timbered, but the Black River Valley, where the town was located, had fertile, cleared farmland. Joe found a little farm for rent near town that had a comfortable dwelling, paid six months' rent with money he had earned helping Gus that summer, and the family moved in.

After seeing Joe and Etta Belle settled, Gus and Lillie turned their horse trading outfit back toward the south. Because of the distractions and delays caused by Joe and Etta Belle's problems, they didn't make it all the way to Oklahoma for the winter. On November 26th, 1904, Lillie gave birth to Edward Albert Fiske in Carroll, a small town in northwest Iowa.

Joe, true to his promise to Etta Belle, began building a future. He bought farm equipment, including a "covered mover's wagon," as described later by the local newspaper, and a nice team of small work horses. He put in time at a lumber mill and ran a dray line, in addition to picking up work occasionally as a mason. He began banking money toward his and Etta Belle's old age, which was rapidly approaching. He'd just passed his fifty-first birthday. Although this was, as far as Etta Belle knew, a potentially permanent arrangement, she made no effort to enroll her four remaining children in school. As hard as it was for Joe to avoid the allure of the congenial crowds in the saloons, he remembered the threat of divorce and kept his promise. For the following three summers the Mecums looked forward to the arrival of Gus and Lillie, who by then had two young sons, Eddie and then Frank, born in January, 1907 in Wichita, Kansas. Etta Belle's fascination with the horse trading profession grew with each visit, especially when it appeared that Gus was making good money. Boredom with farming and her chronic dissatisfaction began to return.

A year after his parents left for Wisconsin, fifteen-year old Charley Mecum launched an enterprise of felony that would last for almost twenty years. He had moved in with his blind uncle John Utter, Etta Belle's brother, when Lillie left with Gus, and soon teamed up with his thirteen-year-old cousin, John's son Claude, to burglarize houses in the quad-cities area. Hitting a house only occasionally, the two soon became emboldened by success. Predictably, they grew careless and greedy, and by the summer of 1905, were robbing several houses a night. The two were arrested in Davenport by a specially-assigned detective on August 13, 1905. They were jailed, and a few weeks later were indicted by a grand jury. Claude, because of his youth and his father's blindness, was given a short sentence in the local jail. Charley, by then approaching the age of eighteen, was sentenced to two years in the men's reformatory at Anamosa.

In February, 1907, when Joe and Etta Belle had been in Wisconsin for two and a half years, they had a surprise guest. A knock on the door woke them at midnight, and on the step stood Charley, now nearly nineteen.

"Hello, Pa."

"Charley! What are you doin' here? We heard you was in jail," Joe exclaimed.

Charley looked at the floor between his prison issued boots. "I got out last week. I rode the cars up from Iowa. You got anything to eat, Ma?"

When Joe had received the news two years ago that his favorite son Charley had been sent to a reformatory for burglary, he was crushed. Now he was at their door, asking sanctuary.

They invited him in and made sleeping space for him, and over the next few days, showered him with attention, offering him help in finding work. Charley's younger brothers and sisters fawned over him, and Joe proudly introduced him to some of his friends, including a new acquaintance and co-worker named Tom Hopkin.

In spite of all the attention and the apparent promise of a stable home, two years in prison had given Charley a restless streak. He started ranging to communities farther from Black River Falls, and within a month of his arrival, Joe and Etta Belle received a letter from the county jail in Winona County, Minnesota, informing them that their son had been arrested in Winona, about fifty miles west of Black River Falls, for stealing a bicycle. He had given Joe's name as nearest kin and someone who might pay the fine so he could avoid jail. Joe refused, and Charley spent the next thirty days in the county jail.

He was released in April, and returned to Black River Falls. "Well, Charley boy, you learned anythin' yet?" Joe asked his son.

"Them guys got no sense of humor, Pa. I was just borrowin' the bike to go a few blocks. I don't even like bikes," Charley commented sheepishly. He promised his parents that his lawless days were over, and started making an honest effort to help Joe with whatever task or employment was at hand.

Joe and Etta Belle were battling again that summer. Joe didn't know that part of the reason for Etta Belle's combative attitude was Joe's good friend Tom Hopkin. He came visiting at the farm whenever Joe and Charley left for work.

Thirty seven years old to Etta Belle's forty five, Tom Hopkin was a "half–breed Indian and a Frenchman," and "a thriftless and labor-fearing individual," according to the local newspapers. He had a criminal record and had served at least two terms in county jails and state prison. The charges usually complained of drunk and disorderly conduct, but he also served time for "adultery."

His prison record gave his last occupation before prison as farm laborer, but he claimed to be a horse trader, wishful thinking on his part. He had little experience or trading stock. Gus Fiske made a comfortable living at horse trading–Hopkin, not so good. The social aspect of the profession attracted Hopkin, along with the possibility of cheating an unsuspecting farmer with a damaged or unhealthy horse.

In July of 1903 while waiting to be sentenced, Tom attempted suicide.

> Badger State Banner
> Black River Falls
> Wisconsin, July 9, 1903
>
> Tom Hopkin, from the town of Brockway, was lodged in the county Jail for being drunk and disorderly, Friday last, and became so despondent that he attempted suicide. He took off his suspenders, tied them together, fastened one end to a beam, made a noose in the other end, and then tried to hang himself. A fellow prisoner observed the act and summoned the sheriff, who arrived none too soon to save the man's life. When the sheriff cut him down he laid on the floor an instant, then gasped and came to. He said he was no good and preferred to die. He evidently changed his mind, however, and will probably try to make himself some good in the future.

The newsman got it wrong. In March, 1904, Tom found himself back in jail. A week later he pled guilty to a charge of adultery, and received a two year sentence in the Wisconsin State prison at Waupun. According to the news accounts, "It was an aggravated case, and could have resulted in a longer term but for the guilty plea." The veiled reference implies a case of rape rather than adultery. The female involved in the incident was not identified. A week later one of his buddies, also in prison, sent Tom a letter which was censored by prison guards and published in the same newspaper:

> Badger State Banner
> March 24, 1904

THOUGHTS FROM THE PEN

General Grant Olson, who is serving a term in Waupun for swindling Jackson County, wrote to Tom Hopkin on March 6, sympathizing with him in his trouble. In it he stated that he had that noon been in [prison] just a year, with another four staring him in the face. He also stated that he heard from Jack Simplot often, and learned that he was enjoying good health and in training to meet Nettleton, the farmer wonder. In the letter he addressed the following rhyme to Hopkin:

It seems so queer to me, Tom
The changes that one year can bring
We three were at the ringside
Each feeling as rich as a king.
Taking those moonlight rambles
Never to bed before ten
But the curtain is up on a far different play
And now we are all in the Pen.

Hopkin served his time, and was released three months early on December 19, 1905. After his release, he picked up work in logging camps and sawmills to support his wife and four children. It was in the logging camps that he met Joe Mecum, and very soon, Joe's wife, Etta Belle.

When Hopkin started hanging around Joe's farm when he was away, he and Etta Belle had plenty of time to put their heads together and discuss horse trading. Both embellished their experience and expertise; Hopkin's was almost non-existent, and Etta Belle's limited to the one summer on the circuit with Gus and Lillie and what she had picked up on their short summer visits. But those shortcomings were no deterrent to a pair bent on larceny. The attention Etta Belle received from this much-younger lady's man played into the needs of her mid-life crisis. She began to entice him with the details of Joe's savings, and her willingness to loot Joe's bank account if Hopkin would join her in their own horse trading venture. By August, 1907, the romance was in full swing, and their plans jelled. Bringing the money, the mover's wagon and team, and a saddle horse, Etta Belle would meet Hopkin in Boscobel, eighty miles straight south of Black River Falls. She would also bring her four children. Florence was by now fourteen, Es was twelve. "They'll be good help," she informed Hopkin.

"If that's the case, I'm bringin' Harvey and Clint, too," stated Hopkin belligerently. His sons were aged sixteen and fourteen. "They'll be better help than Es."

Etta Belle had no choice but agree, but she didn't mention Charley. At nineteen, he was a grown man, far too old for her to manage, and a jailbird to boot. He could stay with his dad. Hopkin would bring his own saddle horse and four other plugs that he had managed to accumulate during his failed horse trading activities.

Etta Belle spent the next few days surreptitiously making a mental list of what she would take from the house and farm–all that she could get into the wagon. She waited until Joe and Charley left for the logging camp. They worked a week at a stretch, then returned to the farm for a few days. She would have plenty of time to put her plan into action. Her first objective was the money. When she visited the bank, she found over $2,000 in the account, Joe's savings from three years of hard work. Gleeful but careful, she made up a story for the banking official that Joe had instructed her to buy a new team and wagon. She left Joe just $100, thinking that small amount would make it impossible for him to mount a search to find her. Feeling as giddy as when she eloped with Joe twenty-eight years before, she threw her possessions into the wagon, hitched the team, mounted Es on the saddle horse, and with Florence and the two youngest children, Elnora and Clifford, set out for Boscobel.

Five days later, Joe and Charley hitched a ride from a fellow logger and arrived back at the deserted farm. At first, Joe was puzzled. From the quiet and lack of activity around the place, he thought Etta Belle and the children had probably gone to town. He could see that the wagon and team was gone, and the saddle horse was probably out in the back lot.

But when he and Charley entered the house, the reality hit him in the gut. It was obvious the house had been empty for several days. He saw empty food shelves and the beds bare. The nails where the children had hung their meager collection of clothes looked stark and rough along the log wall. Charley sank into a kitchen chair while Joe, suddenly furious, charged around the house trying to assess all that Etta Belle had taken. "The bitch! The dirty god-damned bitch!" he bellowed. "Nothin's ever good enough for her!"

Then, overcome with grief and betrayal, he sank into a chair next to Charley. "Where could she go, son? How can she take care of them kids by herself? She's gettin' old!"

His rage returning, he bellowed, "To hell with that god-damned whore! Come on, I'm havin' a drink." He struck out for the nearest saloon and his first drink in nearly three years. He and Charley stayed drunk for three days.

The worst betrayal was yet to come. On the fourth day, Joe partially sobered up, and he and Charley went to the bank to cash their last week's paychecks. "How's that new team and wagon working out?" the banker asked Joe.

"What team and wagon?" Joe responded, dread and a feeling of nausea filling his throat.

"Well, your wife was in here last week for the money to buy a team and wagon. At least that's what she said it was for," the banker said.

"How much is left?" Joe asked, his voice weak.

The banker perused his ledger. "It looks like about a hundred dollars." Joe was speechless. He got unsteadily to his feet and left the bank.

For the next few weeks, nearly paralyzed by Etta Belle's betrayal, Joe retreated back into his jug. Charley got into trouble again. On September 2nd, three weeks after Etta Belle's disappearance with his four sisters and brothers, Charley was arrested in LaCrosse for burglary. He pled not guilty; the end of the month found him in prison at Waupun, Wisconsin, serving a three year sentence. It was nearly 160 miles from LaCrosse to Waupun. When he received the news, Joe hopped a freight to visit his son. His disappointment and heartbreak over this new betrayal from his favorite son was palpable. "Charley, what in the hell were you doin'? How can you be so god-damned stupid?" Joe blustered. Charley, dressed in black and white striped prison garb, hands cuffed and legs shackled, muttered "I dunno, Pa."

"I thought you said you'd turned over a new leaf."

"I guess my leaf turned over just like yours did," Charley said.

"Ain't it enough what your bitch of a mother did? And now you too," Joe said.

"Sorry, Pa."

Joe left the prison and hopped a freight back to Black River Falls. Along the way he picked up a quart of whiskey. He wouldn't see Charley again for three years.

CHAPTER 7

Kansas - 1907

Etta Belle and Tom Hopkin, with her four children and his two teenage boys, headed south, traveling as swiftly as possible in case Joe should decide to follow. In November they reached Beatrice, Nebraska, having covered over five hundred miles in three months. Along the way, Joe's money purchased horses for trade and transportation. Tom Hopkin was no Gus Fiske; he was a poor trader and came out on the losing end of most bargains involving horses. Consequently, more of Joe's money bought the supplies needed to sustain the group of eight people. Most of the country through which they passed was still unfenced, and they grazed their horses along railroad rights-of-way and county roads. They also helped themselves and their horses to the unfenced and verdant crops of Iowa and eastern Nebraska. Etta Belle hoped they would not encounter Gus and Lillie's outfit heading north; she knew that Lillie would be outraged about the stunt she had pulled.

As soon as she had the opportunity, Etta Belle proceeded with the divorce she had sought three years before in Davenport, Iowa. In October, she consulted an attorney in Nebraska. He advised her that she had only one option: filing by mail in Wisconsin, since she hadn't been a resident of Nebraska for the required year. She paid the attorney with more of Joe's money, and he mailed the papers to the Jackson county courthouse in Black River Falls, Wisconsin. To her dismay, a response arrived within a week, asking for money to publish her complaint, since she had stated in her petition that she didn't know where Joe was. Lacking the ability to have papers served on Joe, she would have to divorce him by publication. She realized that if she published her complaint in the newspaper in Wisconsin, Joe might see it and pursue her to Nebraska, or worse, show up to answer the complaint. She abandoned the attempt again.

Early in November, 1907, the group camped near Beatrice, Nebraska, on the property of an acquaintance of Hopkin named John Warren. While Etta Belle and her kids set up camp, the Hopkin men, Tom and his two sons, went into Beatrice for supplies and came back carrying jugs of corn whiskey. During the evening, sitting around the campfire in high spirits, Tom got more and more drunk, while his boys soon passed out. Etta Belle retired to her bed in the wagon, and her four kids crawled into their bedrolls, distributed around the camp near the fire or under the wagon. Tom stayed by the fire, still pulling on the jug. By two o'clock in the morning the camp was quiet. Less than an hour later, the muffled sounds of a struggle and then a piercing scream broke the silence. Fourteen-year-old Florence was struggling with Hopkin, who had crawled into her bedroll naked and was sexually assaulting her. Little Es leaped from his bed and threw himself on Hopkin's back, trying to get the drunken dead weight off his sister. The two Hopkin boys also roused and jumped into the fray, pulling Es away from their father. By then the entire camp was awake and in an uproar.

Furious, Etta Belle lambasted not the rapist, but her daughter. She screamed obscenities at Florence, accusing her of deliberating seducing her new paramour. With Florence sobbing hysterically and denying the accusations, Etta Belle ordered everyone back to bed, including her boyfriend, still nude from the waist down, and told Florence, "I'll deal with you later."

For the next week Etta Belle kept up a relentless barrage of accusations at Florence, alternating between trying to make her confess that the assault had been her fault, and threatening her and Es if they ever told anyone about the incident. Both Florence and Es, acting as a team, refused to give in. Watching Hopkin like a hawk stalking a mouse, Etta Belle saw his glance move often to Florence and linger long enough for her to see the lust in his eyes. It got worse when he was drinking, which was almost every night. She looked on in ever-increasing rage. A plan was forming in her mind. She had to eliminate the witnesses to the rape, end her marriage to Joe, and get Hopkin firmly married.

Ruthless and determined, Etta Belle walked twelve-year-old Es to the depot in Beatrice and bought a train ticket to California. "Jay's in a town called Sacramento," she told him. "You find him, but don't you come back here." As the Beatrice Express newspaper reported it later, "The boy was disposed of by his unnatural mother."

Es arrived in Sacramento, California, penniless and scared. Small for his age and looking like a ten-year-old, he had no idea of how to go about finding his brother, if Jay was even there. It was cold and foggy in the Sacramento valley in November, and he was wet, nearly freezing, and starving. After a week of sleeping in the streets and begging for food, he attracted the notice of Salvation Army workers. He told them his story, including where his father lived in Wisconsin. The kindly missionaries bought a train ticket, and gave him warm clothes and enough food and money to get back to Joe.

Etta Belle was desperate to get rid of Florence, her young and appealing competition, and marry Hopkin. For his part, Hopkin was beginning to get a clear picture of the woman he had taken up with, after he witnessed what had happened to Es. He realized that Etta Belle would do whatever it took to get what she wanted. He didn't relish the specter of another prison sentence like the one he had served in Wisconsin for adultery, should she decide to prosecute him for the rape. Thoroughly cowed, he began to assist her in finding a way to eliminate the problem of Florence. They'd been camped on land belonging to a man named John Warren when the assault on Florence took place. Hopkin learned that the farmer had a brother in Oklahoma near Anadarko named Hugh Warren. He was forty- three years old and a widower. John told Hopkin and Etta Belle that they might be able to work out a trade with Hugh: a very young, attractive wife in exchange for horses to support their budding horse trading business. This sounded ideal to Etta Belle. Anadarko was another three hundred miles from Joe, isolated and surrounded by Indian Country. Just the place to stash the nuisance that Florence had become. No amount of protest and tears could save Florence. Her mother was in charge.

Early in January Etta Belle, Hopkin and their entourage journeyed to Oklahoma to meet Hugh Warren and spend the winter. Undeterred by her failure to obtain a divorce in Wisconsin, Etta Belle stopped in Perry, Oklahoma, to file again. This time she lied about her residency, claiming that she had been a resident of Oklahoma for a year, and again claiming she didn't know how to locate Joe. The lawyer told her it would take several months to work through the details. Meanwhile, Etta Belle thought, she could proceed with her plans for Florence.

The group moved on, from Perry to Anadarko, a dusty little Oklahoma town in the midst of territory assigned to the Kiowa Indians when the government had relocated them nearly thirty years before. Hugh Warren's rented farm was located ten miles east of Anadarko, near the hamlet of Verden. Hopkin and Etta Belle arrived on February 1, and set about getting acquainted with Warren. Etta Belle was building toward the most important horse trade she would ever make. In addition to being thirty years older than Florence—nearly three times her age—Warren was of Canadian / French-Indian descent. That gave him a good deal in common with Tom Hopkin. Etta Belle spent the next three weeks, with terrible resolve, convincing Florence that she had no choice but marry Warren.

"You're ruined now," she told the girl. "No decent man would have you. You can't be choosy." Etta Belle also said she would not be taking Florence any further on the wagon. "I seen the looks you keep givin' Tom," she accused. "You can marry Warren or starve, you little tramp." At the same time, Etta Belle was striking a bargain with Warren.

On February 20th, 1908, Florence and Hugh Warren were married in the County Courthouse at Anadarko. Oklahoma had achieved statehood the previous November 16th. Etta Belle signed the marriage license application, and Tom Hopkin was a witness. After the ceremony, Hopkin and Etta Belle rode away leading a pair of horses, "gifted" to them by her new son-in-law.

The publication for Etta Belle's divorce petition was run two months later, for four consecutive weeks, in the Enterprise Times in Noble County, Oklahoma. She was granted the divorce by default on May 9, since Joe hadn't answered the complaint. Because of the mandatory waiting period in Oklahoma, Etta Belle would not be free to marry Hopkin for another six months. And there was another problem: he already had a wife in Wisconsin. As it turned out, her new marriage never took place. But she had solved the problem of Florence and Es.

Joe had a severe headache. He took a pull of "the hair of the dog that bit him," out of the quart whiskey bottle sitting among the dirty dishes on the cluttered table. God, he felt bad. He had to get goin'. He still worked for the logging company when he wasn't drunk or hung over, and he needed the money to pay the rent on the farm. He still hoped there was some reason Etta Belle had left. Maybe she was just lonesome for her sisters and brothers in Davenport, and went to visit them. She'd be back. She always came back, after she got over her mad-on. He'd been here for three months by himself, waiting for any word from her.

Joe picked up the water bucket and headed out to the well. As he stepped down from the porch, he saw a small forlorn figure wading through the deep snow, up the lane from the county road. He stopped, thinking he was seeing things. Christ! It was Es! How could he be here, all alone? Joe set the bucket down and strode through the snow to the boy. He was a man not given to physical display, but in spite of himself, he gathered the thin little body into his arms. "You got something to tell me, son? Where's your ma?" Joe was almost afraid to ask.

"Oh, yeah, Pa. I got lots to tell you."

Es talked nearly non-stop for the next three days. Joe abandoned liquor during the entire tirade, and as he sobered up, his mind became sharper and more cognizant of what the boy was telling him. Es described the attack on Florence by Hopkin, and his mother's ruthless method of getting rid of him, the most important witness.

Joe's rage and frustration grew until it consumed his mind, waking and sleeping. All he could think about was finding Etta Belle and evening the score. The final straw came when Es told him that he had seen Hopkin's two teenage sons drinking and groping little ten-year-old Elnora during their drunken binges. Wild and reckless with fury, ignoring the specter of the deepening winter, Joe abandoned the rented farm and with Es in tow, set out on the trail of Etta Belle and Hopkin. According to later newspaper interviews with Joe, the two rode in boxcars and hitch-hiked, sleeping in barns and by roadsides and begging food. Joe told his story to anyone who would listen, generating sympathy and outrage from people who could provide food and shelter for him and the boy.

Joe went from Wisconsin straight to Beatrice, Nebraska, where Es had witnessed the rape, and contacted the police chief, one E.G. Moore. Giving Joe the benefit of the doubt, the policeman accompanied Joe and Es to the location where the crime had been committed. According to the Beatrice Express newspaper, "A search of the vicinity of the alleged assault brought to light evidence bearing out the story of the boy." Although a couple of months had passed and Etta Belle and Hopkin were long gone, something about the scene convinced the officers that Es was telling the truth.

Leaving Es with kindly acquaintances in Beatrice, and with the full support of law enforcement, Joe took up the pursuit. He started with information from the post office in Beatrice stating that Etta Belle and Hopkin had asked that their mail be forwarded to Nebraska City, a small town about seventy miles northeast. Again traveling by boxcar and hitching rides, Joe followed. He found that the pair had moved on. For many months, Joe followed the trail of the "elopers" as the paper called them. According to the Beatrice Express, "Every possible clue was followed up." Joe kept up a "constant correspondence" with the Beatrice police chief and the Cowley County sheriff. He traveled to Oklahoma, Missouri, Kansas, Texas, Iowa, and other states, pursuing every lead, and returned to Beatrice a number of times to confer with the police chief and check on Es. During those months, probably from information given by John Warren, the farmer near Beatrice, Joe found Florence in Oklahoma, living with her husband on a creek north of Verden. Now fifteen, she was pregnant. Florence was illiterate like all her brothers and sisters, but coached by Joe and her husband, who knew how to read and write, she signed an affidavit giving all the details of her rape by Hopkin. Florence also affirmed Es's story of how their mother had gotten rid of them after the incident. Triumphant, Joe carried the affidavit back to the sheriff in Beatrice and resumed his search.

Finally, on a Saturday in September, 1908, after nearly a year, three thousand miles of walking, "beating his way in box cars" and begging rides, Joe found Etta Belle and Hopkin camped near Arkansas City, Kansas.

The owner of the livery stable was concerned and helpful. "Didja say she's a white woman travelin' with a bunch of kids and a half-breed? They got a wagon and some horses?" He asked Joe, after Joe had told his story for what seemed like the hundredth time. "That sounds like a pair that was in here yesterday tryin' to sell me a coupla worthless plugs," the man said. "They said they're camped about a mile east of town."

Joe could not contain his elation. This was as close to Tom Hopkin and Etta Belle as he'd been in his long odyssey.

"I gotta get there fast. I don't have a dime to my name," Joe mourned. "Do you think you could loan me a rig. I'd be sure to pay you as soon as I can."

"I'm not in the lending business," the man replied, "but in your case, I'll make an exception." The man had been impressed by Joe's tale of woe, spiced with elopement, adultery, rape and thievery. "You need to get those kids," he told Joe, as he hitched a horse to a small, light buggy.

Joe quietly approached Etta Belle's camp in the middle of the afternoon. He knew he should recruit help from the sheriff in Arkansas City, but after a year in pursuit, he couldn't hold back his fury. He was determined to confront his wife and her lover.

Joe stopped his rig a few hundred yards from the camp. Somewhat apprehensive, but carried forward by resolve, he walked past a string of about ten horses picketed a few yards away, toward the wagon, the one Etta Belle had helped herself to a year before.

"The bitch!" He thought. "She fixed herself up pretty good with my money." He smelled the wood smoke from the campfire mingled with the scent of fresh horse manure. He heard the sound of an axe on wood, back in a grove of trees away from the camp. He was nearly into the camp when he was spotted by his two youngest children sitting on a wagon tongue playing a paddle ball game.

"Papa, Papa!" Elnora and Clifford leaped to their feet and ran to their father.

Etta Belle's head emerged from the wagon covering. Startled, she saw Joe, standing with his arms around his children's shoulders. She recovered quickly. "You kids git back here!" Then to Joe she said, "Well, well, here you are. I heard tell you been followin' us, Joe."

"Yeah, and I finally caught up," Joe said. "You just get yourself ready to come on home now, Etta Belle. You're my wife, and I want my family back."

"Home where, Joe? We ain't never had a home. And I'm not your wife; not since last spring. We is divorced," she said. She stepped down from the wagon.

"How come I never heard nothin' about no divorce," Joe demanded

"Well, maybe you oughta read the Oklahoma newspapers."

"You're lying again! You ain't nothin' but a rotten liar and always have been. An' you ain't gonna get away with it this time." By now Joe was shouting.

"What you gonna do about it, Joe?" Etta Belle shouted back. "Me and the kids is staying right here with Tom."

Tom Hopkin came walking around the wagon, carrying an axe, followed by his two teenage sons. At the sight of him, the pent-up rage that had simmered for a full year burst from Joe. "You no good thievin' sonovabitch!" Joe spat on the ground as if to emphasize the betrayal. "I oughta get me a gun and put a bullet in your god-damned head!" Unable to contain himself, he put down his head and made a run at Hopkin, intending to tackle him and administer a beating. Hopkin's seventeen-year-old son Harvey stepped in front of his father, just as Joe tripped and fell to the ground at his feet. Clint, Hopkin's younger son, stepped up beside his father. "Think you can take us all, old man?"

Joe clambered to his feet as the boys attached themselves to his arms to keep him away from their father. "You better cool off, old man. You're liable to get hurt."

Joe shook them off and backed away. "Well, we'll just see about this. I'll go see what the sheriff has to say about—what do they call it, Tom? Oh yeah, adultery. I'll bet they don't like it any better in Kansas than they did in Wisconsin. Right, Tom? And then we got that problem of you raping my little girl. I don't think the sheriff is gonna like that much. And maybe the newspaperman would like to hear about what you done to Es, sendin' him out to California all by himself. He's just a boy! He came back to Wisconsin and told me all about it. He's a witness, and he ain't got no use for you two. Yep, I guess I'll go see the sheriff."

Turning on his heel, Joe strode back toward his rig. Elnora and Clifford, weeping and forlorn, stood beside their mother watching him go.

Etta Belle realized that Joe fully intended to recruit law enforcement and press charges against them. She sprang into action. "Tom, get the wagon hitched up. We gotta get outta here before he comes back with the Sheriff."

Hopkin and his two sons hurried off to hitch up the team and pull picket stakes, while Etta Belle threw their possessions into the wagon. Within an hour the whole party was packed up and heading east as fast as they could move the horses. Fording creeks slowed them up, and they were just crossing the railroad tracks at Silverdale, five miles east of Arkansas City, when they were apprehended by Sheriff Day, Constable Peek and a triumphant Joe.

Joe had raced into Arkansas City and gone straight to the sheriff's office. The sheriff wired the Beatrice law enforcement in Nebraska to confirm Joe's story. They put their full support behind Joe. The sheriff in Arkansas City had heard Joe's story several times during the past year, and he wasted no time obtaining a fugitive warrant against Hopkin from the local judge, and a second warrant charging Etta Belle with adultery.

The arrest was reported in the Winfield Daily Courier:

> "Mecum apprehended the pair near Arkansas City last Saturday night, when they tried to make their escape eastward. They were caught by law enforcement at the Silverdale crossing. When arrested, the parties were in a covered mover's wagon and had with them two of the children whom Mecum declares are his own."

When the news reached Beatrice of their arrest, the Beatrice Express newspaper reported:

> "Credit for the capture of the man Hopkin is due to Chief Moore, Sheriff Trude, and particularly to Mr. Mecum, who has shown great detective ability in his long search."

Sheriff Day served the warrant on Hopkin, and in handcuffs, Etta Belle's paramour was taken off to jail. She hastily set up a new camp, admonished the Hopkin boys and her two children to stay put, and followed the sheriff's party into Arkansas City. As soon as she entered the sheriff's office, she was served with the arrest warrant for adultery and escorted to a cell, while Hopkin was handcuffed to another prisoner, loaded on the evening train, and taken to Winfield, fifteen miles north, to await the arrival of the sheriff from Beatrice, Nebraska. He was held without bond, since the warrant had designated him a fugitive.

After Hopkin and Etta Belle were arrested, law officers, the county attorney, the deputy county attorney, and the county judge in Beatrice worked far into Saturday night to obtain warrants and extradition papers in both Nebraska and Kansas. The efforts included an emergency trip by the Beatrice sheriff to the Nebraska state capital in Lincoln to obtain the extradition papers. Two days later the Sheriff and police chief from Beatrice arrived in Winfield and took Hopkin back to Nebraska.

On Monday, back in Arkansas City, Etta Belle posted bail. As she left the jail, she stated to reporters, "Them two kids [Florence and Es] ain't testifyin' against Tom. He's my husband now, and their step dad. Joe's lying about Tom raping Florence, just to cause trouble. It's just spite. They won't be testifyin'."

When Etta Belle returned to her hastily assembled camp that day, she found that Joe had taken Elnora and Clifford. He'd had to return the horse and buggy to the livery stable in Arkansas City on Saturday night and he was completely broke, but his resolve had not abated. Full of righteous fury, Joe seized the two children and set out walking north toward Beatrice, over three hundred miles away. Later, the children reported that they had begged food from farmers along their way and slept in barns and stables with no blankets.

Furious and determined to win, Etta Belle stormed back into Arkansas City and demanded an interview with the judge who had issued the warrants. She showed him the papers from the court in Perry, Oklahoma, stating the terms of her divorce and giving her custody of the children. She again told the judge the lie that she was married to Hopkin, but since she could produce no documentation verifying the claim, the judge was skeptical. He sent the sheriff out to find Joe and the two children, with instructions that the sheriff was to turn the children over to the "Probation Officer," when they were found. Joe had made less than twenty miles when they were apprehended by Sheriff Day just east of Winfield. The judge took custody of the children and contacted the probate court, who in turn contacted the Lutheran Children's Friends' Society in Winfield. Elnora and Clifford, terrified and abandoned, were taken to the Lutheran Orphanage.

Two days later, Etta Belle was given a formal hearing in Arkansas City on the charge of adultery. She showed the court her divorce papers, and again insisted that she had married Hopkin in Texas. The judge somehow overlooked the part of the divorce decree stating that the divorce would be final "six months hence," making it November 9 before she could marry Hopkin. She was still legally married to Joe, but the judge accepted her word, dismissed the charges and returned her bail money.

After the children were removed from his custody, Joe was released. He'd run out of options in Winfield. He boarded a boxcar and rode back to Beatrice, where Es was still waiting.

As soon as she was released, Etta Belle's primary goal became freeing her boyfriend, Tom Hopkin. From Arkansas City by telegraph, she wired money to an attorney in Beatrice, along with the message that she would provide proof that the charge of rape was bogus. Dipping into the last of the money she had stolen from Joe a year before, she bought train tickets and sent the Hopkin boys back to their mother in Wisconsin. With all of her responsibilities resolved, she set out alone for Oklahoma and Florence. She had to make sure the girl would never testify against Hopkin.

Meanwhile, Joe had the same idea, only his objective was to make sure that Florence and Es *did* testify. Traveling by freight train, much faster then Etta Belle's team and wagon, he and Es arrived in Oklahoma two days before Etta Belle. Florence assured him that she would appear when the trial took place. At this point, Joe made a major mistake. He underestimated Etta Belle's determination to free Hopkin, and her utter disregard for her children or anyone else who stood in her way. Es, now thirteen, was so happy to see his sister again that he asked Joe for permission to stay with her while he waited for Hopkin's trial to begin. Joe agreed, and feeling secure, he again hopped a freight train and headed back to Nebraska. Ultimately, Es would spend the next two years with Florence.

Joe had no sooner left for Nebraska than Etta Belle arrived at Hugh Warren's farm. Employing the same kind of screaming intimidation she had used on Florence and Es the year before, she launched a new barrage of threats and demands on the two. By the second day, a weeping and thoroughly cowed Florence placed her mark on a paper thrust in front of her by Etta Belle and the County Clerk of Court in Anadarko, which rescinded her previous affidavit. Elated and triumphant, Etta Belle sent the document by overnight mail to Hopkin's attorney in Nebraska. The preliminary hearing for Hopkin was to be held on October 16. By telegraph, Hopkin's attorney advised her that all she had to do now was keep Es and Florence away from Joe and out of Nebraska until after the date of the hearing. Only one four-day continuance was allowed by law. If Joe, as complainant, couldn't locate his two star witnesses by the end of the continuance, the charges against Hopkin would be dismissed.

On September 25th, the Beatrice Express carried the following article:

J.W. MECUM IS HERE

Complaining Witness Reaches City from Oklahoma
to Push Case Against Tom Hopkin.

J.W. Mecum arrived in the city last evening from southern Oklahoma. It was his daughter who was ravished near here last fall for which crime Tom Hopkin now occupies a cell in the county jail awaiting a hearing.

> Mr. Mecum has come to act as complaining witness against Hopkin, whose hearing will probably occur this week. It is understood that Mecum's wife and daughter will reach here in a day or two and that the latter will offer testimony of a very damaging character to Hopkin's interest at the hearing and will doubtless result in his being bound over to the district court.

In truth, Etta Belle had no intention of entering Nebraska, or of letting her two children testify against her lover. Joe found a job in Beatrice and settled down to wait for Etta Belle, Florence and Es to arrive from Oklahoma. A few days later, he was stunned by news from the county attorney. After summarizing the entire story again, the Beatrice Express stated:

> The crime was alleged to have been witnessed by the boy who was sent to California. He was returned to his father through the kindness of the Salvation Army. Upon finally running down Hopkin, Mecum left the boy with his daughter in Oklahoma, thinking he would be able to produce him at the trial. Mr. McGirr, the prosecutor who appeared for the state in open court this morning, stated that the girl upon whom the assault was alleged to have been committed, together with the boy who is alleged to have seen the crime, are now under the control of the mother, who, according to Hopkin is now his wife. [Mr. McGirr] admitted that [the woman has disappeared with the children, and] the state will not be able to procure the attendance of either of these witnesses. From present indications, Hopkin will soon be a free man.
>
> The girl made two affidavits; one giving the details of the alleged crime being in the hands of the county attorney, and still another denying her former story, now in the hands of Mr. Sabin, the attorney for the defendant.
>
> The case is a peculiar one and has cost the county quite a sum of money already. The preliminary hearing must be held [no later than] October 20, the law providing that a preliminary examination cannot be continued longer than four days without the consent of the defendant.

> Mecum is working in this city while his former wife and children cannot be located. Hopkin has been confined in jail for about a month.

Grimly determined but becoming desperately afraid that Etta Belle had gotten the best of him again, Joe attended the long delayed preliminary hearing–arraignment–for Hopkin. According to the Beatrice Express:

> TOM HOPKIN PLEADS NOT GUILTY
> His Hearing is Postponed - Will be Heard October 20 -
> J.W. Mecum, Who Charges Defendant With Crime -
> Unable to Locate Two Important Witnesses
>
> Tom Hopkin was arraigned in county court today and demanded an immediate preliminary hearing, but the state requested a continuance to Tuesday, October 20, and the defendant was remanded to the county jail in default of a $1,000 bond.

Four days later, Joe, exhausted, broke and completely defeated, received the final blow.

> The Beatrice Daily Sun, Wednesday, October 21, 1908.
>
> HOPKIN A FREE MAN
> Dismissed for Lack of Evidence Sufficient to
> Bind Him Over to the District Court
>
> The case of the State against Tom Hopkin was dismissed yesterday in county court when the defendant was called in for a hearing. Hopkin, it will be remembered, is the man arrested on complaint of J.W. Mecum charging him with having criminally assaulted the latter's fifteen-year-old daughter, Florence.
>
> County attorney M.W. Terry entered a dismissal of the complaint for the reason that all the witnesses for the prosecution are non-residents of the state [of Nebraska] out of the jurisdiction of the court, and refused to come voluntarily to this county to testify. There was no means whereby these witnesses could have been

> compelled to come and testify. In addition to the absence of the witnesses there was a likelihood of habeas corpus proceedings being brought by Mr. Sabin, attorney for Hopkin, which would have meant added expense for the county. In the face of these facts, the county attorney found that the only advisable thing to do was to have the case dismissed.

Hopkin's attorney wired the news to Etta Belle in Oklahoma. Leaving Florence and Es permanently with Hugh Warren, she set out for Nebraska to be reunited with Hopkin. Their nomadic life as horse traders would be much easier now; they were rid of six mouths to feed.

While all the legal wrangling about the rape was taking place in the Kansas courts, Clifford and Elnora were in the Lutheran Home in Winfield waiting for their fate to be decided. The case history on record at the orphanage is outrageously incorrect, and puts as much blame on Joe as on Etta Belle for the problems involving the children. The names were confused to the point that much of Hopkin's misbehavior was blamed on Joe in the record. The only part that might have been at least partially accurate was the tale about the children's twenty mile hike from Arkansas City to Winfield with Joe, after Etta Belle and Hopkin were thrown in jail. In part, the record stated:

> [Joe] used the children to beg for him. They would stop near the city limits of a town and Mr. Mecum would write a little message on a slip of paper, saying that they were destitute and starving, ask people to give his children some food or money so that they wouldn't starve, and would send the children around town with this.

Three months after Hopkin was released and he and Etta Belle left the state of Kansas, Elnora and Clifford were permanently committed to the Lutheran Home. According to the written records at the Home, during the half-dozen years they lived there, their mother never visited them, and their dad Joe, only twice. Joe petitioned the court for custody shortly after their confinement, but since he had no home, it was denied.

Etta Belle's affair with Hopkin and their horse trading venture continued for only two more years. By 1910, she lived on a homestead in the Nebraska sand hills, and Tom Hopkin had disappeared from the scene, presumably back to his wife in Wisconsin. Etta Belle took the Hopkin name, and maintained it until her death seven years later, still insisting that she had been married to the man. Hopkin died in California in 1940, reunited with his wife and all four of their children.

Joe's star gradually faded from the fields of family lore. He appeared again briefly during the years Etta Belle was on the Nebraska homestead, racing a big gray horse named John, with his son Es as jockey. Nearly sixty years later, Joe's grand-daughter Lola remembered two occasions when Joe visited Florence, her second husband and her family in Lincoln, Nebraska. At the time, the Sheldon family was living in an area of Lincoln called "Russian Bottom."

"One night dad came home and he had this real old man with him, white hair and real old," Lola said. "He had a bunch of dogs. Dad announced to us kids that he was our grand-dad. That was the first time that I had ever seen my grand-dad [Joe.] This old guy stayed most of the winter then, but he stayed in his wagon with his dogs. He had one team of horses. And in the summer he was gone. I didn't see him again until mama bought a house out in Belmont [a suburb of Lincoln]. He came back and stayed 'til the first of March when we had to give up the house we were in. That time he stayed in the house. He had the back bedroom. He still had his wagon, his horses and his dogs. He didn't make [a fuss] over us kids so we just didn't pay much attention to him. Then he left, and the next time I saw him, Dad and Mama gave him money to get new clothes and a bath. He was real dirty. But he must have taken the money and came on down to St. Joe. I never saw him again."

On October 15, 1927, Florence received a letter from the Chief of Police in St. Joseph, Missouri:

Mrs. Walt Sheldon
Lincoln, Nebraska

Dear Madam:

Mr. Joe Mecum, age seventy eight years, died in April, 1927, at the Noyes hospital where he had been taken, suffering from bronchial pneumonia. He was buried in the City Cemetery.

"Mama was criticized for burying him in Potter's field," Lola said, "but it wasn't her fault. She didn't know he'd died. She had to write letters to find out what happened to him. He probably didn't give much information or who to get hold of [if he was sick or died."]

PART III

BERT AND CHARLIE MECUM

CHAPTER 8

Iowa - 1905

Charley was the fourth child and the second son in Joe and Etta Belle's large brood of children. According to family lore Charley was his dad's favorite "until he screwed up," when he was a teenager. He was born in 1888, in Oquawka, Illinois, two years after his grandfather, Isaac Utter, was run over by a train.

In adulthood, Charley was a slender five feet six or seven inches tall, and had somewhat lighter hair and complexion than most of his siblings. Over the years, Charley collected several prison tattoos thinking they made him look tough. He also bore an array of scars from various misadventures, and he wore eyeglasses occasionally. He was illiterate, like all his brothers and sisters.

When Lillie left Davenport, Iowa, with Gus Fiske in July, 1903, Charley, by now fifteen, moved in with his uncle John Utter. John's son Claude was thirteen, the same age as Charley's brother Bert, who was incarcerated in a reformatory. Charley and Bert had always been close, but when Bert, at age ten, started running away from home for weeks at a time and attracting the attention of the law, Charley chose to stay close to his family. Claude became his surrogate brother. John Utter was blind and beyond charity had no means of income. He was incapable of disciplining two rambunctious teenagers, and Charley and Claude were soon getting into serious trouble.

According to the 1905 Davenport Democrat newspaper account of their arrests, Charley and Claude spent the years between 1903 and 1905 sharpening their skills as burglars and thieves. During the two years, according to the newspaper, they became well known to the police, but efforts to catch them red-handed were unsuccessful.

The boys spent periods of time away from home–time that gradually lengthened into weeks in the summertime. They signed on as roustabouts for circuses, thus obtaining free transportation among neighboring towns, and followed street fairs and carnivals. At other times, they walked or begged rides on drays and freight wagons to get from town to town. The small towns in Iowa, just a few miles apart, all held summer fairs and celebrations on the Fourth of July and other holidays, and each county had an annual fair centered on the local agriculture. These occasions presented perfect opportunities for the boys. They spent the first few days of their stay in each town roaming the streets looking for houses whose occupants were attending the festivities. Unworried about petty crime, virtually no one locked their doors, especially if they were only a few blocks away from home taking part in celebrations. The boys waited until the last day of the event to begin the burglaries, so they would be out of town before the police had a chance to look for them. As brazen as seasoned criminals, they walked up and down alleys and entered homes through unlocked doors, day or night, any time the target seemed safe.

During hot weather, residents moved to their porches when the day started to cool, to catch the evening air. People usually removed their watches and jewelry and emptied purses, reticules and pockets when they were home. The boys began entering houses from the back, so bold that they sometimes entered a home while the occupants were sitting on their front porches. They had a well-practiced routine. Leaving Claude outside as a lookout, Charley eased into the targeted house. Always alert, he made his furtive way through the rooms hoping he didn't step on a squeaky board. He helped himself to whatever booty was available, usually cash, gold watches, jewelry and any item that could be sold quickly in the next town. Then he quietly left the same way he had entered. As time went on, greedy and becoming addicted to the excitement, the boys robbed as many as five homes in one night.

Two years into their career of successful thievery, Claude and Charley were beginning to feel very grown-up and worldly. Now fifteen and seventeen, still too young to shave, they spent some of the loot on baths, haircuts and new clothes. Adopting a worldly swagger, they talked their way into the houses in the red light district–the Tenderloin, as the newspapers called it. They tried impressing the prostitutes with their apparent wealth. They flashed greenbacks, gifted the women with watches and jewelry, and most unwise of all, boasted about their wealth and prospects. This would prove to be the downfall of their little enterprise. But to their chagrin, they weren't able to convince the "ladies of the night" that they were old enough to sample the wares. They kept trying, and each effort required more items with which to bribe the lady of choice.

In the beginning the boys had been clever enough to scatter the burglaries over several cities and towns and not concentrate on any one area, but with success came carelessness. In two days, during the summer of 1905, they committed nine burglaries in Davenport and Moline, Illinois, just across the river. Complaints began to come in at the local Davenport police station, and realizing that these burglaries were probably connected, the department assigned a special detective to the case.

Charley and Claude were arrested at 10:00 on a sweltering night in August, 1905. During one burglary, Charley had helped himself to a full box of expensive Cuban cigars. When he realized the cigars' value–too much for smoking them himself–he tried to find a buyer. The person they approached with the cigars notified the police and gave a description of the boys. The detective assigned to the case made a tour of the red light district, stopping occasionally at a brothel for information, and found his quarry standing on a street corner, making no effort to hide or evade him. He brought the pair to the station and subjected them an interrogation that lasted all night. Finally, early in the morning, Claude broke down and admitted to all nine of the most recent burglaries. He gave a complete accounting of the plunder and where they had disposed of it. Most of the stolen items and some of the cash were recovered.

The Sunday, August 13, 1905, Davenport Democrat trumpeted the story of the arrest:

DARING THIEVES CAUGHT AFTER MANY BURGLARIES

Police Made a Good Catch in East End Friday Evening

Two Young Boys with Much Money and Jewelry Prove to be Thieves

> With their pockets filled with jewelry and a goodly supply of money, two boys, the youngest and most daring thieves that have operated in this city and vicinity for some time, were arrested by Captain Mullaine on Second and Rock streets about 10 o'clock Friday night. The names of the lads are Charley Mecum and Claude Utter, aged seventeen and fifteen years respectively. They reside on the west end of the city, when at home, and are well known in police circles. For the past two years they have been seeing the country and undoubtedly have been working at and living off the fruits of their daring and unlawful business.

The boys assured the officials that they were really decent folks who were simply down on their luck. They had intended to take the proceeds from the burglaries and "go straight." They were signed on with a street fair company to open their own "African Dodger" stand in Anamosa, about 100 miles northwest of Davenport.

In the days of Jim Crow, entertainment like the African Dodger and a similar game called "Hit the Coon" were popular in the traveling fairs. A Negro (or a white man in black face) thrust his head through a hole in a board and taunted the onlookers who would pay a nickel to throw baseballs at him. He could pull his head back through the hole if he was fast enough, but frequently he wasn't fast enough. After a few years, simply throwing baseballs wasn't enough for some of the sadistic customers, so they brought wooden or iron balls when a carnival was in town with the intent to inflict injury. Supposedly, only black men or white men with black-face makeup could be "Dodgers," because bruises didn't show.

The boys implied they had planned to purchase the materials needed for the venture with the money from their thefts, and hire their black man with more of the money. But that story didn't agree with the facts: they had been squandering their loot as fast as they hi-jacked it. The officials in Davenport were unimpressed by the explanation. The boys were indicted by a grand jury, and pled guilty thinking they would get lighter sentences. In spite of sympathy for their youth, the judge handed out stiff sentences–two years each in the reformatory at Anamosa, a prison that at the time housed both youths and seasoned criminals, and would figure prominently in Charley's future. Joe and Etta Belle and their children had briefly lived in the area of the prison a few years before.

One ironic outcome of Charley's sentence was his reunion with his brother Bert, whose most recent sentence for burglary overlapped his by a year. During that time, Bert made himself important as the experienced jailbird, and he set about impressing his big brother with his apparent skills at outwitting guards and plotting escapes. At the end of his sentence, as he was about to depart the prison on foot carrying everything he owned in a cloth wrapped bundle, Bert, now seventeen years old, told Charley, "I'm think I'm gonna find me a job and try goin' straight for awhile. I'll get word to you where I'm at. You only got another year. Come see me when you get out. We'll have a drink and bullshit awhile."

When he was released six months later, Charley could find no trace of his brother. He didn't know that Bert had adopted another alias and disappeared into the countryside. With his new name, "Conroy Wilson," he was impossible to find.

Charley was discharged from Anamosa six months early, at age nineteen, on February 18, 1907. After searching for Bert for a few days without success, he headed for his parents' rented farm in Black River Falls, Wisconsin. When he was caught a month later for stealing the bike, he served his sentence under the alias "Bert Demon." He was beginning to learn from Bert.

He swore to his parents that he'd stay out of trouble, and made their rented farm his base of operations for the next nine months. But Joe and Etta Belle's behavior seemed to affect his ability to stay out of trouble. When Joe and Etta Belle separated in Davenport in 1904, Charley and Claude started their burglaries. Within days of Etta Belle's elopement with Tom Hopkin in 1907, Charley was burglarizing homes in the area of Black River Falls. A month later he was arrested in LaCrosse County, and sent to Waupun Prison in Wisconsin with a sentence of three years. He served two and a half years, and was released February 10, 1910. By then Joe and Etta Belle were long gone from Wisconsin.

As the day of his prison release arrived, Charley remembered Bert's invitation from three years before. He caught a freight train going west, and then made his way down the Mississippi to Davenport for a get-together with the Utter family members who remained there—aunts, uncles and cousins. He figured his relatives would know how to find Bert.

They welcomed him like a prodigal son, and caught him up on family news. Bert was in Fulton, Illinois, a little town just across the river from Clinton, Iowa, thirty miles north of Davenport. Etta Belle was homesteading in Nebraska and Joe was in Lincoln trying to get into horse racing. They didn't know where Jay or Sophie were, and hadn't heard from the two littlest Mecums, still in the orphanage in Kansas, in years. As far as they knew, Florence and Es were still on the Indian reservation in Oklahoma with Hugh Warren.

Charley set out for Fulton at once and found the farm where Bert worked as a field hand. Bert had stuck with the job for nearly three years, and in that time had saved most of his wages. Again, reunion with his big brother gave him a feeling of importance. He boasted expansively about his affluence, throwing in tidbits about what an accomplished criminal he was—at age twenty. He was compulsive in his need to impress Charley.

It took only a short time of listening to Bert before Charley was restless again. He hopped another freight heading west, following the route taken by newly wed Joe and Etta Belle thirty years before, and headed to Greeley, a small town northeast of Kearny, Nebraska. On the way he stopped in Lincoln and hunted up Joe, who was living in a covered wagon at the county fairgrounds. Over a bottle of Jack Daniels they commiserated about all the things that had happened since that summer of 1907 in Wisconsin.

"Well, Charley, you turnin' over a new leaf' again?" Joe asked.

"Yeah Pa. I'm sure sick of jail cells."

After his crushing defeat by Etta Belle and Hopkin in Kansas, Joe had become the go-between for the family the last few years, hopping freights or buying train tickets when he had the money, to visit and carry family news to his scattered offspring. On his last visit to Oklahoma he had told Florence that Etta Belle's romance with Tom Hopkin had fallen apart and she was homesteading in Nebraska. "That half-breed had no use for hard work," he said. "She spent the money she stole from me, and now she's got nothin'."

A few days after leaving Joe, Charley arrived on foot at Etta Belle's Nebraska sand hill homestead. It was early May. To his great surprise he found both Es and Florence, along with Florence's baby Lola, sharing the sod house with Etta Belle.

Florence at seventeen was a much more assertive woman than she'd been at fifteen when Etta Belle had bullied her into marrying Hugh Warren. Making her own decisions became an attraction. After sticking it out in misery in the hill country of the Oklahoma Indian Reservation for two years, she had abandoned her aging husband. Warren, she had learned, like her father and stepfather, liked his liquor, and she came to believe he was drinking himself to death. With Es, who had been living with her the entire time, she boarded a train for Nebraska. When the pair showed up at the door of Etta Belle's sod house in the spring of 1910, Florence was defiant and out for revenge. "After what you done to me, Ma, you owe me. Me and Es is staying here whether you like it or not." She thrust the baby Lola at Etta Belle. "Here's what I got from your little war with Pa. She needs a diaper change. Matter of fact, she needs diapers." So the battle was resumed.

When Charley arrived in early May, it was obvious there was no room for another person in the little one room sod house. After two days' visit and reunion, Charley persuaded his brother and sister to go with him back to Lincoln to see Joe.

"Es, Pa's got a big gray gelding he calls John, a real runner. He needs a jockey. I think you could make some money," he told his little brother. Es was fifteen years old, but was still small and thin, barely 100 pounds. Charley neglected to tell Es that John was such an enthusiastic runner that he ran out from under all the jockeys who'd been brave enough to mount him, and constantly "jumped the gun" at the starting line. Joe had developed a system of backing John up to the starting line with a blind over his eyes. When the gun sounded, Joe jerked off the blind. John whirled and leaped after the competing horses, which were already several lengths in the lead. Unless the jockey was tied to the saddle, he found himself dumped on his head in the dirt. Consequently, jockeys quit after one race. In spite of the handicaps and starting the races backward, John consistently won his races.

Assuring Etta Belle that she'd be back in a few days, Florence left the baby Lola with Etta Belle and she, Charley and Es boarded a passenger train headed back to Lincoln. It would be more than twenty years before Charley saw Lola again–as a full grown woman–through very different eyes.

Joe welcomed his children with enthusiasm. Es remembered the close relationship he and Joe had developed during the year they pursued Etta Belle and Hopkin and greeted Joe warmly. He declared himself eager to help with the risky business of racing John, even if he had to be tied onto the horse's back.

After a day of gossiping about family, Charley and Florence decided to visit the Iowa relatives in Davenport, leaving Es with Joe. This time the tickets were paid for by their dad. They didn't make it all the way to Davenport. Charley had another idea.

The horses were tired. Charley drew back his arm for the hundredth time and lashed the sweat covered rumps in front of him. They were beautiful matched bays, pulling a sporty, shiny black buggy at breakneck speed down the dusty Iowa road, rutted from the recent heavy June rains, toward the Mississippi River. It was still over fifty miles to Davenport, where he planned to cross the river, turn north, ride another fifty miles and meet Florence in a couple days in Fulton, Illinois, near where Bert had been working for a farmer for the last three years. She'd be coming cross country with the other rig. It hadn't been hard to talk Florence into a little turn at "horse trading." She'd been stuck on that reservation down in Oklahoma for two years and now she was ripe for some excitement.

Sometimes he wondered if there wasn't a better way to make a living. Ever since they'd left Lincoln in May, they had been making good money at their version of "horse trading." They had found a nice team and buggy tied to a hitching rail in Anamosa. It wasn't much trouble to walk them out of town and slip away in the darkness. The team wasn't matched, so Charley drove them to Marion, split them up and sold one to a horse trader and the other one to a Norwegian farmer. He got $100 apiece for the horses and another thirty for the buggy at a livery barn. It was safer to split up a rig before selling it; harder to trace and identify. He and Florence were jubilant at the money they were making, but it was turning out to be hard work–a lot harder than the way he'd made a living before. Burglary was a slow way to get rich but not much work. Horse stealing was risky, but a guy sure made money quicker, if he was smart and didn't get caught.

With pockets full of greenbacks from selling the first rig, they had picked up second team and buggy tied to a hitching rack in Marion and headed southwest to where he'd heard Gus and Lillie were camped outside Marengo. It was the middle of June and they were headed north toward Minnesota on their regular circuit. Charley thought maybe Gus and his horse trading outfit might be a way to get rid of the team. It was funny how the word got around when a horse trader was in the country. Gus stood out among horse traders. He had a downright beautiful pair of matched three-year-old sorrel fillies and a flashy black top-buggy that he drove around to farms to let people know he was in the area with good horses to trade. He always dressed like a businessman, with a collar and necktie, and his little show team of hot-blooded fillies was always curried and trimmed. He looked so respectable it was hard for a farmer to argue with him when he was working on a trade.

It took Charley and Florence better than half a day to get to Gus's camp from Marion. They spent the rest of the day visiting and getting caught up on news. The little boys were really growing. Eddie was six and Frank was three. Lillie kept Frank's hair in long curls and he looked girlie, and Eddie bullied the little one when he was out of his dad's sight. Lillie still talked about homesteading, but Gus just ignored her. She was really getting sick of being a nomad. She'd always been different from the rest of the family; she acted kind of ashamed of the shenanigans her brothers and sisters–and even her mother–got into. She didn't say much while Charley showed Gus the new rig and talked about a trade, but he was pretty sure she was suspicious. She knew he'd only been out of prison for a few months and couldn't have earned that much honest money. He had to find another way to get rid of the team and buggy.

Charley and Florence stayed around Gus's camp overnight, and the next morning they quietly talked between themselves about heading back toward Cedar Rapids. Then Charley changed his mind. Bert might have an idea about where to sell the rig at a profit. Florence could take the second team and buggy to Fulton and wait until Charley got there. He'd find another easy piece of merchandise and then he'd high-tail it for the Mississippi and meet her in Fulton. This would be the last one for awhile. They'd have a good start, and could do whatever they wanted. Florence had been saying she thought maybe she should get back to Nebraska and get the baby, Lola, and now she'd have some money to maybe take up a homestead near Etta Belle.

Florence dropped Charley off outside of Marengo when they were safely a few miles away from Gus's horse trading stand. He said goodbye and told her it wouldn't be more than a couple days until he'd show up in Fulton. She drove away toward the east. On foot, Charley hiked into the village. It was about noon, and the warm June sun made him sleepy. He took a nap under a tree away from the dirt and dust of Main Street, and woke up when a bum yellow dog started sniffing around. Hungry, he found a saloon that sold meals. The barkeep tried to strike up a conversation, but Charley responded with grunts and pretty soon the guy gave up. Charley didn't want to be saying anything the bartender might remember.

After a few beers, he stepped out into late afternoon sun and strolled up the street, looking for his chance. He almost couldn't believe what he was seeing. The dumb bastard who left his rig while he bull-shitted in the telephone office was just asking for it to be "borrowed." Charley was never one to pass up an opportunity like that. There sat the buggy and the bays, tied to a rail and ready to go. He looked around. Not a soul on the deserted street. He casually untied the halter rope from the rail, climbed into the buggy, turned the team and quietly walked them out of town, drawing no attention. Once outside the city limits, he slashed the horses with the buggy whip and headed east. He couldn't help gloating; he'd scored three rigs in three days. This was the way to make money.

According to later newspapers, the team and rig belonged to a local government official. The man came out of the telephone office at about 4:15 in the afternoon and found the team missing, but didn't feel any alarm for at least an hour. He thought a friend had borrowed it, and would soon bring it back. When he did realize it was missing, he had all the contacts he needed to find the culprit.

Most of Iowa's new telephones were small local party lines with virtually no long distance service, but still, word got around by primitive telephone much faster than a horse could travel. By nine o'clock the next morning, citizens and law officers for fifty miles had been alerted to watch for the stolen rig.

Charley had thirty miles ahead of him, from Marengo due east to West Liberty. He decided he'd stop there for the night, let the horses rest in the livery barn and go on in the morning. It got dark halfway to West Liberty, still a long way from the Mississippi. The night sky was moonless and inky, the countryside around him obscured except for an occasional faint light from a kerosene lamp shining from a farmhouse window. None of the farms and only the bigger towns had electricity. The horses raced through the darkness along the two wheel tracks that passed for a county road.

He pulled into the livery barn in the tiny town of West Liberty after midnight, the horses heaving and flecked with foam and sweat. He flipped a coin to the sleepy attendant and started to unhitch the team. The horses pawed and tossed their heads restlessly, trying to get to the water and feed troughs. "Them horses are pretty hot. You better cool 'em down before you feed or water 'em," the man told Charley.

"Sure they're hot. I come near thirty miles this afternoon. I'm too god-damn tired to do any hot-walkin'," Charley replied. "I gotta be outta here at sunup. Jest give 'em some oats." Shaking his head and muttering under his breath the man obeyed. Charley grabbed a lap robe out of the buggy and started to bed down in the soft hay.

"It'll be another dime if you're sleepin' here," the attendant grumbled.

"I'll tend to it in the mornin'." Charley turned his back and was soon snoring.

He rose with the sun and sneaked out of the livery before the owner woke, without paying the extra ten cents. By 5:30 he was again barreling down the road toward Illinois. Within an hour, the team was lathered and laboring, the one on the right having a hard time staying even with the other big bay. Charley pulled the team down to a slow trot, thinking he had gotten away clean and there was no need to hurry.

Thanks to all the new telephones, a dragnet of automobiles reached out in all directions from Marengo, hot on his trail. Three hours after Charley left West Liberty, the sheriff in Marengo received word by telephone that Charley had spent the night in the livery stable and had left at 5:30. So far, law enforcement was chasing the team and buggy without knowing who the driver was. Once they picked up his trail, telephones alerted sheriffs and police ahead of Charley, along his apparent route. In the communities ahead of him, law officers were on high alert.

He made it all the way to the Mississippi and crossed into Rock Island, Illinois, twelve hours after he left West Liberty. The horses were in bad shape, exhausted and blown. On June 22, The Marengo Republican described the capture:

> The capture of the team and driver was made by a Rock Island policeman shortly before the arrival there of Sheriff Owen and his party. This policeman was watching through a window for [another fugitive] when he saw the team go by and recognized it from the description he had received [by telephone] just a little while before. He had to go to the rear of the building to get out and by the time he was on the street the team was two blocks away. He impressed into service a passing automobile. They overtook the team and ran the auto in front of the team while the policeman covered the driver with his revolver. The driver threw up his hands. He had a revolver on the seat beside him, but had no time to get it.
>
> On Monday evening, Sheriff Owen had the fellow in the Iowa County jail, bringing him back in an automobile. Mr. Thompson's horses were brought home this morning on the five o'clock freight

> [from Rock Island.] One of the horses is in fairly good shape, but the other is badly foundered and stiffened. It was apparently injured by being fed while too hot. This was a fine driving team of bays, seven or eight years old, weighing 1100 pounds each. Mr. Thompson had refused $400 for [the pair.]
>
> The prisoner gives his name as Charles B. Smitch, although he had told the Rock Island police it was Charley Hopkin. He says he was born in Peoria, Illinois, and has no home. When asked his business, he said it had been principally lying around in county jails. He says he was never in Marengo before and that a man in Oxford had hired him to drive this team to Moline, which he was doing when arrested. He does not explain why he offered to sell this team in Rock Island shortly before his arrest, a fact which Sheriff Owen discovered.

In addition to lying to the Rockford, Illinois, police, Charley compounded his crime by giving up his sister. Certain that he could generate sympathy and convince the police he was innocent, he inserted seventeen-year-old Florence into the plot. "My sister Florence's been travelin' with me," Charley protested. "She can tell you I didn't steal the rig. I been takin' care of her."

"Did she help you steal the rig?" the Rockford detective asked.

"Course not! I didn't steal it." Waiting for the arrival of the Iowa sheriff, Charley invented stories and protested his innocence.

"If she can back up your story, where do we find her?"

"She's heading for Fulton drivin' my rig. I told you, I was only drivin' this one for pay, 'cause that guy hired me. I don't need to steal a rig. I got my own," he lied. He volunteered a full description of Florence and the rig she drove toward Illinois.

A week later, on a plea of not guilty, a judge offered Charley bail of $2500, which he could not produce. Awaiting arraignment by a grand jury, he stayed in the Iowa County jail for the next four months.

On October 19th, the Marengo Republican published another news item:

PLEADS GUILTY AND GOES TO THE PEN

> Charles B. Smitch, who has been in jail since June for stealing J.W. Thompson's team, was indicted by the grand jury last week, and pled guilty yesterday just as his case was being opened for trial to a jury. He received a sentence of five years, the full limit of the law, and was assigned to Anamosa. It is expected, however, that he will be transferred to Fort Madison soon, as it was learned that this is not his first offense. Only first termers are allowed to remain at Anamosa, that being more of a reformatory. Smitch, whose other name is Charley Mecum, has served sentences in at least two other penitentiaries. While at the depot last evening in charge of a deputy warden of Anamosa, he confessed to having been in Marengo the afternoon the team was stolen, and, with a partner, stealing the team.

After she said goodbye to Charley, Florence, alone with the horses and buggy, struck out due east from Marengo, over the wild and rough terrain of eastern Iowa. She stayed well south of Cedar Rapids, away from people and law enforcement. It took two full days, stopping only once to water and feed the team and sleep on the buggy seat for a few hours, to drive the horses and buggy the sixty miles across Iowa toward Clinton. She crossed the Mississippi River into Illinois and made her way to the little town of Fulton on the east bank. She put up the tired team in a livery stable and found a rooming house in a poor section of town where she could spend the night. She went back to tell the livery attendant where she was staying, and settled in to wait for Charley.

She started to worry. This latest caper involved two rigs at once. The venture was getting out of hand; too big, too busy. They'd left Lincoln, Nebraska only a few weeks ago, and they'd already stolen three rigs. They were sure to get caught, no matter what Charley said to the contrary. When he showed up the next day, they would get a hold of Bert and see about selling their booty. Then she was definitely going to quit and go back to Nebraska. Charley, her big brother by five years, had made this sound like an easy and grand adventure when he first convinced her to help him in his little "horse trading" scheme. Now she was remembering the years he had spent in jail, in Iowa and Wisconsin.

The next day, Florence picked up her rig at the livery and drove out of town a mile to the farm where Bert worked. It took her a while to convince him that she was his sister and what she was doing there. She hadn't seen him since they were little kids, although he was only two years older. When he finally believed her, they stood leaning on the buggy and talking about Charley's plans. She voiced her concerns and worries about Charley getting caught. Animated and excited about Charley possibly making a big "score," Bert dismissed her apprehension.

"I'm sick of stayin' here on this place, slopping hogs and chopping corn," he said. "I got me some greenbacks saved up. I'll throw in with you guys and we'll do a little horsetradin'. When Charley gets here, I'll collect my time, and we'll go travelin'." He fairly boiled over with enthusiasm.

"What if we get caught?" she fretted again.

"Don't you worry, little sister. If they try to send us up again, we'll get out. I got ways. Me and Charley know that joint at Anamosa pretty well. Ain't no way they can hold us."

Florence drove back to town, anxious and fearful that things had just gotten worse, with Bert buying in.

The second morning, a bright and sunny June day, she heard a knock at the door of the rooming house. As the housekeeper opened the door, Florence, relieved and excited, hurried down the stairs. Instead of Charley, a pair of tall, stern-looking men stood on the stoop.

"Is your name Florence Mecum?" one of the men asked. Terrified, forgetting her married name, Florence could only nod slowly. "The sister of one Charley Mecum?" She nodded again.

"We're from the Rock Island police department. Joe Green, down at the livery, tells us that you left a team and buggy there yesterday. That right?" Again, Florence nodded.

"Did you know that rig belongs to a fella over in Iowa, at Marion?" She just stared at them, mute.

"I'm sorry, but you're going to have to come with us. There's a sheriff's deputy from Iowa waiting at the station house." Numb, she gathered up her few possessions and followed them.

"Florry, what am I going to do with you?" The magistrate looked at her sadly. "I see you've pled guilty to horse stealing. Here you are, only seventeen years old, and a woman at that. And you tell me there's a little girl waiting for you over in Nebraska?" Florence nodded.

She stood in the Linn County courtroom in Marion, Iowa. Behind the high bench sat a gloomy, white haired man. Florid jowls and drooping eyes gave him the mournful look of a scolded beagle.

"We are not accustomed to seeing a woman standing here," the judge went on, "especially one as young as you. Our criminal system isn't well prepared for women. Do you hear what I'm saying?" She slowly nodded again, hoping that he was saying he was going to go easy on her.

"But my hands are tied. The law is the law. I have to punish you for what you did, even though I think your brother should be ashamed of himself, getting you into this."

She hung her head, wishing she could tell the judge what she thought of her sonovabitch brother for giving her up.

"The only place we have for you to serve a prison term is the reformatory over in Anamosa," the judge said. "It's not going to be nice for you. You could be there all alone. Like I said, we don't have many women go through here."

In spite of his protestations on the "unnatural occurrence" of imprisoning a woman, the judge sentenced Florence to eighteen months in the women's "department" at Anamosa. Because of her youth and gender and for the sake of her daughter, the judge said, in a burst of chivalry, he would keep the information about her arrest and incarceration out of the record and the newspapers. "Your little girl will never know her mother was a convict," he scolded. "I hope no court ever sees your face again."

In 1872, the citizens of Anamosa, Iowa, had donated fifteen acres of land within the city limits, plus sixty-one acres of pastureland nearby for a new state prison. One of the reasons the site was chosen by the State of Iowa was the location of three nearby quarries that supplied enough high quality limestone to fulfill all the state's demands for the construction of public buildings. The quarries kept the inmates busy and tired enough not to cause trouble. The first inmates were admitted in 1873. In 1907, a new by-law changed the institution from a penitentiary to a reformatory for first time offenders.

Starting in 1900, the prison adopted a Grade System or a designation of different privilege levels. Prisoners were divided into first, second and third grades. One and two grades wore clothes in respectable gray instead of black and white prison stripes, and ate together in the dining hall. Third grade prisoners, those being disciplined, wore stripes and ate alone in their cells. The prisoners were controlled by their desire to gain higher grade levels, and the system aided in maintaining discipline.

In 1886, an area for women was walled off, with its own yard and entrance, but no opening or access to the rest of the prison. By 1917, a total of only fifteen females had ever served time at Anamosa, fewer than one per year. The rare woman incarcerated there found herself isolated and friendless. Male and female prisoners didn't mix. With no prison-mates, good behavior was easy for Florence, and lonely, solitary meals, in her "respectable" gray dress, her only option. Only once during her sentence did she have company, a thirty-five year old prostitute who confided that she had picked the pocket of one of her customers. Prostitution did not engender a prison sentence, but theft did. In six months she was gone, and Florence was alone again. Even though Charley served his sentence just beyond her wall, she never saw him during her entire prison stay.

Boredom became her worst enemy. She walked in the ten by twenty foot exercise yard just outside her cell when the weather allowed. Day-to-day chores of kitchen and laundry work that helped keep the male prisoners busy on their side of the prison, she easily completed in less than an hour a day. From the men's side of the prison guards brought three frugal meals a day, cold by the time they arrived. Warned by the prison warden to keep their distance from female prisoners, the guards did not chat with her, or pass on news she might have missed because she couldn't read. Two taciturn, stern-faced older women took turns at day and night shifts as prison matrons, but they provided no companionship for the girl.

Wild with boredom, Florence asked for extra chores. Finally the matrons complied by giving her the task of sewing: hemming sheets and other bedding for the men's division, mending prison uniforms and other tasks that she performed meticulously with small, even hand-stitching. Her perfect work eventually brought her a reward: a Singer sewing machine. It was treadle-powered and sewed a lock stitch, so much better and faster than hand sewing.

Day after day, her routine didn't change. Later, she remembered those months at Anamosa as the loneliest time in her life. In return for good behavior, her sentence was shortened to one year. When she walked out of the prison, she vowed she would never see the inside of such a place again. She started making her way back to Nebraska. Two months later, Bert broke Charley out of prison.

Bert was the first Mecum to bear the trademark "Mecum upper lip," inherited from his father Joe, and his front teeth were so crooked they were "on edge," twisted sideways, according to one of his rap sheets. From the time he was a little kid, Bert had been a loner. He later said he ran away from home in 1900 to "fend for himself." Fending meant thievery. Etta Belle and Joe were still living together as a family at the time–the year that Bert's youngest brother Clifford was born. Bert didn't limit himself to Iowa in exploring the criminal life. He came back to Joe and Etta Belle from time-to-time, usually to hide out, but he didn't stay long. He ranged in wider circles, visiting towns up and down the Mississippi and practicing his burglary and thievery skills. Twice, his extreme youth served him when authorities caught him and held him in county jails for short terms. Each time he used aliases, cannily insisting that he was an orphan and there were no parents for the officials to contact. By the age of thirteen, he was in prison in Jefferson City, Missouri, under an alias, serving two years for burglary.

The Missouri State Penitentiary was initially built in 1835, when state legislators decided that the new industry would help the struggling small town of Jefferson City. Over the years, the prison grew like misshapen mushroom without adequate planning or design. By 1888 the hodgepodge of buildings had been declared the largest prison in the world. In that era, no provision was made for separating juvenile offenders from the general prison population. Young offenders, to protect them from seasoned and hardened inmates, were usually given suspended sentences after a brief stay in city or county jails and sent home to their parents. In Bert's case, at thirteen it was obvious that he was approaching incorrigible status, and he continued to maintain to authorities that he had no parents to go home to. By getting into trouble in Missouri with a prior criminal record, he condemned himself to the facilities in Jefferson City. The prison, in addition to being the largest in the world, was also the most violent. Time Magazine eventually called the prison the "bloodiest forty-seven acres in America."

Bert's stay in the prison had been one of terror and training. With thousands of inmates crowded into tight quarters, stabbings and assaults were common, and screams in the night became commonplace. Because of his slight build and his youth, Bert was the target of sexual assaults and bullying. By the time he was released at age fifteen, Bert was a hardened, committed criminal, robbed of any childhood innocence he might have had. He migrated back to Iowa, and within six months he was arrested again. The authorities sentenced him to two years at the Iowa Penitentiary at Anamosa. There, a year later, Bert and Charley had their reunion. It wasn't until after his release that Anamosa became a "reformatory," reserved for first-time offenders.

After he left Anamosa Bert drifted through Mississippi river towns in Iowa and Illinois. Temptation to use his well-honed criminal skills presented itself frequently, but Bert was in the mood for a change from prison. He needed to find a way to try the straight life for awhile. Under various aliases, he took temporary work to survive, and finally, during the summer of 1907, he found a job working for a farmer in Fulton, Illinois, the little town just across the river from Clinton, Iowa. He used the alias "Conroy Wilson," a combination of the name of a small Iowa town where he had lived briefly, and his grandmother Mary Ann's second married name. He remained at the farm for three years, from 1907 through 1910, the longest period of time in his life he had stayed out of trouble and out of prison.

When Charley and Florence didn't show up at the farm with the horses and buggies, Bert realized that they'd been caught. After Florence's visit, he'd been unable to contain his excitement and anticipation, and he foolishly notified the farmer that he was quitting and left the farm. Now he was at loose ends, but the pull of easy money and thrills had been revived. For a few months he drifted from town to town, restless and eager for action. Being illiterate had its definite drawbacks–he couldn't write letters to Charley, and Charley couldn't have replied anyway. But he could send telegrams, because the telegraph operator typed whatever Bert told him, and the receiver on Charley's end read the message to him. At Anamosa, inmates were allowed to respond to telegrams. After he established that Charley was indeed back at Anamosa, Bert sent telegrams every so often telling Charley where he was and how to get in touch. He didn't dare go to the prison for visits because he didn't want to show his face to the guards and the warden, some of whom had been there during his last stay. He couldn't put anything in the telegrams that he didn't want the warden to see, so he tried to use codes to suggest that they stage a break-out. His codes didn't work, or at least Charley didn't appear to understand because he didn't react. Bert had learned to use that new-fangled contraption called the telephone, but that had its shortcomings too. A caller had to shout to be heard on the other end, and everybody within two blocks on his end heard his conversation. That wouldn't be good for Charley, inside the prison.

When Charley had been in jail in Anamosa for nine months, he received earthshaking news. Anamosa had become a reformatory, and since he was not a first-time offender, he would be transferred to the Iowa State Penitentiary at Fort Madison. When he and Bert had been thrown into Anamosa's general population of hardened criminals, the two teenagers as a team had managed to fend off the worst sexual attacks and physical brutality. After Bert had been discharged, Charley faced six months without an ally. It had been a terrible ordeal, one that still haunted his dreams. The prison at Waupun in Wisconsin, where he'd landed a few months after leaving Anamosa, had also been a penitentiary, but by then Charley was nineteen and nearly as hard and mean as the rest of the inmates, better able to protect himself. Still, he could not face the idea of three years in Fort Madison. From Anamosa, he sent a telegram to Bert, asking him to come to the prison to talk to Charley about their "sick uncle."

CHAPTER 9

Anamosa - 1911

"Bert, I gotta get outta here!" Charley was desperate. "I just heard they're going to send me to the Big House at Fort Madison. They don't keep guys here for more than one stay. They found out I'd been in here before, and about those other deals I was into before, up in Wisconsin. I can't go to the Pen. You know what the State Pen does to a guy."

Bert nodded, his expression grim. "I been thinkin' on this since last fall when I found out you was in here," he told his brother. "It'll be easy, with everthin' you and me know about this place. I'll do some more thinkin', and get ready."

"Well, think on it fast," Charley said. "They're gonna move me in a month."

"I'll be back in a week or so," Bert told him.

Two weeks later, on Monday evening, August 7th, 1911, Bert came into Anamosa on the evening train. He registered at a little local hotel under his real name, Bert Mecum. He had no suitcase, but the clerk didn't seem to find that strange. Bert wasn't worried about being identified as Charley's brother, because Charley was serving his term under the alias "Charles Smitch."

He walked the half mile up to the prison and told the guard at the gate he needed to see Charley. "I'm his lawyer," he said. "He's got a dyin' uncle that's gonna be leavin' him some property." Bert had shaved and dressed in a cheap but clean business suit. He wore a white paper collar over his wrinkled shirt and a golf cap sat on his straight black hair. The guard at the gate was not suspicious. He called another guard, and told him to escort Bert into the visitor's room. Charley was brought in. His heart lurched with excitement when he saw his brother waiting for him.

"It's about god-damn time you got here," he blustered at Bert in a loud whisper. "I was startin' to think you wasn't comin." Charley wore the black and white stripes of a Grade 3 inmate, indicating that he had committed some infraction to the rules and was being disciplined. He worked every day but Sunday in the lime quarry west of town. The inmates were walked the two miles out to the quarry each morning, where they dug rock with picks and shovels all day long and then were marched back to the prison before dark.

"I think maybe I got an idea," Bert told Charley. "A guy was tellin' me last week that up in Canada, a town called Winnipeg, the law has set aside part of town for people that don't necessarily follow the law, if you know what I mean. The guy said that if you lay low, the cops kind of ignore what goes on, like the fancy ladies and the guys that like to go see 'em. If we can get across the border we'll be fixed."

"Okay, here's what I been figurin'," Charley told Bert.

The place to stage the breakout, he said, was the wild, rough country along the two-mile track out to the quarry. "We can get rid of all but one guard by getting me sent back to the prison. I've seen 'em bring a prisoner back for one reason or another in the daytime, and it's always just one guard that brings him back. You can use the lawyer story again to get me sent back," Charley told Bert. Along the track were a number of remote sites that they could use to spring Charley. The two were familiar with the whole area. In addition to spending many months of their lives within the walls of the prison and walking back and forth to work at the quarry, they had lived, many years before with Joe and Etta Belle and the rest of their brood, in an area across the creek called "Strawberry Hill." The house they had rented was still there.

Bert decided that Friday, the 11th of August would be the big day. He would get weapons in Cedar Rapids, two .44s for each of them, he bragged expansively.

"God damn, Bert! .44 Colts cost fifteen or twenty dollars apiece," Charley said.

"I know some guys," Bert responded. "Don't you worry, I'll get 'em. We gotta make sure to do this right."

Bert would bring clothes for Charley and the equipment needed to tie and gag the guard. "Here's how it'll go down," Bert told his brother.

"I'll come in Thursday and stay over at the hotel. I'll rent a rig and drive out along that track that goes out to the quarry where you guys walk to work. I'll find a place to set this operation up. In the mornin' I'll rent the rig again and drive along the tracks just when you guys are goin' to the quarry," he said. "When you see me, you'll know I've got it all set up. If I'm not there, then you'll know we have to wait a day or two."

Bert said that he would rent a second rig and have it waiting at the other livery stable, in case the first horse was tired and to confuse any pursuers. If they tied up the guard and gagged him properly, he wouldn't be able to sound the alarm for several hours, after they were long gone. The pair agreed that the plan would work, and said goodbye in a state of high anticipation.

Following the plan, Bert was back in Anamosa on Thursday evening. This time he registered at the hotel as "Wilson"–again using his grandmother's married name. Lucky for him there was a different clerk at the desk. The other guy would surely have recognized him from Monday night and realized he was using an alias. He had covered a lot of ground in that short time. He'd still had some of the money from his job with the farmer, and in Cedar Rapids he'd managed to find a pair of .44 Smith and Wesson pistols for ten bucks apiece. They were nickel plated and looked big enough to scare the shit out of anybody he pointed them at. He might never have to fire them. He had some civilian clothes for Charley in a little canvas tote, and some rope and a blanket that they might need to subdue the guard. Also in the tote, which the newspapers later called a "telescope," was another revolver for Charley. Bert had been forced to economize and buy a .38 for five bucks, instead of the second pair of 44s he'd promised. It would do; it looked like serious business, and Charley probably wouldn't have to use it anyway.

Bert left the equipment and guns under the bed in his room and walked down the street from the hotel to the Henrickson Livery. He rented a horse and buggy, chatting amiably with the attendant, even though his heart pounded with excitement. Keeping out of sight behind the buggy, he waited until the work detail passed on its way from the quarry back to the prison. Then he drove out along the railroad tracks, back and forth along the road from the prison to the quarry that paralleled the tracks, looking for the best site to stage Charley's escape. It took Bert a couple of hours to get familiar with the terrain, but he was finally satisfied with a spot where he could wait concealed behind a big boulder, right near the embankment where the train tracks crossed the Wapsi river. He could conceal the horse and buggy under the railroad trestle. Just as he got back to the hotel, a cloudburst rain started. "That's good," he thought. "There won't be any tracks left." The rain was over by morning.

Rising early on Friday morning, Bert grabbed a quick breakfast in the hotel dining room, and walked down to the same livery stable to get a horse and buggy. The attendant thought it a bit strange that he seemed nervous and impatient when he'd been so relaxed the night before. Bert urged the man to hurry with hitching the horse he wanted. "God damn," he thought to himself. "I gotta get out there before those guys do." He was afraid the work detail would pass beyond where he could get the prearranged signal to Charley. Finally the attendant extended the reins. Bert leaped into the buggy and sped out of town toward the prison. He met the prison gang walking toward the quarry, and crossed the railroad tracks right in front of them. A guard noticed him but didn't recognize him from his visits to the prison. Charley also saw him, and knew the escape was on track.

Bert went back to town and stopped in front of another livery stable–the Dunlap–and ordered another team and buggy. He told the livery attendant that he would pick it up in a few hours. At around 8:30 A.M, he walked into the Hines grocery store and called the prison warden's office. "I'm Smitch's attorney," he told the warden. "Charley has just inherited some money from an uncle who died, and I need to talk to him about what to do with it." He said he had come in on the 7:45 passenger train from Cedar Rapids, and he wanted to return on the 10:00, so he needed to see Charley as soon as possible.

Sensing nothing out of order, the warden told Bert he thought he could have Charley at the prison and ready for an interview in about forty five minutes. The warden sent a messenger out to the quarry to have Charley brought back to the prison. The roads were a muddy mess because of the rain the night before, and it took the messenger's horse twenty minutes to slog through two miles of mud out to the quarry. Behind the hotel, holding the rented rig, Bert waited until he saw the messenger going along the track toward the quarry. He knew his brother would soon be walking back to the prison with a single guard.

Agitated and nervous, Bert drove to the spot he had picked the night before. He eased the horse and buggy down the embankment and tied it under the railroad trestle. He climbed up the embankment and squatted down behind the big boulder, breathing hard. He guessed it might take fifteen minutes or so before Charley and the guard came walking from the quarry.

The country surrounding Bert's hiding place about a mile from Anamosa Prison was wild and lonely, laced with steep ravines filled with clumps of brush which were nearly impassable, rugged hills, rocky ledges, weed grown valleys, heavy cornfields, and occasionally, deserted buildings. A sparsely traveled trail ran alongside, then crossed the railroad tracks a short distance away, a "public highway," navigable only by horse or on foot. Boulders, brush and a curve in the trail concealed the ambush site from the Anderson homestead, a residence and a mill several hundred yards away. Bert waited, fidgeting, not daring to chance revealing himself by looking up the muddy road toward the quarry. The messenger came riding by, back to the prison. Bert ducked his head, and still he waited. Minutes passed. At last, he heard the sound of voices approaching.

As Charley and Guard Alan Hamaker came to the spot just across the trestle bridge on the Wapsipinicon River, Bert crouched behind a big boulder with the two .44 pistols. He worried that he was not very well hidden, and as it turned out, he was right. Hamaker saw him, and even worse, recognized him from his visit to the prison two weeks before. The guard knew instantly that he was in serious trouble. Bert rose to full height and aimed both of the huge pistols at the guard. "Put up your hands. I just want your prisoner. I don't want to hurt you unless I have to."

The young guard made the mistake of trying to be a hero. He fumbled with the revolver that he carried on his belt. Bert fired one shot, which went wild and nicked Charley in the soft tissue between the thumb and forefinger of his left hand. He howled in protest. The distraction gave Hamaker time to pull his revolver and fire off a shot at Bert. The bullet missed. Bert fired again, and the bullet hit Hamaker in the abdomen. The guard fell to the ground, unconscious. Charley, his hand gushing blood, jumped on him and wrenched the pistol from his hand.

"You stupid sonovabitch! You shot me!" he screamed at Bert.

"Shut up, god-damn it! You know damn well I didn't mean to," Bert grated back. "Change your clothes while I cover him." Charley stripped off his black and white prison garb and grabbed the "telescope" suitcase, pulling on the civilian clothes he found there. He started to put the prison clothes, now splattered with his own blood, into the suitcase. "No!" Bert yelled. "We'll ditch those somewhere."

"Okay, now what do we do?" Charley demanded of his younger brother.

"I've got a rope in the buggy," Bert replied. "Help me drag him down the bank." While the guard lay unconscious on the muddy ground, Bert tied his hands. Nursing his wounded hand, Charley helped Bert drag the critically wounded man down the thirty foot embankment, past the horse and buggy and several yards into the woods along the creek. The guard slowly regained consciousness.

Bert and Charley were starting to feel euphoric and powerful. "I told you I'd get even for that day you reported me to the warden," Charley exulted to the guard. The hapless Hamaker had been responsible for Charley's demotion weeks ago to Grade 3 inmate. Now he could get back at the guard.

Bert gloated to Hamaker, "I aimed to kill you. It's lucky for you I aimed too low. If you hadn't grabbed your gun I wouldn't have shot you."

Charley, his wounded hand making him clumsy, attempted to apply a gag. As he stuffed a handkerchief into the guard's mouth, Hamaker thrust his tongue forward and closed his teeth part way, so the gag couldn't go fully into his mouth. With the pain from the damaged hand distracting him, Charley didn't notice. He tried to secure the gag with another handkerchief, but botched tying the knot, leaving it too loose to be effective. He tied a blindfold over the guard's eyes. Then the pair untied the badly wounded guard's hands, stood him up and forced his arms into an awkward embrace around a large tree, pressing him tightly against the rough bark. They tied his hands together on the opposite side of the tree, and then wrapped the rope around and around the tree and the man, mummy style. Finished, they told him in the most threatening tones that they were leaving, and if they heard any noise from him, they'd come back and kill him. Even after they were in the buggy, several hundred yards away, they stopped and shouted back at him to be quiet. It didn't occur to them that shouting at the wounded man might attract attention they didn't want.

Tied to the tree, Allan Hamaker fought to remain conscious. Closing his eyes behind the blindfold, he tried to guess when the convicts had actually left the scene. Time passed, his pain making it seem like hours, and he heard nothing. Maybe they were gone. He felt himself growing weaker, and knew he was probably bleeding to death. He rubbed his face against the rough bark of the tree, scraping skin and flesh but gradually working loose the cloth that bound the gag into his mouth. He relaxed his clenched jaw and with his tongue pushed out the handkerchief. Through strength grown from desperation, he began shouting for help. He was afraid he would lose consciousness and he knew if he did, he would die. He said silent prayers between periods of gathering strength to shout. He was beginning to give up hope of anyone hearing him when he heard two young voices, "Hey mister! Are you hurt, Mister?"

Breathing a silent prayer of thanks, Allen Hamaker called weakly, "Please! I'm shot. Please help me." He heard rustling in the brush, and then felt the blindfold being untied.

"Geez, mister, you're really bloody." The boys didn't know that most of the blood they saw had come from the wounded hand of one of the guard's attackers. Hamaker's bleeding was inside.

The boys hastily unwrapped the rope binding the wounded man to the tree and rubbed the circulation back into his arms. "Can you walk, mister? We can help you over to Anderson's place and get help."

"I can try," Hamaker replied. The boys draped the man's arms over their shoulders and half carried him the 300 yards to the Anderson homestead.

"Get help!" they shouted as they approached the house. "We got a shot man here!"

Mr. Anderson emerged from the mill adjacent to the house and saw the guard's pasty face and the bullet wound leaking blood. Alarmed, he took charge. "Please," Hamaker got out, as Anderson drew the wounded man's arm over his stocky shoulders, "Telephone the prison and tell the warden that Charles Smitch is loose. His brother shot me."

Anderson helped Hamaker into the house and laid him on a bed. He picked up the telephone and alerted the prison that a prisoner had escaped. Then he ran out to his barn and hitched up a team and wagon. With the help of the two boys and his wife, he loaded Hamaker into the wagon and tried to make him comfortable. He drove as quickly as he could, trying to avoid causing the guard additional pain, to the only medical facility available, a small hospital that the community called "The Sanitarium," which was run by a nursing order of Catholic nuns.

Iowa's abundance of telephones served the critically wounded Hamaker well. The supervisor at the Sanitarium called a doctor in Cedar Rapids, twenty miles to the west, and told him that he was needed in Anamosa. Hamaker could not be moved to Cedar Rapids without endangered his life further. "I'm sorry to tell you, sir, that there are no trains coming this way any time soon, and the roads are too muddy for an automobile to bring you here. You'll have to come by horse and buggy."

Dr. Crawford spit out an oath. "What else can go wrong for this poor fellow?" he lamented. A specialist in surgery, Dr. Crawford visited at the Anamosa Sanitarium on a regular basis. "With this mud, it'll take me several hours, but I'll leave right now," he shouted into the primitive telephone.

After one o'clock in the afternoon, more than five hours after Hamaker was shot, the mud-splattered doctor arrived in Anamosa to find the guard in critical condition, in great pain and barely conscious. "I have to go in after that bullet," he told the nurse.

Surgery in 1911 was a grim prospect. Louis Pasteur and Joseph Lister had established the facts on germs and bacteria twenty years before, but infection was still the greatest concern for surgeons. Sulpha drugs and penicillin were decades in the future. The only safeguard against infection for Dr. Crawford, and consequently for Allen Hamaker, were soap and water and liberal doses of carbolic acid sprayed on the wound and surrounding area—an effective disinfectant, but a skin irritant and deadly poison when ingested. Instruments were dipped in carbolic acid, and bandages were boiled or baked in an electric oven. Debris carried into the wound by the bullet—scraps of cloth from the guard's uniform, bacteria or other contaminants on his skin—presented a hazard of infection with no sure solution. Whiskey, the product used for both antiseptic and anesthesia by the western cowboy, was deemed to present its own special perils. It was used by doctors only in emergencies.

The prison warden hovered outside the door of Hamaker's room. "What's it look like, Doc?"

"Very serious. He might not make it," the doctor replied.

"Doc, I have to question him. I know it sounds hard, but I have to get his statement in writing, so we can go after these murdering bastards."

The guard passed in and out of consciousness as the warden tried to question him. He managed to say that the same man who came to the prison to visit Smitch two weeks before had shot him and escaped with Smitch in a horse and buggy. "I recognized him the minute he stepped from behind the boulder." He could barely get the words out, grimacing with every labored, shallow breath.

"Warden, I have to operate. Now!" The doctor wheeled his patient into the operating room.

Crawford's white clad nurse stood by the operating table holding a cloth mask. The administration of anesthesia for surgery was not a medical specialty in 1911, and was routinely done by nurses. It helped patients pass quickly into comfortable unconsciousness, and doctors were convinced that the process was safe. Overdose was not a serious consideration at the time; the fear that the patient might "wake up" during surgery was a bigger concern. Crawford's nurse, one of the Catholic nuns, was assigned to place the ether-soaked cloth mask over Hamaker's face.

Ether had been in use for nearly sixty years. Before its acceptance in the mid-1800s, opium and alcohol were the common methods used to anesthetize a patient for dental work or surgery. The Mayo brothers in Rochester, Minnesota, had pioneered and standardized many procedures for surgery–including anesthesia–over the past fifteen years, with great success in increasing surgical patient survival rates. They had quickly abandoned the use of chloroform years before when it caused increased patient mortality due to heart failure. Dr. Crawford had used ether successfully for several years.

At the operating table, Dr. Crawford cut away the guard's ruined uniform. His abdomen was distended and hard to the touch. Dark blood oozed from the round black hole in his belly. "It looks like his liver was hit. He's bleeding inside," the doctor told the nurse. "Get some clean cloth. There's going to be a lot of blood." He poised his scalpel over the bullet hole.

Within ten minutes, after draining and mopping several pints of dark, venous blood from Hamaker's abdominal cavity, the operating room looked like the kill-floor of an abattoir, but the doctor was relived to see that the only organ that had been perforated was the liver. The bullet had by-passed the intestines and stomach–organs that surely would have released bacteria into the blood-stream and doomed the man to fatal infection–and passing through the liver, nicked the diaphragm and lodged in the muscles of his back. The injury to his diaphragm caused the guard extreme pain and difficulty breathing. Good news was that the bleeding from the liver had subsided. The doctor made the decision to leave the bullet where it was until Hamaker had recovered and regained his strength, when, as the news accounts stated, "Xray and the knife will make [removing the bullet] a minor operation." He irrigated the abdominal cavity with water sterilized by boiling, stitched the incision and told the nurse to remove the ether mask. "He's in the hands of the Almighty now," Dr. Crawford said. "The liver is very adept at healing itself, if only he doesn't develop infection."

Reporters from both Cedar Rapids met the doctor outside the hospital, inquiring about the condition of his patient. He told them, "He has a chance to live, but at best only a fighting chance, because there are possibilities of serious complications."

While the drama played out at the Anamosa Sanitarium, uproar engulfed the prison and newspaper reporters went on high alert. All three area papers–Anamosa, Viola and Cedar Falls–published special editions covering the prison break by the suddenly notorious brothers, now the most famous in the Midwest since Frank and Jesse James. An informal posse quickly formed. As reported by the Anamosa Eureka:

> [When notice of the escape was received at the prison] the shuffle of revolvers and rifles and the rapid step of determined men sounded about the corridors of the administration building as one party after another was made up and took to the trail. The bandits had chosen their time well; heavy rains of the night before had left the roads rutted and slippery and well nigh impassable for autos, though several took to the chase. Within a few moments, telephones were jingling all over this section of the state. The grim looks and muttered words of those who followed each other into the chase indicated that the fugitives would be given scant quarter if overtaken.
>
> Prisoners were locked in their cells and every available guard was spared to engage in the manhunt, which was participated in by officers and citizens as well. It is safe to say that within a few hours fifty armed men were seeking the desperados who had gained something like an hour's head start. Sheriff Hogan and Yardmaster Taylor [from the prison] were among the first to leave. They were perhaps the closest upon the trail, and it is thought that they were within thirty minutes of the fleeing men. They were thrown off the trail by a youth whom they met along the road [who gave bad information], and pulled into Viola along

> with others, about two hours behind Mecum and "Smitch." In the meantime, telegrams were written and sent to every nearby town. Deputy Bean took his bicycle and raced to the train station where he caught the westbound train to Marion and Cedar Rapids. Other deputies [and] peace officers joined the manhunt, which lasted all day and is still in progress. The numbers grew as the day progressed, and during the afternoon fully two hundred men and boys were engaged in the exciting chase.

The posse following Bert and Charley picked up their trail at the site of the incident, and were soon puzzled by their meandering path. Pulling out from under the trestle in the buggy, with Bert driving, the pair headed west, cross-country toward Viola, a little hamlet five miles west of Anamosa. Charley's hand, wrapped in a corner of the blanket, had stopped bleeding and he realized it was only a flesh wound that would soon heal. He was pretty sure he'd still be able use the hand to wield the .38 that Bert had given him, if necessary. Now he also had Hamaker's police issue pistol, another .38.

According to the Anamosa Eureka, the Mecums traced and re-traced their path several times.

> "They crossed Buffalo creek and followed the Stone City road, then headed northwest on the Ridge Road. At the Hart place, they turned south, crossed the "Wapsie" at the Matsell Bridge and approached Viola from the west. They stopped and talked to people along the way. Fortunately for them, the households did not have telephones and hadn't heard about the jail break. They stopped at a house near Viola that afternoon and inquired at length about trains. At the Taylor farm, also near Viola, they stopped and asked for a bandage for Smitch's hand. Just before they reached Viola, they stopped at another farmhouse and asked the time of day. When they were asked if they were trying to make the Cedar Rapids train, they replied "yes" and drove rapidly away.

In spite of all the publicity and 200 men and boys in the woods looking for them, their luck held. The people they encountered in their aimless flight knew nothing about them, but by now, the horse pulling the buggy through the muddy rutted roads was exhausted.

What Bert had considered careful planning was in shambles. To the pursuing posse, their route seemed to be unplanned and disjointed. They were seen by an unsuspecting mailman driving back and forth on the road to Viola several times, seemingly undecided what direction to take. On the final trip, before they reached Viola they turned south along the railroad tracks and were seen–by passengers on the west bound twelve o'clock train–heading down a grass lane toward an old lime kiln. The posse later found the horse and buggy tied at the lime kiln, the horse exhausted and the bandits gone. In the buggy were the canvas "telescope" and a blanket that was "covered with blood." The only tracks found in the mud near the buggy were footprints leading into deep woods. They were less than five miles from where they had been nearly five hours before.

The Anamosa Eureka story continued:

> The manhunt continued with a futile attempt to discover a trail in the brush and rocks near Viola. A posse from Marion and the chief of police and several men from Cedar Rapids were on the ground. The surrounding country is certainly favorable to the bandits. Clumps of brush through which a man can hardly find a way, rugged hills and weed-grown valleys give evidence to being friendly to the purpose of the escaping men.
>
> During the afternoon the bloodhounds of Sheriff Bill Loftus were brought from Marion. The dogs failed to take the scent, and their actions proved to the onlookers that the dogs belong strictly to the Bertch show class. After a random beating of the bushes and surrounding hills that lasted through the afternoon, the approach of darkness brought no clue. The hunters returned from the chase, leaving guards at those railroad stations towards which the fugitives might be attracted in an effort to leave the country. Sheriff Hogan is in the search with a huge force of deputies. Farmers from the surrounding country have formed into a posse that is watching, or trying to watch, every foot of territory between Viola and the east Marion railroad yards.

"Charley, I know a place we can hole up 'til dark. Remember that old barn of Stout's? You and I used to play in the haymow when we lived over on Strawberry Hill." Bert said.

"Sure I remember it. What's your idea?"

"We can hole up there, then after dark we'll head north and circle around west to Marion and hop a freight in the yards."

"God damn it, Bert, that's fifteen miles. Ain't no way we're gonna make fifteen miles walkin' without gettin' caught."

"Who said anything about walkin'," Bert said grimly. "Ain't you this famous horse thief? I'm damn sure we can find transportation up north."

The pair skulked toward the barn, at the end of a long ravine shadowed by trees and brush. Behind the structure they opened a pair of shutters. As Bert crawled through the window, his collar caught on a protruding nail. His collar button snapped off and landed on the floor unnoticed. He stood up and looked around. The old barn was dimly lit in the stifling August heat and dust motes floated in the few streaks of sunlight shining through cracks in the board walls. Up a flight of wooden stairs, a haymow stretched along one side, and in one area, a few rotted boards were thrown over the hay. The area was concealed from the big front doors, where men of the posse would surely enter if they came looking for the Mecums.

"There, Charley. We'll dig some hay out of there and crawl in and then pull the hay back in around us."

Helping Bert dig the nest, Charley accidentally kicked the cover off a bin of oats positioned over the feed troughs below. Sweating and miserable with his throbbing hand, Charley ignored it. They crawled into the hay and pulled as much as they could reach back into the hole with them. Exhausted with exertion and spent adrenaline, in spite of the August heat, they both fell into a light slumber.

"Charley, wake up!" Bert was shaking him. Charley was drenched in sweat, and his hand had stiffened and hurt like hell. The chaff from the hay had worked into his collar and he itched all over. "Yeah, yeah! Whatsa matter?" he snarled.

"I think the posse's gone the other way," Bert said. "I can't hear those hounds anymore, or those guys hollerin' at each other. They probably think we're still over south in the woods."

"What're you thinkin'?"

"Well, in an hour or so it'll be dark enough to give 'em the slip. We'll take off walkin' north. We can stay away from the roads, and find a horse or a rig at one of those farms," Bert said.

"We better reload the guns," Charley told him. "We might need all our shots if we run into that posse."

Charley ejected the single empty cartridge from the guard's .38 caliber revolver into the hay. Search as he might, he couldn't find it. "Oh hell, what's the difference," he thought. They were in such deep trouble one empty cartridge wouldn't change things.

As dark approached, the pair crawled out, stuffed hay back into their makeshift bed, crept back out the barn window and struck off to the north. Once again, luck prevailed. They had walked through the deepening twilight for only about an hour and a half, when they saw a farmhouse with a hitched team and wagon tied in front of the adjacent barn. The owner must be inside at supper. They couldn't believe their luck. In spite of the quiet of the rural landscape where any barking dog could give them away, they crept up to the horses and soundlessly mounted the wagon driver's seat. They quietly walked the horses away from the farmhouse and headed west. It was ten more miles to Marion, where the extensive railroad yards and switching stations were full of freight cars. They made the trip entirely without incident in less than two hours, in spite of the darkness. On the way, they saw not one person. "They must still be lookin' over there in the woods to the south," Bert said.

Leaving the horses and wagon grazing on the right-of-way, they approached the rail yard cautiously, on the lookout for the dogs sometimes used by yard bulls. Undetected, they found an idled freight train that would soon be heading north, and clutching their weapons, they slid into an open car and moved far back into a dark corner. They had reached sanctuary a scant hour before law enforcement officials posted guards in the rail yards. They were hungry and thirsty, but euphoric. By

8:00 on Saturday morning, they were in Waterloo, sixty miles away from Marion, Iowa, heading for Shangri-la in Winnipeg.

Saturday morning, the owner of the barn, the farmer, Stout, called a reporter for the Anamosa Eureka, telling him he had clues to the men's whereabouts. He had found an empty .38 cartridge in his haymow, a shoe print outside the barn window, a collar button, loose hay on the barn floor, and a displaced feed box cover. The farmer pointed out a shallow hole in the hay beneath some lumber where he thought the men had spent their time in the barn. The newspaper reporter remained skeptical. He assessed the hole as far too small for two men. If they did spend Friday afternoon in the barn, the 200 man posse had been for many hours looking in the wrong place–in the woods–a possibility the reporter was not willing to support or report. While authorities and the media spent valuable time arguing and speculating, Bert and Charley made good their escape.

A week after the escape, the newspapers published follow-up articles. After recounting the entire incident a reporter gave this opinion:

> August 17, 1911
> The Anamosa Eureka
>
> During the past days there have been numerous stories, many clues have been given and the presence of the bandits has been reported in many localities. The stories have been as many and varied as the individuals making the reports.
>
> However the men may have eluded their pursuers, it is certain that they are well out of the country. They will probably not be recaptured until they again fall into trouble. One has done time in prison and the Bertillion records of his physical makeup are complete and accurate. When he falls into a police court where such records are kept he will be apprehended. Both are criminal in disposition, and can be depended upon to again reach the courts. Reasoning along this line, their apprehension is merely a matter of time.

The Bertillion records referred to the criminal identification system called anthropometry, developed by a French law enforcement officer and records clerk named Alphonse Bertillion. Using this system, a person was identified by body measurement of the head and body, along with individual markings–scars, tattoos–and personality characteristics. The measurements were made into a formula that would apply only to one person and would not change. Bertillion used it in 1884 to identify 241 multiple offenders, and the system was soon widely adopted by American and British police forces. The system made it possible to sift through a large number of records quickly, allowing law enforcement to narrow the pool of possible offenders. The system was later found to be flawed, and replaced with fingerprinting by the early 1900s. But parts of the system were still used far into the twentieth century on wanted posters. In Charley and Bert's era, the Bertillion system was combined with photographs for positive identification.

August 17, 1911
The Cedar Rapids Republic

Des Moines, Iowa. Governor Carroll tonight announced that a reward of $950 would be offered for Charles Smitch who escaped from the Anamosa prison last week, and his companion who shot and seriously wounded Guard Hamaker. Prison officials have [also] offered a reward, and the state will pay [another] $300 for the capture of Smitch and $500 for the capture of his companion, who is said to be Smitch's brother. Physicians who are attending Hamaker, now in a Cedar Rapids hospital, believe he will recover.

En route toward Canada, Bert and Charley had no information or knowledge of whether their victim had survived.

CHAPTER 10

Manitoba - 1912

It was a long way to Winnipeg–over 800 miles, riding in box cars halfway across Iowa, all the way across Minnesota, and more than 100 miles into Manitoba. Bert had a few dollars left, Charley had none. The brothers had to get off the trains from time to time to find water and food, but always found another train and continued their journey.

They reached Winnipeg with a primary goal of obtaining money. Charley's hand had started to heal, and as they rode, he had practiced with it, handling and mock firing Allen Hamaker's police revolver. They had accepted the fact that they were probably murderers, so their options had been significantly reduced in number. As they saw it, there was little reason to avoid resuming their criminal activities.

Winnipeg in 1911 was a haven for people like Charley and Bert. Several times the city government had changed policies on the problem of rampant prostitution. Finally, an agreement between the city council and the police department had given the police the right to regulate the profession at their discretion. The police department's solution had been to set aside several city blocks, a "segregated area" near the Canadian Pacific railroad station, to put the prostitutes and their clients into an enclave where few questions would be asked. They called it "Point Douglas," an area where, amid charges of police corruption and moral decay, brothels were ignored or even allowed. It became "the first stop for drifters, transients and out-of town criminals" coming in on trains, according the news accounts, and a "hot-bed of criminal activity which included drunkenness and general rowdy-ism." By 1910, more than fifty reported brothels operated on two parallel streets in Point Douglas. Most residents of Winnipeg seemed to prefer that the criminal element, including prostitutes, be confined to this segregated area rather than spread through town, so they looked the other way.

Trying not to draw attention to themselves, Bert and Charley roamed the Point Douglas area until they got the "lay of the land" and settled in the red light district, sleeping in an abandoned building the first night and avoiding the constables. The second night, August 19th, they broke into a house about half a mile from their lair in a more affluent neighborhood. That crime netted only a few dollars, watches and silverware. They had no way to "fence" the valuables, so they traded the loot for liquor and used the cash to buy food and rent a room in a flea bag rooming house. Two days later, August 20th, they tried another house with the same results. On August 21st, Bert told Charley, "We gotta make a bigger score, and that means usin' the guns."

"What the hell," Charley replied, thinking of the guard they had left for dead in Iowa. "We got nothin' to lose."

They identified a neighborhood grocery store that seemed to have a lot of customers. Near closing time, they sidled in the door and waited until the last customer left. Holding the clerk at gunpoint, they cleaned out the cash register, netting over $100. This was more like it.

They spent some of the loot on new clothes and a shave, paid rent on a better room, and partied for the next two days, drunkenly bragging about their exploits, claiming that they had killed a prison guard in Iowa. For all they knew, they could have been telling the truth, since they hadn't heard anything about Hamaker since leaving him tied to the tree. They continued their pattern of burglaries, hitting a house nearly every night.

Citizen complaints started to reach the police constables, alerting them that the area around Point Douglas was being subjected to an unusually high number of break-ins. Shortly after five o'clock on August 23, 1911, a woman ran to a beat cop named MacKenzie and informed him that a house had just been broken into a few blocks away. MacKenzie rushed to the Central Police Station to report the incident. The Police Dispatcher sent another constable, William Patrick Traynor, to the scene on an Indian motorcycle.

Constable Traynor was twenty-seven years old, married with three small children. He had emigrated from Ireland, and in 1905 at age twenty-one, had joined the Brandon, Manitoba, police department. Two years later, in July, 1907, he moved to the Winnipeg police force.

At the time, Winnipeg police did not allow its officers to carry firearms during a day shift, but equipped them with only a "billy-club" or truncheon. In a quote, one officer defended this policy, saying, "A revolver is a very dangerous weapon, even in the hands of an experienced man." They were about to find out just how dangerous.

Constable Traynor had been reprimanded a short time before the August 23rd Mecum incident for letting an armed suspect escape. Acting on a tip, Traynor had politely asked the suspect to accompany him to the police station for an interview. The suspect, named Copeland, pulled a gun and fired at Traynor repeatedly, while the constable pursued him more than half a mile. The suspect escaped by hiding in a railway yard. Traynor was suspended by the police department for several days, until the thief was accosted and charged with eight armed robberies in Winnipeg and a nearby town. A newspaperman later reported overhearing Traynor say "I will never be afraid of being shot at again."

As Constable Traynor interviewed the female witness to the break-in and received a description of the thieves, she sighted the Mecums on the approach to a railroad bridge over the Assiniboine River and excitedly pointed them out. Moving cautiously, Traynor approached the two and tried to arrest them. They pulled their guns and fled over the bridge toward a lumber yard. Traynor pursued them, and managed to knock Charley to the ground with his billy club before any shots were fired.

As the constable prepared to handcuff him, Bert raced back to his brother and aimed both his pistols at Traynor. "Let him go!" he shouted at Traynor. The constable hesitated, remembering the run-in with Copeland a few weeks before. "I said let him go!" Bert pulled back the hammers of both .44 pistols. "I don't want ta' shoot you, but I will if I have to."

Reluctantly, the constable threw up his hands and released Charley, who scooped up the two .38s he had dropped when Traynor clubbed him. The two men turned and ran back into the lumber yard, quickly disappearing among high stacks of sawn lumber and logs.

Constable Traynor dashed into the lumberyard office. "Do you have a firearm here?" he demanded of the owner.

Intimidated by the sight of the constable obviously in full chase mode, the owner reached into a drawer. "It only holds one shot," he quavered.

"Those bandits don't know that," said Traynor as he seized the weapon. He left the office just as Charley and Bert ran out the far side of the lumber stacks and into the street. Traynor followed, soon joined in the chase by three more constables. They pursued the men into the segregated area at a safe distance, until they saw the Mecums run into the back of a brothel owned by a madam known as Olga Ross. Two of the constables, without hesitation, dashed in the back door after the heavily armed bandits, hoping to flush them out, while Traynor went around to the front and a very young Constable Brown stayed near the back door to prevent the Mecums' escape. Inside the house, the two pursuing constables ran directly into the muzzles of four loaded hand-guns. "I guess you fellas better stop right there," Bert grinned menacingly at them. "Come on, boys. Get yourselves into the crapper there," he gestured toward the bathroom at the end of the hall.

The constables backed down the hall, watching for an opportunity to rush the bandits, but with four guns pointed at them, they had no options. Bert shoved them into the bathroom, and slammed and locked the door. He and Charley turned and raced out the front door, not expecting to see a police officer in front of the house. Constable Traynor, on guard near the front door, retreated behind a tree and fired his one shot from the borrowed pistol. He missed both targets. Bert and Charley opened fire, one round from each of the four pistols. One of the .44 slugs hit Traynor in the side, penetrated his lung and lodged in his liver.

Constables MacKenzie and Scott broke out of the bathroom and followed, just as Traynor fell. Constable MacKenzie stayed with the wounded Traynor while Constables Brown and Scott continued the pursuit of the suspects, armed only with their billy clubs and a handful of rocks. Nineteen-year-old Constable Brown pursued the pair through several yards and back lanes, throwing rocks at them and dodging the return fire, while Scott followed on the street. Later the Winnipeg newspapers reported an estimate by the constables that the Mecums fired thirty five shots during the entire episode, at least seven of which were directed at Constable Brown. With five shots in each of four pistols, they had to reload all their weapons at least once, if the count was accurate.

The pair ran onto Sutherland Avenue, the street car line, still firing over their shoulders at the pursuing police. While onlookers scattered and took cover in doorways, the Mecums leaped onto a moving electric trolley car.

The trolley cars operated with a staff of two, a motorman—or driver—and a conductor, either of whom could operate the coach. The cars had long poles on swivels mounted on the roof, at the end of which were wheels, or "trolleys," that followed overhead electric cables and conducted power to the car.

Holding their four guns on the driver, the Mecums demanded that he accelerate. At the rear of the car, the conductor saw what was happening and twisted a lever that pulled the car free from its trolleys. He jumped off as the street car screeched to a stop, followed by most of the passengers. Bert reluctantly dropped his weapons onto an empty seat and struggled to put the trolleys back on the overhead cables, cursing at the conductor, their bad luck, and Charley, who held his pistols on the driver and watched for the constables. The driver threw his handheld controller out the window and also jumped off the streetcar, followed by all the remaining passengers who weren't hiding under seats. Constable Brown arrived at a run to see the driver abandon the streetcar. Still unarmed, he bounded onto the car amid a hail of gunfire. With no way to re-start the streetcar, Bert and Charley backed off the coach still firing at the young constable. Bert grabbed the halter of a passing horse and buggy as its driver whipped his horse and tried desperately to get away. Charley leaped into the buggy and put his gun to the driver's head. Bert jumped on the other side and pressed a second pistol on the man's head, shouting that he "get us outta here or I'll shoot ya." A teenage youth dove off the streetcar and grabbed the horse's head. Charley swung his pistol and fired at the teenager. The boy ducked under the horse's neck to the other side. Charley fired at him again. The horse reared and tossed its head, trying to get away from the youth holding its bridle and the gunfire. Charley fired again and hit the horse in the neck just behind his ears. The horse dropped like a rock, exposing the youth to the bandits' gunfire. As the horse fell dead, with the bandits still firing at the boy, Constables Brown and MacKenzie jumped onto the buggy and knocked Charley unconscious with their billy clubs. Two big strapping civilians who had joined the constables during the thirty minute chase through the streets and alleys, grabbed Bert and physically subdued him. The constables then, according to the newspaper, "released their pent up tension and frustration through the liberal application of their truncheons on the heads and backs of their now captive quarry."

Meanwhile, at Olga Ross's, Constable Traynor had been given immediate first aid by a doctor who had been making a house call in the vicinity. He was taken by ambulance to a hospital, where the staff surgeon, after exploratory surgery to locate the bullet, announced to the police and the press that his condition was serious, with "little hope for his life." Police detectives had followed the ambulance and hovered outside the operating room. When the surgeon notified them of the constable's precarious condition, the detectives persuaded the doctors to allow them to hold a live line-up at his bedside, so they would have the suspects positively identified in case of his death.

Each flanked by burly constables, bleeding and bruised by the stout hickory truncheons and barely conscious, Charley and Bert now sported leg irons and manacles. The constables dragged the pair up the steps of the hospital, through the doors and down the hallway to Traynor's room, and stood them up like mannequins at his bedside. "Are these the men you tried to arrest, Constable Traynor?" asked the detective. Traynor nodded. "Did these same men open fire on numerous pursuing constables, resist arrest and attempt to murder the constables?" Again he nodded. "Are these the men who shot you?" Rallying his strength, he was able to whisper, "Yes, they're the ones." just before he lapsed into unconsciousness.

With all the bullets that flew during the gun battle and the constables having no arms, the newspapers marveled, "It is nearly unbelievable that only one person, Constable Traynor, was hit."

During interrogation and later through their attorney, Bert and Charley took credit. "We could have shot them all, if we'd really intended to kill anyone. We was just trying to scare them into lettin' us go," Bert told the Winnipeg Free Press. "That kid cop [Constable Brown] was just too brave to kill. There's sure no yellow in him." The "kid cop" was only two years younger than Bert.

According to the Iowa newspapers that received dispatches from Winnipeg shortly after the Mecums were in custody, Bert and Charley had shown very bad judgment by crossing the border into Canada and not staying out of trouble. Commented one reporter for the Anamosa Eureka:

> "There is little regret in Iowa that through the insistence of the Dominion police, the Mecums will not be surrendered to Iowa law enforcement. It is recognized that the Canadian courts of justice will deal far more summarily with them than would be possible in the local courts. It is also recognized that the Canadian prisons are of a sort that make the Iowa institutions seem like parlors of delight."

The prisoners were taken to the local station house, where, in Canada, the authorities had the legal right to inflict "Third Degree" questioning. The Third Degree referred to a ritual of the Freemason Society used to illustrate that right overcomes wrong. In police terms, it was a harsh and grueling process of extracting information or a confession. The Canadian police had virtually no limits on the methods that they could use.

The constables separated Charley and Bert into interrogation rooms close enough to hear what was going on next door. Bert remained arrogant and defiant, but Charley, according to police dispatches, seemed "nervous" and the constables decided that he would be the easiest to break. They needed a full confession. At first Charley refused to answer questions, so the constables started to take turns on him with their police batons. Each time they paused, they asked him again, "What is your name? Where are you from? What are you doing in Canada? Which one of you shot Constable Traynor?"

Eventually, badly beaten, Charley confessed to the jail break in Iowa; that they had shot a guard at Anamosa; and that Bert, not he, had shot the constable. Taken to the hospital, a week later he had recovered enough to walk, and the pair landed in a local jail. The charges would be attempted murder or murder, depending on the outcome of Traynor's wounds. Charley was booked as "Frank Jones" and Bert became "Harry Kelley."

On September 13, 1911, about three weeks later, the bullet still lodged in his liver, Constable Traynor was released from the hospital, in frail condition but healthy enough to save Bert and Charley from a murder charge. During the trial of the Mecums, he suffered a relapse and was unable to attend the trial. He returned to work on October 30, nearly ten weeks after the shooting.

In the provincial jail in Winnipeg, waiting for trial, Bert and Charley continued to be incorrigible. Before the days of "prisoners' rights" jails were a grim place. Confined to six by eight foot cells, taking their meals in the cells, and using "night jars" for sanitation, the Mecums were confined for two months with only one respite, the day in mid-September when they were taken to the courthouse for arraignment.

For the arraignment hearing, Bert and Charley were clean-shaven and feeling expansive in the face of the volumes of media attention they were getting. The newspaper stated, "The men are not in the least disturbed over the predicament in which they find themselves. They both apparently enjoy the notoriety gained."

The pair was neatly dressed in the clothes they had bought with proceeds from their burglaries, and a news article stated, "Although neither man wore a collar, they both looked spruce." Disposable paper or celluloid collars could be obtained by the dozen for just pennies, and were considered a requirement for the well-dressed man.

Charley and Bert had spent much of their ample "leisure" time in jail concocting ways to baffle or mislead their captors. One of their scams was convincing officials and the public that they knew sign language. The reporter for the Winnipeg Tribune, eager to add spice to his story and to the Mecum mystique, reported:

> "The deep cunning of the men is apparent. They chatted gaily while waiting for the proceedings to begin. When they realized an officer of the court was near enough to hear what they were talking about, they at once stopped and a few seconds later held a rapid conversation on their fingers. Both are experts at the deaf and dumb language, judging from the speed with which they can converse. At the conclusion of one of the talks, Kelley [Bert's alias] laughed silently and heartily."

In reality, Bert and Charley were experts at nothing beyond cons, lies and criminal activity. They had been inventing elaborate stories for prostitutes and petty criminals and concocting lies since childhood, and each success encouraged them to broaden the scope of their fantasies. Fanning their fingers at each other pretending to converse seemed like an entertaining game. They would soon find that their new hosts in the Canadian penal system were not amused nor impressed by their scams, and had limited tolerance.

While in the provincial jail, belligerent and bellicose to the last, Bert bragged to anyone who would listen that there was no jail on the continent (meaning Canada or the U.S.) that could hold him for six years. (That seems to have been the sentence he expected.) "Convicts have to go out of the prison for work, and the guards are always armed. There is bound to come one second when the guards will not be watching us, while I am always watching them. One smash over the head with a rock or a shovel is all that's necessary. With the guard gone, the rest will be easy."

In an interview with the press, Bert claimed to have had a good education. The newsman asked, "Why couldn't you put it to better use than being an outlaw?"

Bert replied, "Your legislatures make laws which permit the selling of whiskey, and very bad whiskey at that. Someone has to be found to drink it and there you are."

The brothers told the court that they could get $6,000 to pay an attorney, and unlimited funds to fight any conviction. This must have been partially true – although the amount was almost surely a lie – because when they went to trial a month later, they had retained an attorney or had been appointed one by the court. At the arraignment, they pled guilty to all charges except the two attempted murder charges.

After their arraignment, and before returning to the provincial jail, they complained bitterly about not being together and nearly begged to be able to share a cell. Their pleas were ignored. They also coaxed the court to tell them where they would be sent if they were convicted. Again they were ignored, and by this time they had no counsel to apprise them of the options. They were bound over for the "assizes," the Canadian equivalent of district court, to await trial on the attempted murder charges three weeks later.

News coverage during the few weeks between the arraignment and the trial in October reported outrageous behavior from the two. They may have been protesting the refusal to allow them to share a jail cell and not being told where their sentences would be served after the trial, but whatever the cause, they continued to dig themselves into deeper and deeper troubles. Headlines in the Anamosa Eureka read, "Mecums Act Like Wild Men."

It seems that the two decided to cause as much trouble as possible. During one incident, Charley was allowed out of his cell for exercise in the corridor. When he saw his brother in the corridor, Bert began to destroy his bed and bedding, although just how he accomplished it with bare hands was not discussed in the paper. When Charley saw what was happening, he began to dismantle the walls of the corridor, "tearing down the iron strips that form one side of the corridor where he exercises." The guards, armed again with the trusty billy clubs, rushed in and beat the pair senseless. Until the date of the trial, three weeks later, Bert slept on the ruins of his bedding, and both convicts were handcuffed day and night. They were promised much more severe actions if their disruptive behavior continued.

On October 25th, with Constable Traynor still among the living, the brothers finally came to trial in the Canadian district court, the Assizes, on the charge of attempted murder. The Winnipeg Free Press wrote that when they were brought into the courthouse, extra precautions were taken.

> "The rule is usually to send a single officer to bring a prisoner from the jail to the courthouse. In the case of the Mecums, three officers were sent. They were brought into the courthouse heavily chained and each handcuffed to a 250-pound constable. At the foot of the stairway leading up to the courtroom, Kelley [Bert] decided to balk. He refused to mount the stairs. Considerable time was spent with the billies getting him in the spirit of moving."

When Charley and Bert were put on the stand, they once again took control and waxed eloquent and expansive. According to the newspaper, "They were remarkably frank in their statements, and told a story of the chase and their capture." The only excuse they offered was alcohol, and said they didn't recognize the constables as police officers. The constables involved in the chase had been in full uniform, including high bowler hats with huge police shields and lower lip straps that could indicate nothing but a drum major or a policeman.

When it was Charley's turn to take the stand, he freely admitted being committed to the Anamosa prison in Iowa a year before for stealing a horse and buggy. He also admitted the escape where the prison guard, Allen Hamaker, was shot, but invented a fantastic story about a third brother named "Mike" being the person who broke him out of prison. He denied that Bert had anything to do with it. He also testified that he himself was involved in the "scuffle" where Hamaker was shot, but that Hamaker had shot himself. "I was holding the guard by the wrist to keep him from shooting me," he asserted. "His gun was pressed against his stomach, and when he tried to get away from me, he accidentally pulled the trigger and shot himself," he insisted.

When Bert took the stand, he insisted that he had never served time in Canada or in Illinois. This might have been the truth, because his known prison terms were served in Iowa and Missouri. Charley had been in jail in Waupun, Wisconsin, before being committed to Anamosa the second time.

The trial lasted only one day. The jury returned a guilty verdict on each attempted murder charge in less than thirty minutes. The next day, Friday, October 27th, 1911, the judge sentenced them to ten years on each attempted murder charge, to be served concurrently. Their tenure in the provincial jail in Winnipeg was over. They were taken to Stony Mountain federal penitentiary north of Winnipeg to start their sentences.

When they pled guilty to the burglary charges after their initial arraignment in September, they had been promised that with good behavior, those charges would be withdrawn. The news reports stated, "The burglary charges were kept on the police docket from week to week pending the behavior of the prisoners in the penitentiary. It was understood that if their conduct was good the charges would be withdrawn." In spite of another heavy sentence hanging over them, the two continued to be incorrigible and defied the rules of the institution.

In November, they appeared back in Winnipeg for their final sentencing for the re-instituted burglary charges. The two appeared in the "dock," the Canadian equivalent of the witness stand, in baggy grey uniforms with crimson stripes and rough prison boots. Pasty-faced from months of confinement, their heads shaven against head lice, they wore double handcuffs and leg shackles, and were handcuffed to each other, with a prison guard on each side. The judge was succinct in his sentencing. "There is no point in lecturing you," he said. "You knew the consequences of your behavior and you chose the disruptions anyway." The judge instituted the five year sentences for burglary that had been held in abeyance, and added two years for bad behavior. With the previous convictions for attempted murder, they each would serve seventeen years.

Charley and Bert, according to news accounts, were "extremely surprised at the heaviness of the sentence." Apparently they thought they could behave any way they chose with no consequences, but the Canadian authorities intended to show them the realities.

Back in his cell, defiant to the end, Bert loudly claimed, "Them sonsabitches said that all charges would be dropped if we pleaded guilty. Well, they ain't seen nothin' yet!"

When the Mecums returned to Stony Mountain prison, they launched a campaign of rebellion. They took every opportunity to disrupt the everyday operation of the prison–destroying property, starting fights and fires and refusing orders–which led to stays in the infirmary healing up from encounters with the billy clubs, and days of solitary confinement in shackles and handcuffs.

Less than four months later, the Canadian authorities had had enough. On the fifth of March, 1912, seven months after the original jail-break in Iowa, the pair was ordered moved to the federal prison at Kingston, Ontario.

CHAPTER 11

Ontario - 1913

In Winnipeg, the guards from Stony Mountain loaded Charley and Bert, dressed in their rough Canadian prison garb, into a horse drawn paddy wagon and hauled them to the railway station. Taking pride in now being known as "the Brothers Mecum," the pair shuffled aboard a passenger train for the fifteen hundred mile trip to Kingston, Ontario, home of the toughest prison in Canada. They, along with two convicts named George Brown and Arthur Bonner, made the trip adorned with manacles and leg irons, shackled to each other and to their seats with sturdy chains. Brown and Bonner had joined them in some of their escapades at Stony Mountain and had earned the same punishment.

The first leg of the trip, from Winnipeg to Thunder Bay, Ontario, a distance of 420 miles, took three days and nights. Winter had not loosed its grip on central Canada, and deep black forests fortified with massive snowdrifts and frozen lakes dominated the landscape. Moose, wildlife and drifts on the tracks slowed their progress. Depots and settlements lay many miles apart as the train skirted the northern rims of Lake Superior and Lake Huron on its way to Toronto. Charley and Bert had not earned the comforts other passengers enjoyed. In wooden cars heated with pot bellied, coal and wood-burning heaters, they couldn't move from their seats, so they alternately froze and roasted, depending upon the frequency with which the guards stoked the fires. Not allowed to de-train, they again had to use buckets for sanitary needs while wearing the handcuffs and leg-irons. The guards brought cold meals from vendors at the depots where the train stopped along the way. With no provisions for sleeping comfortably, they dozed, slumped in their chains, upright on unpadded bench seats.

"Charley! Wake up!" Bert shook Charley from his doze. "We're gonna be in a place called Toronto soon," he whispered. I heard them guards talkin'. We need to get up a little surprise for the bulls."

Bert outlined his plans. "When we pull into the station and stop, I'll be watchin' for my chance. You just take your cue from me. I'm gonna kill me a bull before I die."

They didn't tell Brown or Bonner their plans.

The train pulled into Toronto, less than 200 miles from their destination, on March 12th. After over a week on the train without incident, the guards had begun to relax their vigilance, and to neglect chaining the prisoners to their seats immediately after toilet breaks. In Toronto it took nearly an hour for crews to load fuel and water, and allow the passengers to partake of a noon meal in the depot. The guards allowed the prisoners to use the toilet buckets and again handed them cold sandwiches. Bert waited until the train began to slowly pull out of the depot to begin the final leg to the journey to Kingston. He watched the guards closely. In a careless moment, the guards walked too close to the convicts while they were still unchained from their seats. He gave Charley the signal.

Springing to his feet, Bert swung the heavy manacles and hit one guard on the side of his head. As he fell at the convict's feet, Bert clutched both ends of a loop in the chain and managed to slip it over the guard's head. Twisting the chain, he heaved himself backward in an attempt to garrote the man. At the same time, Charley attacked the other guard and knocked him to the floor, then leaping astride his back, hammered his head with the manacles.

According to accounts in the Toronto newspapers, "The two brothers nearly murdered their guards with their fists and shackles." Passengers in an adjoining car saw the attack and began to scream for help. The conductor pulled the emergency brake cable and the train screeched to a stop. Hearing the commotion, three Toronto police officers who had stood on the platform watching the train leave leaped aboard with their two-foot hickory truncheons. Again, Bert and Charley were beaten senseless.

"The officers [showed] no restraint, and a short time later the convicts lay bleeding on the floor of the car," stated the newspapers.

They were still a full day's travel from the Kingston prison. Charley and Bert were left lying on the floor of the car the entire way, and given no food or water. At the prison, still in full restraints, they were thrown into the back of a freight wagon and hauled to the infirmary, where they were shackled to hospital beds.

A month later, they were barely out of the infirmary when, on April 15, the passenger ship Titanic went down in the Atlantic Ocean. They knew or cared nothing of the event. They had healed from the beating on the train and were once again relocated to prison cells.

Two weeks later, on April 29th' 1912, they resumed their rebellion. The Mecums, along with Brown and Bonner, were housed in the same cell block, an area called the "Prison of Isolation," where the most desperate criminals were kept away from the general prison population. This was a strategic error on the part of the prison administration. Instead of solitary confinement, the arrangement allowed these four men, who had been operating in concert since the incarceration in Manitoba, to put their heads together and plan anew.

Bert was no sooner locked into his cell than he started planning his next jail break. First he needed a weapon. Through the open bars of the cells it was easy for him to talk to his cohorts and develop his plan. A guard named Davis, and a "keeper" named Madden usually stayed at their station outside the door of the cellblock, a room divided into cells, each occupied by one inmate. Convict workers, or "Trustees," came in from time to time to haul out the night wastes and mop the corridors. Bert began to befriend one trustee, Vincent McNeil, who he thought could be trusted because of his constant profane complaining while he performed his janitorial services.

Finally, Bert decided they were ready. On the chosen day, the only person present inside the ward besides the four prisoners was the trustee McNeil, who was sweeping between the cells. At eleven o'clock that morning, Bert got his attention.

"Vince, come here. I gotta talk to you."

The trustee, looking cautiously around to see who might be watching, sidled nearer to Bert's cell. "Whaddaya want, Mecum?"

Bert, speaking in low confidential tones, told him, "I got a surefire plan to get us outta here. For a little help I'd let you in on it."

Wary, the man replied ,"I don't know about that, Mecum. I don't have it so bad, and I'd hate to be where you are."

"Come on, Vince. Don'tcha wanta get out of this shit detail and breathe some free air? This plan of mine will work. All I need is for you to do a couple things."

"What kinda things?" McNeil was cagey.

Bert brought his hand from behind his back and extended it through the bars. He held an eighteen inch piece of angle iron. "I did a little repair work on my bed, and I had this piece left over," he smirked. "All you need to do is get Davis in here, give him a little tap on the head, and then open the cells for us."

McNeil thought about it briefly. "At least I won't have to dump your honey buckets anymore," he conceded. He turned and walked to the door of the ward, holding the angle iron behind him. "Davis!" he called through the door. "Come in here. I got a problem." He stood where he would be concealed when the door swung into the corridor.

As Davis stepped through, McNeil pushed the door shut and brought the iron bar crashing down on the man's head, inflicting a critical wound and dropping him like a stone. McNeil retrieved the guard's keys, seized the man's ankles and dragged him into an empty cell.

Fueled by adrenaline, he unlocked the cell doors of the Mecums, Brown and Bonner. Outside the door, the ward-keeper Madden heard suspicious sounds from the cell block and stepped into the ward to check on Davis. The five convicts overpowered him and dragged him into the cell where Davis was still unconscious. Charley and Bert stripped Davis and Madden of their uniforms, doffed their prison clothes and tried on the uniforms. Six months of prison, innumerable beatings and days of restricted diets in two prisons had turned the Mecums thin and haggard, and the shaven heads looked skeletal. The guards' uniforms hung like rags on their bony frames, a dead giveaway. They passed the uniforms to Bonner and Brown. The fit convinced Bert, in complete charge of the operation, that the guards outside would not take notice. He and Charley threw their prison clothes back on.

The convicts searched the guards and ransacked the ward for weapons, but guards for the most dangerous felons carried only billy clubs–no firearms or other weapons that could fall into the hands of the prisoners. They were still searching when the prison surgeon, a doctor named Phelan, knocked on the door to the ward, the usual procedure for an outsider to be admitted. Alarmed, Bert motioned for the others to get out of sight. Bonner, dressed in the guard Davis' uniform, opened the door into the corridor. As soon as the unsuspecting doctor entered, Bonner closed and locked the door. With the iron bar as a weapon, Bert ordered Phelan to undress. The doctor complied without argument. He was a much smaller man than the two burly guards, so Charley dressed in his civilian clothes. Bert locked the doctor in the cell with the two guards.

The five convicts, two of them dressed in guards' uniforms, one in the doctor's civilian clothes and two still in their prison garb, walked out of the cell block toward the front gate, posing as a normal prison detail. The tower guard paid no attention to them. As they approached the towering steel front gate, one of the convicts dressed as a guard signaled the gatekeeper, named Rutherford, to open the gates. A later prison dispatch read: "Seeing the brass buttons [on the bogus guards' uniforms], and assuming this was an ordinary party of guards bringing convicts for some special work detail, the gatekeeper complied." With his attention focused on the opening gates, Rutherford didn't see Bonner come up behind him. The convict struck him viciously on the head with the steel bed leg, knocking him unconscious. Bert armed himself with the man's truncheon. The second gatekeeper was occupied inside the gatehouse with a drayman bringing supplies into the prison and didn't see what had happened.

The prisoners passed out of the opened gate, crossed the street in front of the prison and started past the warden's residence, still trying to appear as a work detail. Right in front of the warden's house, the group met an assistant farm director named McCarthy, a man responsible for managing prisoners who worked on the prison farm. With one glance, the director realized something was wrong, and he called out a challenge. Bonner delivered a brutal blow to the director's head with the iron bar, knocking him unconscious. The five prisoners ran across the warden's yard and scaled a low rock wall that enclosed a small field.

By now, an alarm had been sounded, and several officers from the prison were in hot pursuit of the escaping convicts. The dispatch stated, "They very foolishly headed toward the prison quarry and were spotted by a prison scout." The scout called out a challenge, and facing the scout's loaded pistol, Brown surrendered and was brought back to the prison. Bert was the next to be apprehended, hiding in a shed, and was brought in by a single armed guard. Bonner and the trustee, McNeil, made for a bridge that would be the first leg of a short twenty mile trip to the U.S border and New York State. Two prison guards had reached the bridge first, and waited with weapons drawn when Bonner emerged from the bulrushes beside the river and prepared to swim across. The dispatch related that "Hennessy sent a few bullets near his head and he signaled submission at once." Another guard got the drop on McNeil up on the bridge, and he surrendered. The two were marched back to the prison.

Charley was the last to be captured. By this time, "all the boys in the neighborhood" had joined the prison guards in their search. A guard named O'Driscoll, conducting a house to house search, was advised of a man hiding in a nearby barn. The guard shouted at Charley to "come out with your hands up. You are surrounded," and Charley complied.

A prison dispatch sent by the warden of Kingston Prison to the Inspector of Penitentiaries in Ottawa the next day noted that the entire escape lasted only a little over two hours. He commended his officers, saying, "The spirit and determination manifested by the officers in pursuit excelled anything I have ever witnessed on such occasions. Few horses were available, and only one borrowed automobile, but bicycles and legs were used to best advantage so that the hiding places were covered by the pursuers before the refugees could escape into the bush."

The escaping convicts left a trail of four injured guards. The farm instructor, McCarthy and the first guard to be felled, Davis, were seriously injured. Fortunately the two survived, but suffered from the head injuries for the rest of their lives. Charley and Bert once again avoided murder charges.

His career embarrassed and threatened by the prison break, the prison warden set out to contain and subdue the "Brothers Mecum." In his dispatch to the Inspector of Penitentiaries, he stated, "The five chief actors in the affair are in the punishment cells and will be presented with Oregon Boots tomorrow."

The "Oregon Boot," or Gardner Shackle as it was properly known, was patented in 1866 by the Oregon State Penitentiary Warden, J.C. Gardner, just seven years after Oregon's Statehood. Each shackle consisted of a heavy iron band that locked around one ankle. The band was supported by another iron ring and braces which attached to the heel of a boot. The shackle weighed between five and twenty-eight pounds, depending upon the severity of the restraint required for the particular prisoner. It extended as far as eight inches below the instep, causing the inmate to have to lift the heavy device vertically to take a step, putting the weight on the knee and hip joint. The "Boot" was placed on one leg only, keeping the inmate off balance and depriving him of agility. Adding insult to injury, prisoners were put to work manufacturing the shackles.

At the time the Oregon Boot was invented, the Oregon Territorial Prison and later the State Penitentiary had an enormous escape problem. Warden Gardner and subsequent wardens felt that the inmate population could not be adequately controlled without using the Gardner Shackle on each and every prisoner. Wearing the shackle for extended periods of time caused physical damage to hips, knees and ankles. Inmates would be bedridden for weeks at a time in extreme pain. The Gardner Shackle became known as a man-killer to the prisoners who wore them. Most states and countries began to curtail the use of the "Boot" in the early 1900s, deeming it overly cruel punishment. But for severe discipline problems it was still used occasionally through the 1930s.

When Gardner was replaced as the warden of the Oregon Penitentiary, he obtained a court order preventing the use of the shackle without payment to him. That same year, the Oregon Legislature authorized paying his royalties.

The Canadian prisons were not constrained by Gardner's patent or the U.S. court order requiring that he be paid royalties. They used the Oregon Boot regularly to control incorrigible prisoners, and Charley and Bert, along with their three cronies, certainly fit that description. From the day that they became acquainted with the Boot, Charley and Bert made no more newspaper headlines. They were put to work in the prison bakery, and required to endure their new footwear day and night. Some incorrigible inmates were able to have the burden lifted gradually to the minimum five pounds and finally have it taken off completely as a reward for good behavior and a new attitude. Charley and Bert's history of violence and treachery and the trail of wounded men they left behind kept the Boot in their lives and on their ankles for the next five years. The pain they endured from the Shackle put to shame the beatings they had earned early in their criminal careers. They were virtually crippled, but still required to do their regular work and chores while dragging and lifting the heavy shackle. The device apparently accomplished what innumerable beatings, bread and water diet, and all other resources couldn't: It finally brought an end to their rebellion and defiance.

CHAPTER 12

Anamosa II - 1917

On October 15, 1917, just five and half years after the prison break in Kingston, Ontario – six years into their seventeen year sentence – Charley and Bert were deported back to the U.S. At Windsor, Ontario, across the border from Detroit, they were turned over to Jones County, Iowa, officials. They faced sentencing for the prison break from Anamosa prison and the shooting of the guard, Allen Hamaker. They still had long prison terms ahead. That June, four months before their extradition, their mother, Etta Belle, had passed away at the age of fifty-four in Colorado. Lillie and Gus Fiske had left in 1912 for Montana to take up a homestead, and Florence had married Walt Sheldon, a man more than twenty years her senior. With the help of authorities in Nebraska, she had finally wrested custody of her four-year-old daughter Lola away from Etta Belle, who had been determined to keep the little girl, and had succeeded for more than two years.

By the time Bert and Charley returned to Iowa, Anamosa prison had again begun accepting long term prisoners. Bert pled guilty to the charge of Assisting a Prisoner to Escape, and was sentenced to Anamosa for an indefinite term. He was also ordered to pay for the costs of his extradition and prosecution, $1500. In lieu of paying the fine, he served five years. He was discharged from Anamosa and was sent to Fort Madison Penitentiary for Assault with the Intent to do Great Bodily Harm, for the shooting of Allan Hamaker. He served nine months, and was discharged on August 2, 1923. He was thirty-one years old and had spent nearly his entire life from the age of twelve in reformatories or prison.

Ten months later he was arrested in Hennepin County, Minnesota, near Minneapolis, for burglary and sentenced to two years. This time he was alone. A year later, in August, 1925, he applied for parole and was denied. He applied again in February, 1926, and was again denied. The second denial was reversed, and he was discharged from the Hennepin County Jail the next day. Bert was never heard from again, in spite of a concerted effort in 1934 to find him when one of his sisters became ill. He is buried somewhere in the Midwest, undoubtedly in an unmarked grave, or with a marker bearing another of his many aliases, and thus forever lost to posterity.

While Bert continued his life of crime, Charley worked on abandoning his lawless ways. He also was sentenced to five years for the prison escape and through good behavior, served only three years at Anamosa. He was discharged two years before Bert, on April first, 1920, because he wasn't the one who had shot both Traynor and Hamaker. He turned thirty-three a month later. Although he had been in prison almost continuously since the age of seventeen, Charley was never in trouble again.

Of all the officers and guards Bert and Charley left wounded and bleeding in their wake, the most tragic was Constable Traynor, the Winnipeg municipal policeman. With the bullet still in his liver, he was unable to return to his motorcycle beat on the streets, a job he loved, and was assigned to Acting Desk Sergeant duties at the Central Police Station.

In late 1911, the Winnipeg Police Commission submitted a recommendation that Constables Traynor and Brown be awarded the King's Police Medal for bravery. In 1912, both officers were selected for the medal and the announcement was officially published on January 1, 1913, in the London Gazette's New Year's Honors List. Arrangements were made for the medals to be awarded on May 28 at the Annual Police Inspection and Parade in Winnipeg.

In early May, 1913, still in fragile health twenty months after the shooting, Constable Traynor contracted typhoid fever. On May 11, weakened by his injuries, Traynor died at 4:20 in the afternoon. He was 29 years old, and left a widow and three small children, aged five, three and one year old.

During the annual Police Inspection and Parade, Constables Traynor — posthumously — and Brown were awarded the Kings Police Medal for bravery. Traynor's was the first such medal awarded in Canada.

Traynor's widow was left in extreme financial distress. She received a lump sum of $550 from the police commission for her husband's years of service: $250 for the first year and $60 for each additional year. The record shows that the widow made numerous appeals to the Police Commission for further compensation, but they were denied as there "was no provision for such situations." Traynor had joined the IOOF (Independent Order of Odd Fellows) in 1906, and had been a member for seven years. At the time, police officers, firemen and other such public servants did not have unions or associations to protect their families in time of crisis, so they joined benevolent organizations like IOOF to provide extra safety and insurance against injury and death. The Traynors received a total of $29.10 from the IOOF while the constable was convalescing, and an additional $21.10 to pay for his nursing care. The Lodge paid another $113.25 in sick benefits, funeral expenses and financial aid after his death. The IOOF continued to pay Mrs. Traynor $50 per year in widow's benefits and "other financial relief" in later years, according to Lodge records. All told, the widow collected less than $1000 for medical bills and the loss of her husband and her children's father, while Charley and Bert lived on, Bert for at least thirteen years and Charley, nearly fifty.

The shooting of Constable Traynor brought about significant changes in the Winnipeg Police Department, and consequently in other municipalities in the province. In 1917, the members of the police department formed their own union, and affiliated with the Winnipeg Trades and Labor Council to handle situations like that of Traynor and his survivors.

After the shooting, there rose such a public outcry from the citizens of Winnipeg concerning the vulnerability of the city to armed gunmen from the United States, that the Police Commission held a special meeting two days after the incident to discuss the matter of arming the police. At the meeting, the Police Commission authorized Acting Chief Newton to purchase Colt automatic police revolvers for use by day-shift personnel.

Since the Mecum brothers had been holed up in the "segregated area," as the red-light district was known, and had in fact shot Constable Traynor from the front of one of the brothels, the shooting also contributed to the cleanup of the area. A few days after the shooting, the Winnipeg Tribune stated that "the shooting of Constable Traynor may mean the end of Winnipeg's Red Light District. Many of the women are preparing to seek new pastures where there will not be so much notoriety."

Subsequent articles followed the progress made by the City and the police department. The officers objected to the size and weight of the initial purchase of weapons, and they were gradually replaced with smaller and lighter revolvers. The "shady ladies" gradually left town, and those few who remained were greatly restricted. "The women now remaining can be relied on by the police to run fairly decent houses, as such decency goes," stated the Tribune.

In 1995, Traynor's youngest son presented his father's medal for bravery to the Winnipeg Police Museum for permanent display.

Without a doubt, the entire law enforcement organization of Winnipeg was deeply impacted by the brief tenure of the Mecums. It was miraculous that, in spite of the viciousness of the brothers' attacks on the guards and police officers, as well as all the on-lookers put in jeopardy during the unrestrained gunfire in the streets of Winnipeg, no one was killed, except for the indirect death of Traynor nearly two years after the gunshot wound. Alan Hamaker, the Iowa prison guard, carried his injuries throughout his life, and the guards who received the business end of the steel bar in Kingston didn't escape without long term effects. But Charley and Bert were extraordinarily lucky that they didn't kill any of the people they attacked, since the Canadian authorities had no compunction about inflicting maximum punishment when necessary to subdue or rid society of a hardened criminal.

CHAPTER 13

Nebraska - 1930

The man mounted the wooden board steps at the back door of the house in Lincoln, Nebraska, and knocked. The door opened and a little boy about ten years old stood there. The man asked, "Is your dad home?"

"Pa!" the boy called over his shoulder. "Man wants ta see you."

Walt Sheldon, followed by his wife Florence, came through the kitchen to the back door. The man was standing with his back to the door, surveying the yard.

"Help you?" Walt Sheldon spoke with a flat midwestern accent. Florence peered over his shoulder at the man.

The man turned. "Don'tcha know me, Florry? I'm Charley." Florence stared at him, stunned. "Guess it's been quite awhile," he said. Enormously pregnant, she pushed back the three small children staring at him from behind her skirts.

She recovered her voice. "About twenty years! The last time I saw you was in '11." Her wary face seemed to say, *"What're you doing here?"* "This here's my husband, Walt Sheldon," she said, reluctant to act friendly to the man who had cost her a year in prison.

Charley dipped his chin at Walt. "I come to buy a team and wagon, if you got one for sale. I hear you deal in horses and rigs sometimes."

"Mostly I move houses," Walt said, "but I do have one team I could let you have, and a little wagon. Come on in." Unabashed by Florence's reserve, Charley followed Walt into the house. On a chair in the small sitting room sat a beautiful young woman just out of her teens, a school book in her lap. She was dark-skinned and petite, with black hair and deep brown eyes. The sight of her stopped Charley in his tracks, and he stared at her wordlessly. "This here's Lola. You remember her, don'tcha?"

Florence was right on his heels. "She wasn't even two the last time you seen her, at Ma's homestead over at Greeley."

At a loss for words, Charley nodded to the girl and sat down at the table with Walt. He positioned himself in a way that allowed him to sneak glances at Lola. "How you gonna get this rig 500 miles back to Chicago, Charley?" Walt asked. "Ain't there horses for sale closer?"

"I can put it in a boxcar," Charley answered. "Nebrasky's always had better horses, and I thought I might look up some family."

The men discussed purchase arrangements for a few minutes, then Florence said, "Lola, go get me a pail of water and I'll make us some coffee."

Lola rose and walked into the kitchen. As she picked up the empty water pail, Charley sprang to his feet. "I'll help you," he said. He took the pail and followed her out the door.

Lola told the story later. *"He followed me out to the well and pumped the water for me. I just took one look at him and thought to myself, 'What a man!' From then on, I never looked at anybody else."* The fact that Charley was her uncle, twenty-one years older and already married made absolutely no difference to Lola. She saw what she wanted, and in true Mecum fashion, simply took it.

Lola had been a baby the last time Charley saw her. She was now a woman–beautiful, willful and obstinate. At nearly twenty-two, she was almost four years late graduating from high school. Still, it was quite an accomplishment, when none of her aunts and uncles on the Mecum side except Elnora and Clifford had ever learned to read or write. She was in her last year of high school in 1929, when she met her uncle Charley.

In April, 1920, after his final discharge from Anamosa, Charley was thirty-three, penniless and untrained for any job but stealing and prison baking. While he'd been in prison a World War had killed nine million people, another half a million people in the U.S. had died of the "Spanish Flu," and women had won the right to vote. The Panama Canal had opened, Lawrence of Arabia led a revolt against the Turks, communism had taken over Russia and the Chicago Black Sox had scandalized baseball. Thirteen years of Prohibition took root the year he was discharged from Anamosa. But Charley was not interested in the big money he could earn as a criminal. He was ready to find another way to live.

Hoping for a new start, he left Iowa and headed for Chicago. Because of his prison experience as a baker, he landed a job with the Calumet Baking Powder Company, and within a few months, he met and married a redhead named Mabel Howe. She was twenty two years old, ten years younger than Charley, and had a somewhat questionable history. This was the first serious relationship with a woman that Charley had ever had. For the next nine years, Charley's life was somewhat serene, except for one unfortunate problem. As a result of working in bakeries and inhaling baking ingredients for nearly fifteen years, Charley had developed "Baker's Consumption," a lung disease similar to tuberculosis that afflicted as many as seventy-five percent of all volume bakers. Early in 1929, Charley found a new job, working for Miller Rubber Company, whose main product at the time was automobile tires.

When he arrived at Florence's house in Lincoln, Charley had not divulged to anyone, not even Mabel, the details of a private meeting he'd had just weeks before, with a shift foreman from the Miller Rubber Company in Chicago.

"Charley, I need to see you in my office." Charley's heart gave an uneasy bump. After nearly ten years of freedom, he still shrank from close encounters with people in charge. As he walked warily into the office, the foreman shook his hand and greeted him cordially, then closed the door.

"Charley, you've been here–how long? A year or so?"

"Guess so," Charley mumbled in reply.

"And you've put in your shifts, kept your nose clean, and don't spend a lot of time talking about yourself, right?"

"Not much to say." Charley was beginning to believe this was not going to be a reprimand of any kind. In fact, the guy was downright friendly.

"That's what leads me to believe you're a guy who can be trusted to be careful talking about his work. Am I right?"

"I'd say so, right."

"We're looking for some good men to help us get out a new product we're working on. How do you think you might like sales, and maybe owning your own business?"

"Sales? I ain't never sold nothing. And I don't have the money to be startin' no business."

"Oh, we'd help you with that. And this product would sell itself."

"What kind of a new product are you talkin' about?" Skeptical, Charley thought this was starting to sound too good to be true.

"Before I get into that, I need to know that you can keep this conversation to yourself. I'm giving you the chance to get in on the ground floor of something that could make you a lot of money, but I don't want other people, like the competition, to hear about it just yet."

"I don't talk much about nothin'. You know that," Charley responded.

"Yes, I guess I do," said the foreman. He gave Charley a penetrating look and began the briefing, telling Charley what he needed to know.

Charley's employer, the Miller Rubber Company, based in Akron, Ohio, needed sales representatives, who would also act as delivery men. Backed by the company, the salesmen would be self-employed, buying inventory from the company on credit and paying after the product was sold. For public scrutiny, the job description would be "working among the farmers" selling and repairing tires. He would have a regular route, traveling and serving customers door to door. It would be up to him to make the contacts and deliver the products.

The reality of the proposal was this: In the 1920s, the Miller Rubber Company had begun manufacturing latex condoms. The pesky little problem was that the product was illegal in the United States.

In 1873, the Comstock Law made it illegal to advertise or ship through the U.S. Mail any kind of birth control. In spite of the law, rubber companies surreptitiously researched new products to fulfill demand that they knew existed. By 1929 condoms were vastly improved by the invention of very thin and very strong latex, and the demand exploded. For the most part, local law enforcement officials simply ignored the burgeoning industry. But when the product was shipped through the U.S. mail it became a federal offense and legal action had to be taken. The Miller Rubber Company's distribution solution was to hire traveling salesmen, who could deliver the product in person. It turned out to be such a lucrative market–one of very few left when the country entered the Great Depression–that fourteen other companies soon joined in manufacturing, and by the mid-1930s these fifteen makers were producing 1.5 million condoms per day. The only way to buy them was from the door-to-door salesmen or the outlets, like pharmacy back rooms, that they supplied.

With Charley's prison record, the idea of taking on the sales of an illegal product was dicey at best. The irresistible element for Charley was that he could make as much as $50 per day–over $1500 per month–an amount that would become a veritable fortune in the 1930s. Condoms were expensive, partly because they were illegal, but the alternatives–unwanted children and STDs–were even more expensive.

It didn't take long for Charley to make the decision, and begin telling his friends and acquaintances–and his wife–a carefully memorized story: "I work for Miller Rubber Company in tires. I have my own business, working amongst the farmers."

After his first visit to buy the horses and wagon, Charley returned to Lincoln in September, soon after Lola's senior year in high school started. He brought a gift. Excited, she ripped the paper off of a new leather school bag. "You need somethin' nice to carry your books," he told her. "You're the first person in this family to get schoolin'."

Lola ran her hand over the smooth leather case, a rich Oxblood color. The shoulder strap and brass buckles were elegant. "Oh, Charley, I do believe this is the nicest thing I ever had," she cooed. Florence stood behind her, a tense disapproving grimace on her face.

"How'd you like to go see a picture show?" Charley grinned at Lola. "Charlie Chaplin's showin' at the Paramount." She nodded and with a big smile, jumped to her feet.

Florence glowered at Lola. "Don't you have some schoolwork or somethin'?"

"Nope. Finished it," Lola was already reaching for her jacket. She hurried out the door and stopped in her tracks. Sitting at the curb was a shiny black Ford car.

"Charley! Is that yours?"

Charley's grin was full of self-satisfaction. "It's one of them new ones, a Model A," he bragged.

"How can you afford somethin' like that?" Lola said.

"I have my own business," he said, his voice taking on the flat tone of a memorized speech. "I work amongst the farmers."

"What is it you do amongst the farmers?" She was intensely curious.

"I sell and fix tires and such. Come on; we don't wanna be late." He hurried her into the car, before she could ask any more questions.

After the movie, Charley drove her home and when he saw Florence waiting at the door, clearly hopping mad, he quickly drove away. "Just what do you think you're doin'?" Florence sputtered at Lola. "You're makin' a scandal, a downright scandal!"

"What's so bad about Charley takin' me to the show, mama?"

"He's your uncle, an' I seen you flappin' your eyelids at him. That's just plain disgustin'. Ain't you got no sense at all?"

"It's all in your mind, ma. He treats me good, and besides, he's making lots of money. I like havin' fun."

"Some things is more important than big money and havin' fun, Lola. You're gonna be sorry about all this when the old hen comes home to roost," Florence said, as Lola closed her bedroom door with a slam.

After Christmas, early in 1930, Charley was again in Lincoln, calling at Florence and Walt Sheldon's home. This time, he arrived in a Model T Ford. "Come on, Lola. Wanna learn how to drive?" With Charley at the wheel, they left the city limits of Lincoln and drove alongside snow-covered fields at a break-neck speed of thirty-five miles an hour. Fortunately, automobile and truck traffic had beaten a trail through the snow, so the little "Tin Lizzie" had no trouble navigating the primitive road. About fifteen miles out of town, Charley turned the car around, aimed it back toward Lincoln and shut off the engine. "Your turn," he said. He walked to the passenger's side of the car. Excited, Lola hopped out and struggled through the process of cranking the engine with a hand crank inserted below the radiator, leaping into the driver's seat and engaging the clutch. By the time they arrived back at home, she was nearly frozen, but fairly adept at handling the car. She shut it off and looked at Charley, her cheeks and her eyes glowing. "That was SO much fun!" she gushed.

"You like this little Lizzie?" he asked. She nodded eagerly.

"It's all yours. I'm goin' back to Chicago tomorrow."

"What're you talkin' about? I can't drive that good yet!"

"It just won't do to have you walkin' to school in this weather," he said. Lola was beginning to get excited. "Oh Charley, you are so good to me," she gushed. "Maybe someday I can drive it to Chicago to see you." Charley winced, thinking of Mabel waiting at home.

Inside the house, Charley tried to soothe Florence's objections. "Oh now, Florry. She's doin' a good job, gettin' her schooling. It only cost a few hundred, and I can afford it. My business is doin' real good."

Florence protested, "How's we gonna buy tires and gas for that thing? Times is gettin' tough."

He said. "No reason Lola can't have a car when she needs it. I sell tires for a livin', and gas don't cost much." He pulled a twenty dollar bill out of his pocket and handed it to Lola. "Here, this is for gas," he said. "Just don't forget to check the water and oil sometimes."

Many years later, Lola continued the story, demonstrating a capable and independent nature much like her grandmother, Etta Belle. "The next morning [after Charley left] I took my car to school. I didn't have a driver's license; I didn't have nothin'. I guess you didn't need a driver's license back in them days. Only thing Charley told me, he said, 'Don't take any side streets or you'll get stuck in the snow. Just go with the traffic and you'll be all right.' So then it went down to fourteen below zero, and you know them old Model Ts—wouldn't start when it was cold, but I had a remedy. I would jack up that hind wheel on the driver's side and check to make sure the spark was up, and tromp the ole brake down. Then I'd set the paper my lunch was wrapped in on fire under the carburetor, the car would start and I'd take off for home. I got a write-up in the school paper over it–me startin' my car with the rest of them settin' there. Lookin' back, I don't know why I didn't blow the car up, with that fire under the carburetor."

In the spring of 1930, at age twenty two, Lola graduated from high school. For the next two years she stayed with her parents, stepfather Walt Sheldon and mother Florence. Her mother had given birth to eight more children with Walt, and depended on Lola's help. Florence had given birth to her youngest child, Rosalie, while Lola was finishing her senior year. During those two years, Lola lived only for Charley's visits. Florence watched helplessly as the romance between her daughter and her brother flourished. They went to "picture shows," on picnics, long drives and spent a good deal of time in Florence's basement kitchen, with Charley "teaching" Lola to bake. Charley showered Lola with gifts and money, making fewer and fewer trips home to Chicago and his wife, Mabel. He began building a "route" for his product in the Iowa / Nebraska area.

In 1932, Lola, at age twenty four, found out purely by accident that Walt Sheldon was not her biological father. As she told the story, "I'd started playin' with a Ouija board, and was still pretty skeptical, but it was kinda fun."

One day, in a session with a neighbor, in order to test the veracity of the board, she queried it with a question she thought had an obvious answer. She asked the name of her father. The board spelled out "Hugh Warren."

"Well I was looking for Walt Sheldon," she said, "so I asked it again, and then again. Darn, the third time it got mad at me, so I said to the neighbor, it sure ain't telling the truth is it?

"So then I went downstairs and I told my mother about it. I said, 'Well, maybe [that Ouija board] isn't right because it told me my dad's name is Hugh Warren and that's not right. I know who my dad is.'

"She said, 'Sure you know who your dad is.' So we let it go.

"We had lunch and then I was cleaning up the table. Daddy always went in [the sitting room] to get noon markets and stuff off'n our 'lil ole radio. We didn't have a TV or nothin'. I watched Momma go in to [sit with] Daddy and I heard her tell him, 'There must be something to that weejee board that told Lola her Dad's name.'

"Now what could I think? I [lost all] faith in my mother after I confronted her. I said, 'Mama, why don't you tell me who my dad is? Have I got any brothers or sisters that I don't know about?'

"She said, 'Ain't you happy? Why don't you just leave well enough alone?' I asked her two or three times, but she took to the grave what I would like to know today, and why? Who could it hurt? I would love to have my school records fixed. I would love to put my own name on my diploma." Her high school diploma was issued to "Lola Sheldon."

The incident put resentment and a feeling of betrayal in Lola's heart, which worked into her decision to leave with Charley and Mabel a few weeks later.

In 1932, Mabel developed an illness that required extensive surgery and a long convalescence. It was a perfect opportunity for Lola to get away from her parents. Charley had bought a camping trailer that he pulled with his Model A and lived in while on his sales circuits. He "hired" Lola to go on the road with him, supposedly to help take care of Mabel during her recovery. For the next year the trio lived in the trailer and traveled all over the Midwest, mostly in Missouri, but also in Nebraska, Iowa, Minnesota and Kansas. When she left with Charley and Mabel, Lola took her youngest half-sister, two-year-old Rosalie with her, partly to placate Florence for leaving her when she so badly needed help. The little girl would be five before Lola returned her to Florence.

During those years, Lola later admitted, she started a campaign to take Charley away from Mabel. "He was just too good a man for her," she declared. "She was nothing but a hooker, and I unhooked her," a fairly typical statement for "the other woman" trying to justify her behavior. Sometime within those years, the pair made the decision to take their relationship to the next level: they started having sex. In spite of his endless supply of birth control, Charley worried about pregnancy. He knew that if anyone, including Florence or Mabel, found out about the true nature of the relationship, he would very likely be sent back to prison for incest. In 1933, Mabel went back to Chicago, but Lola stayed with Charley. Her campaign had worked, but it had dire consequences.

In early 1935, the worst thing possible happened: In spite of Charley faithfully using his product, Lola learned that she was pregnant. Suddenly the specter of prison again reared its ugly head. The couple told no one in the family about the pregnancy, they simply continued living as they had for the last three years but avoiding family. In October, 1935, in Spirit Lake, Iowa, Lola gave birth to a baby girl that she named Lulubelle. Charley was forty eight and Lola, twenty seven. The child bore Lola's maiden name, Warren.

At Christmas that year, Lola began to long for her family back in Nebraska. Although she hadn't seen them for three years, she knew that the family had by now figured out the true nature of her relationship with Charley. She persuaded Charley that if the family had not yet turned them in to the authorities, they probably never would. Taking a big chance, he agreed to drive her to Lincoln to see her parents and introduce them to the baby, Lulubelle

Lola told the story: "I had Lulubelle and I didn't know how Mama would take it. Charley and I, we'd been in Iowa and the northern states 'cause Charley worked amongst the farmers and we made good money. We come back from Minnesota after Lulubelle was born in October. It was Christmas. When we got to Mama's house, Charley says, 'I won't go in with you. I'll wait on the corner and if they won't let you in then you just forget about them.'

"So I went up to the front door and I rapped and Daddy came to the door. He let out a scream and he hollered, 'Mama, Mama, come see what I've got.' And he grabbed Lulubelle. We didn't have no big welcome–he just had his arms open, you know. That's why I can't say that I had a bad stepdad; I didn't. I never knew any other daddy. So he held Lulubelle, and that broke the ice."

For the next four years, relations between the two families progressed smoothly. Then an incident happened that caused a twenty year rift. By that time, Florence had recovered her health and taken a job with the Burlington Northern Railroad in the maintenance shop. During a visit, Lulubelle and one of Lola's half sisters got into a childish argument over a guitar. Charley and Will got into the fight, each defending his own child.

Lola told the story many years later: "The next morning we left. I told Mama before she left for work that I'd leave my address in a glass dish on top of the cupboard. I did, but never heard from her. It was just a stupid thing, but I never heard or saw nothin' from them for twenty years. My brothers and sisters grew up from little kids into men and women.

With growing boldness, Charley and Lola began to live more and more like a legitimate family. Lola said later, "In the winter Charley didn't want to fight those roads. He'd go out into an area where he knew he could get out several days a week and make enough to live on, and that's where we'd stay for the winter. Then when spring got there, we'd hit the road again to make more money."

They began presenting themselves as husband and wife, inventing a marriage ceremony in Clinton, Iowa. In 1941, their first son, Charley Mecum, Jr., was born in Muscatine, Iowa. This time the baby bore his father's surname. The six year gap in the succession of children would indicate that during that time Charley made good use of his product. As years went by with no repercussions from Mabel or Florence, he began to feel confident. The babies began to appear more frequently, three girls and three boys born after Lulubelle, between 1941 and 1950.

In 1941, Charley's business came to an abrupt end. According to Lola, gas rationing during World War II made it impossible for Charley to get enough gas to take care of his "tire business amongst the farmers." That might have been a problem, but a much bigger one was that the government, not wanting a repeat of the STD crisis of World War I when seventy percent of the American soldiers contracted sexually transmitted diseases, began issuing condoms in the soldiers' kit bags and changed the laws to allow condoms to be sold in pharmacies. This brought Charley's condom business to an abrupt end. He had to find a different job, so he went to work for the government in the war industry.

Charley worked in a bomber plant in Lincoln, Nebraska, spraying the inside of war planes with insulation and sound proofing. The job aggravated the problems he had with his lungs from the "Baker's Consumption," but he stuck with it until the job was phased out. Then he got another government job in Kansas City putting the roofing on airplane hangers. The way Lola reported it, "After he finished up in Nebraska there wasn't no more work there so the government offered to send him either to Denver or Kansas City. I remembered the dime stores here, Woolworth's and Ben Franklin, so I says, 'Let's go to Kansas City,' so that's where we went and this is where we've been." After the war, he secured a permanent job as a custodian at a local high school.

Charley, Jr., was not quite two and another boy, born in Lincoln, was 3 months old when the family moved to Kansas City. All the other children were born there, when Charley was in his fifties and sixties. "Charley died here in Kansas City, right over in Bethel," Lola said. He died in 1961 at age seventy three.

After Charley's death, with no visible means of support and no job skills, Lola hastened to the local Social Security office and applied for benefits under Charley's employment record. She was met with bitter news. Mabel had never divorced Charley and had not legally remarried, so Lola could not claim a common-law marriage or Charley's Social Security benefits. Mabel had beaten her to the draw.

Lola did, however, still have five minor children at home, and their social security payments helped her from becoming destitute. It would be more than ten years before she could draw on her own social security, and as each child reached eighteen and became ineligible for benefits, life grew harder and harder for her. Lola harbored a great deal of bitterness against Mabel, even though Mabel had spent fifteen years as Charley's legal wife before he left her for his niece. Mabel had never forsaken the Mecum name, to which she was legally entitled. Lola invented fantastic stories about Mabel having married "at least three different men without divorcing any of them," implying that she didn't have a right to Charley's

Social Security benefits. Lola's children were true believers, and she succeeded in building a bulwark of fabrications that protected them from the seedier side of the Mecum history.

Years later Lola, speaking of Mabel and the estrangement from her family, said, "She supposedly married that other guy but she always carried the name Mecum. She always went to Mama with all her sob stories and on and on. And that caused trouble for me. That's why twenty years just slipped down the toilet. Mama thought I was a naughty girl before anything even started. When Charley would take me to the show, why, that was terrible. Well, if goin' to the show was terrible, I was gonna do something really terrible. I have never confessed to too many people that I married my uncle. But then I thought 'Lola, you confess.' It don't make any difference to me anymore. Who would I hurt? Nobody but myself, because he's gone. Can't hurt him."

"The time he came to Lincoln to buy the horses, that was the first time I'd seen Charley, and I guess it wouldn't have made no difference from then on, you know what I mean. Love at first sight. Just him pumpin' a pail of water for me, and to this day–now this might be childish–but I've never seen another man like him. Courteous, considerate and on and on. In a roundabout way, I know'd he was my uncle, but when you're headstrong you don't care. That day, I'd never seen him before; he was like a stranger. I never seen another man yet that could hold a candle to him. There's no way I'd change my life. We were together thirty two years."

PART IV

GUS AND LILLIE FISKE

Lille
ca. 1930

CHAPTER 14

Montana - 1912

"Gus, me and the boys are going to Montana to homestead. You can come along if you want to." Lillie set her lips in a firm line, her chin held high and her voice defiant.

The warm Oklahoma sun shone on the sleek coats of the horses milling around the hay wagon—black, sorrel, bay and buckskin. Early March gave them mild weather, and Gus had built a string of horses to start his annual trading circuit. Lillie had moved all their household goods from the rented house where they had lived since December, into the "gypsy wagon" that sat in the yard, ready to be hooked up to the work team. Eddie, nearly eight, and Frank, age five, dashed around in a state of high anticipation, "helping" their mother pack the wagon and getting in her way.

Gus laughed. "Sure you are, Lil. What the hell brought this on?"

"I been thinkin' about it for awhile. I'm sick of people callin' us gypsies and throwin' off on us. When we come around they hide their kids like we got a disease or something. That's not good for the boys."

"Lil, we been doing this for nigh on ten years," Gus said. "You knew what this business was like when you came with me."

"I knew some of it, but there was a lot I didn't know, too."

"Like what?"

"Like you havin' an eye for the ladies," Lillie told her tall, handsome, auburn-haired husband.

"Aw, come on Lil. It was just that one time."

"Right, and if there's ever another time, you won't be seein' me and the boys again," she stated. "Anyway, we should be tryin' to set a better example for the boys than this family is doin'."

Lillie worried about the effect her brothers might have on her sons, especially Eddie, who had always looked up to Charley. She feared that if he found out the truth about Bert and Charley, he would grow up thinking their behavior was acceptable. She'd been able to keep some of the secrets hidden, like Etta Belle's conduct that ended with the permanent loss of her two youngest children, Clifford and Elnora. The boys didn't know about the time their other aunts and uncles had spent in jail. She wasn't sure how long she could keep such things from them.

"I'm takin' these boys to Montana so they can go to school and learn to be somebody besides jailbirds," she told Gus.

"Well, that's your family, not mine," Gus protested. "It ain't my fault I married into a bunch like the Mecums."

Stung, Lillie retorted, "Ain't you forgettin' about your brother Ed, the nigger killer? You namin' Eddie after him sure helps the boy figure out what's right and wrong, doesn't it."

"You sure got a burr under your blanket, don'tcha?" Gus said.

"Call it what you want," Lillie said. "I'm just lettin' you know, we ain't goin' to Minnesota this year. We're goin' to Montana, me and the boys."

Gus and Lillie's first son had been born in Carroll, Iowa, a year and a half after their marriage, and Gus named him for his oldest brother. Gus's family, the Fiskes, were a well- respected family, pillars of the community of Delavan, Illinois, except for this black sheep named Edward. By trade he was a housepainter and paper hanger. He liked alcohol and when drunk was an aggressive bully, but he also showed symptoms of being a coward. During one drunken fight in 1901, he had seized an iron poker and from behind, while his target was occupied by the fists of a cohort named Frank Wiseman, he had nearly killed a man with four vicious blows to the head. He was not arrested or prosecuted, but Wiseman was found guilty of assault.

After several more scrapes with the law for assault and other troublemaking, Ed finally committed murder. On September 2, 1905, The Delavan, Illinois, "Times" reported:

> The record of a Fair week unmarred by a disturbance of any kind was [destroyed] in the closing hours by a bloody crime. At an early hour Saturday morning, Bert Green, a colored man of Terre Haute, Indiana, was shot and killed by Ed Fiske of this city. The killing took place at the fairgrounds. The fatal shot was fired close to 1 o'clock in the morning. The victim died at the New Delavan Hotel, where he had been taken after the shooting.
>
> "Fiske was born in Delavan and has lived here most of his life. He is aged about thirty-six years and is unmarried. His family connections are all of the most respectable kind, being held in the highest esteem by all who know them, but Fiske himself has for years borne a bad reputation. He is a drinking man, and when under the influence of liquor is quarrelsome and even dangerous."

The night the murder occurred, Ed and Frank Wiseman had driven, via horse and buggy, to the nearby hamlet of San Jose to drink and buy jugs of what the newspapers referred to as "rattlesnake gargle." When they returned to Delavan about ten thirty at night, the county fair was just winding down. The pair continued drinking for the next two hours, wandering the fairgrounds and making frequent trips back to the buggy for pulls on the whiskey bottles.

Earlier in the week, Ed and Wiseman had spotted a light-skinned black man accompanied by an even lighter-skinned woman who they decided was white, running a concession stand on the midway. This offended their bigoted sensibilities.

By 1:00 A.M., Ed had reached the state of drunkenness where he was looking for trouble. He decided that he and Wiseman would go to the concession stand and "have a little fun with the coon." On the way there, they encountered a special policeman serving as a guard. Feigning congenial interest, Ed asked if he might examine the revolver the guard carried. Foolishly, the guard handed him the pistol. Ed immediately turned the gun on the guard and demanded that he hand over his uniform coat and his badge. Intimidated, the guard complied.

Ed and Wiseman approached the tent of the Greens, who were in the midst of packing up their possessions to move to another fair the next day, along with a friend named Naughten. Barging into the tent with Wiseman, Ed pretended to be a policeman there to arrest them. Neither fooled by nor afraid of the pair, Mrs. Green ordered them out of the tent. Her husband repeated the demand. Naughten got into a scuffle with Wiseman, and received a blow to the head. Seeing that their ruse was not working, Ed and Wiseman left the tent, but on the way out, Ed spitefully kicked out a couple of tent pegs, causing the tent to partially collapse on the people inside.

Green picked up a lantern, Naughten a soft drink bottle, and the wife a pistol, and the trio went outside the tent to reset the pegs. Ed stepped out from behind a tree where he had been hiding and fired one shot. It hit Green over one eye and passed through his brain. His wife fired two shots at Ed, which both missed, and she dropped to her knees to attend to her dying husband. Ed and Wiseman ran. They stopped long enough to return the guard's uniform and revolver; then Ed disappeared and Wiseman went home to bed.

Reported the Times:

> "The crime seems to have been committed in a purely wanton spirit, the victim having been quiet and inoffensive in his conduct and having furnished no known provocation. The alleged slayer, Ed Fiske, immediately disappeared, and from that day to this no clue has been discovered as to his whereabouts."

And, indeed, "Uncle Ed" was never heard from again. About six weeks after the murder, a farmer found a makeshift cave-like dwelling in a cornfield near the railroad tracks. Assumed to be the murderer's temporary hideout, it was abandoned. A later genealogy search indicated that there had been an "Edward Fiske" living in Pensacola, Florida, in 1896, nine years before the incident in Delavan, Illinois. This may or may not have been the same man, but no trace of him was found after 1905.

Ed and Gus's father, Albert, had died two years before the incident. The murder created such shame that their mother Mary put her home up for sale and moved to Chicago with her only daughter, Anna, who had married a doctor named McCabe in 1893. Later, her daughter's family, along with Mary, moved to Oregon, where Mary lived to the ripe old age of eighty seven, passing away February 25th, 1921.

By 1912, Gus and Lillie had been married and following a horse trading circuit for nine years. Gus' marriage proposal to Lillie, delivered at the front door of her rented house in Davenport, Iowa, in July, 1903, had been somewhat short of romantic. Gus had become acquainted with Lillie's brother Jay, who had served his sentence for horse stealing and decided to try becoming a horse trader. He had seen Gus as a mentor and a quick way to launch his own string. He first brought Gus around to the little house in the alley in Davenport where Lillie lived with her dad and Charley, when Lillie was sixteen. Gus, twenty six, had already established himself as a successful horse trader. He was a frequent visitor for the next year.

"I'm leavin' today, Lil. Are you coming with me or are you staying here?" Gus sat on the padded seat of his gleaming black buggy. The flashy matched sorrel fillies, freshly curried and their white blaze faces washed clean, danced impatiently. Lillie was not completely surprised by the question. Gus had been coming around daily for the past two weeks, and they'd known each other more than a year. She knew the nature of his business–that he was constantly "moving on."

"I guess I'm going with you," she responded, and went inside to pack her trunk.

When Gus Fiske entered the Mecum family by marrying Lillie, the whole family became enamored with horse trading, a profession that fitted right into their lifestyle of thievery, prevarication and skullduggery. In the late 1800s, itinerant horse traders became an integral part of the agricultural community of the Midwest, filling a role almost identical to the used car salesmen who emerged into the economy half a century later. It was more a barter system than outright sell/purchase. When asked how he put a value on his horse in a trade Gus answered, "That part is easy. Keep talking until you get a horse as good or better than the one you're trading, and the price of him to boot." Boot was the difference between the values of the horses, and Gus cleverly convinced the buyer that Gus's horse had the higher value, so cash would change hands. He'd trade for one that had been worked hard and worn down so it was thin and looked poor, and he'd give one that he'd had for awhile and had fattened up. His looked so much better that he got the price of the thin one as boot–in cash. It was the "boot" that the trader used to support himself and his family. After he fattened the new acquisition and gave it time to rest, he sold it at a profit.

Gus's outfit consisted of thirty to fifty head of horses–his "string"–and a haywagon that had twelve "stanchions" or openings, allowing the trading stock to feed directly out of the wagon. The new acquisitions he was fattening up also received oats. The horses foraged for grass along railroad and county rights-of-way, as well as numerous corn fields that bordered the roadways–out of the sight of the farmers. When set up for trading, Gus tied his mares at the stanchions around the wagon, and the rest of the string, composed mainly of bigger geldings, were content to stay around the mares and not stray, removing the need for a corral. Gus didn't often trade in mules or lactating mares, and never in stallions. He employed a man to travel with him who wore several different hats–serving as an outrider to keep the horse herd under control, a groom, a cook and myriad other responsibilities. The hired man rode a horse and before Gus's marriage, they both slept in tents. Gus himself traveled in what was called a "top buggy," a shiny black, well-maintained conveyance pulled by two young, trim, matched mares that he trained himself. He trusted them to help him present the impression of a successful and honest businessman. Perfectly matched sets of horses were uncommon and exceedingly desirable, more valuable than teams of similar horses of different colors. Owning such a pair added to his image. Gus kept himself clean shaven, well groomed and neatly dressed. A master storyteller, he loved to talk.

Gus usually wintered in Oklahoma or Arkansas, and during colder months he rented a house, warmer and more comfortable than the tents. He started his nine-month trading circuit every spring, with a string of what he called "southern chunks," short, stocky mares that were used by cotton farmers in Oklahoma and Arkansas, for breeding with donkeys to produce mules. It was a lucrative market, since mules were born sterile–unable to reproduce. Each new mule colt came from a female horse. As he proceeded northward, he began trading the mares for longer-legged and more powerful geldings, which would be traded to corn farmers in Iowa and Nebraska and loggers working in the woods of northern Minnesota and Wisconsin. Moving in increments of about twenty miles, he set up for business in what he called a "stand." After set-up, the hired man stayed with the outfit while Gus roamed the countryside in his top buggy, announcing to farmers and businessmen that he was "in the country" and ready to trade. Sometimes a stand lasted a week or more, and sometimes, if the trades ran out, they loaded up and moved another twenty miles within a couple of days. The mid-season destination, Wisconsin or Minnesota, changed from year to year. After a week or so in the woods the "outfit" started south again, trading along the way, again seeking "southern chunks," with the objective of reaching southern climes before frigid weather set in.

Roger Welsch, historian with the University of Nebraska, wrote, "When the work of the world was done with genuine horsepower and men traveled in the saddle, a sound knowledge of horseflesh was serious business. It was a ready source of entertainment, too. Working with horses every day, most men fancied themselves experts, and few could resist the challenge of a trade. Trading horses was a kind of recreation, like betting on races, and as Mark Twain said of horse races, it was a difference of opinion that made horse trades."

Wrote Welsch, A hundred years ago farmers on the Great Plains lived a life of isolation. Back then, only three or four strange faces might appear in a year, and the sight of a stranger entering the farmyard–once it was determined that he was not an immediate danger–was a rare and exciting occurrence. When the stranger was an itinerant horse trader, offering not only a social exchange but also the opportunity for a battle of wits, the possibility of financial gain, and the certainty of some horse talk, his appearance took on the importance of a first-rate social event."

And Gus Fiske did not disappoint. In addition to maintaining his image as a clean and honest businessman–and later as a family man–he was adept at methods that made his string look healthy and well trained. Those methods included doping and any number of skillful tricks, chemicals and props to conceal defects, injuries and disease in the horses he traded. At the time, these schemes were not considered felonious in the field of horse trading–they were just part of the game. The trader knew that his buyer would be employing exactly the same methods to dispose of animals that no longer served his needs. It was the duty of each party to protect himself and get the better end of whatever bargain was reached.

Gus's genial personality and gregarious nature made the bargaining part of a trade easy for him. Never in a hurry, he appeared to have unlimited time to visit and swap stories with all comers. Later in life, after his trading days were over, he could captivate an audience for hours with his colorful, hilarious, and detailed stories of more than twenty years of getting the best of an opponent in a trade. His story telling ability along with his appearance of casual affluence captured the interest of the Mecums and persuaded several to try their hands at his profession, beginning with Jay. Gus's gift of gab was especially appealing to people like the illiterate Mecums, who grew up before invention of the radio and couldn't read. Story tellers like Gus were one of their important forms of entertainment.

After Lillie joined his operation in 1903, Gus added a "gypsy wagon," which could be compared to one of the camping trailers pulled by automobiles that began to emerge in the 1920s. Driving the wagon pulled by a team of large horses, Lillie became adept at controlling the powerful animals, while Gus ranged farther afield with his top buggy and smaller mares. Kept attractively painted and in good condition, the wagon made the nomadic horse trading life more acceptable for a woman, although cooking, laundry and other housekeeping activities had to be performed out of doors, over a campfire. The wagon provided a comfortable bed, privacy, a storage place for personal possessions, and with its hard roof, protection from the weather. The wagon made Lillie feel as if she had a home of sorts. The lifestyle was hard and the work heavy for a woman just over five feet tall and weighing one hundred pounds. She had learned to hitch up a team and the tedious job of setting up and breaking camp, as well as washing clothes with lye soap in a big iron kettle over the campfire and cooking with equipment like the camp cooks on the ranches and trail drives had used.

But after following horse herds across six or seven states for nine years, and now raising two boys in a wagon, Lillie was tired of the nomadic life. Her second son, Charles Franklin, called Frank, had been born January 15, 1907, in Wichita, Kansas. Gus could read and write and she realized the importance of educating the boys.

Seeing that Lillie was determined to undertake the new venture, Gus reluctantly conceded, and the family started north toward Montana, a trip of nearly fifteen hundred miles. Before they left Oklahoma, Lillie arranged to have the family sit for a formal portrait. In that picture, the group is presented as a reasonably affluent middleclass family. Gus, approaching forty years old, wears a natty three piece suit with a fashionable thigh length jacket, soft button up boots and a silk necktie. Not yet thirty, Lillie stands behind him, dressed in a lacy high-necked white blouse, a white belt around her slim waist, and a dark skirt brushing her boot-tops. Her face is full and youthful, her long dark hair is done up in a modified Gibson style. Her dark eyes stare at the camera with a defiant expression mirrored by her determined, straight mouth. The boys are decked out in suits and ties, with knee pants and high laced shoes. Eddie, his upper lip an exact replica of his Uncle Bert Mecum, is wary, while five year old Frank seems merely interested and slightly bored. In the upcoming years, Lillie sat for at least two more formal portraits. A scant fifteen years later, her hair gray and chopped to the ear lobes, she appears thin and wrinkled, looking like her own grandmother.

After crossing the Missouri River by ferry at Omaha, Nebraska, thus avoiding the Platte, Gus headed his outfit northwest along the eastern bank of the Missouri. He realized that by taking this route they would need to cross the river again in Montana, but he still had a horse herd to disperse and there were many more homesteaders on the east side of the Missouri through South and North Dakota. These farmers constituted the potential of more trades than he might find west of the river. Anyway, they wouldn't reach Montana until some time in August, when the river was low and easier to ford.

In 1912, most of the Missouri River was a free flowing stream. Two "run of the river" dams had been constructed near Great Falls–the Black Eagle in 1891 and the Rainbow in 1910–to generate electricity, and the Hauser near Helena had gone into operation in 1907. But these did little to change the flow level of the great river. Spring run-off engorged the river in all downstream areas, cutting off travel for weeks, but by August and September, especially in years of low rainfall, the river could be forded in certain locations. The massive Fort Peck dam, which would permanently alter the flow of the river, was twenty-five years in the future when Gus and Lillie arrived in Montana.

Fifty miles north of Omaha, the family reached Vermillion, South Dakota, in an area Gus had never, in all his nomadic years of horse trading, explored. After a few days of serious selling to thin his string of horses, they traveled north along the Missouri, through the grasslands of South and North Dakota. In the thirty-odd years since the decimation of the great bison herds, the tall and short grasses indigenous to the Midwest–the mixed prairies–had grown unchecked, except for occasional lightening-caused prairie fires. The sheer numbers of bison, with their massive weight and sharp hooves, had for thousands of years kept the surface vegetation at bay, allowing the curly black root of the short grasses–buffalo grass and blue grama–to spread and secure the topsoil. Without the bison, and with a few years of abundant rainfall, the grasses had thrived, year after year, until in many places the prairies the Fiskes crossed were covered with deep layers of dead grass. The plows of the homesteaders would institute a further cataclysmic change when they rooted out the soil-saving grasses to cultivate their fields, and released the topsoil to the devastating erosion of the 1930s.

In the 1890s the Great Northern and Northern Pacific railroads had pushed their way across Montana. By 1910 the Milwaukee Railroad had passed through central Montana following the current route of U.S. Highway 200, and nearly all the branch lines that would ever be built in Montana were finished. With all these travel opportunities, immigrants poured into the Dakota and Montana prairies from all over the world. As Gus and Lillie trekked north through the Dakotas, they saw shanties and sod houses dotting the prairie, along with tiny hamlets and towns along the railroads. The dry season upon them, the prairies toasted brown in the hot sun, taking many homesteaders' sparse crops along.

That summer, 1912, instead of trading for geldings for the Wisconsin and Minnesota woods the way he usually did, Gus sold his horses outright or traded for milk cows and items that they needed for homesteading. From government literature that Gus had obtained and read to Lillie, they had reached agreement on a destination–an area in Montana where they wanted to settle and approximately the piece of land that they wanted to file on. They chose a site about fifteen miles south of Wolf Point, across the Missouri near a new community called Terrace, in Dawson County. In the next few years as further divisions occurred, it would become Richland County, and then McCone County. Another small town near Terrace, to be named Vida, was not yet established.

Ed was seventy four years old when he described his memories of the trip and the first years on the homestead:

"Somebody asked me one time if I was scared of Indians when we come to this country in 1912. I said, 'No, but we sure would have liked to see Henry Plummer and all them road agents.' We'd been told about him when people heard we was comin' to Montana.

"On that trip up here [from Vermillion] I drove the buggy with the saddle horse [tied on behind.] I was 8 years old. Dad drove the wagon. Once in awhile Mother'd come back and drive the buggy and I'd get up in the wagon and take a nap. My brother Frank was five.

"These guys'd have a hard time makin' these books about the west interestin' to me. I got in on a lot of that. I saw some of it. This was all CK territory then. That guy who lived in Miles City, what was his name? Yeah, Huffman. He traveled around on CK roundups. Took good clear pictures and wrote interestin' stuff about them. Up around Bear Creek and Shade Creek and the Big Dry. Said the CK had 12,000 head of cattle in there then. It was all free range. They just run 'em loose all over the country. They had 2,000 head of cows and 10,000 steers. The cows would calve and hang around the calves, and the steers would hang around the cows. But one time after a big blizzard [1889] they was findin' CK beef clear down in the Black Hills [in South Dakota.]

"Them homesteaders, we called 'em honyockers, they lived high butchering CK beef. They [the CK bosses] talked to George Clark one time. They was gonna hire him to go up along the river there—yeah, the Missouri. Wanted him to spy on them people, the homesteaders, and bring back evidence that they was stealin' beef. Ol' George tol' me, 'What'd I wanta do that for? Why, them was some of the nicest people I ever met. In the first place, when they butchered, they'd get a big one so they wouldn't have to kill so often. And when ya came around, they'd put ya up for the night, serve ya the best steak for supper and breakfast, and always invite ya back. Why, I went all the way up that river, and came back without any evidence a-tall.'

"Yeah, it was the homesteadin' that killed the big ranches. They was sellin' out the CK herd when we come to the country in '12. Some of 'em come in '10, but most of us come in '12. Just down east of here in Dakota, at Minot, we sold some horses and bought three cows. Dad tied one on each side of the team [pulling the wagon] and led one behind, or sometimes he'd tie 'em to the buggy.

"We pulled inta Poplar and there was an Indian fair goin' on. We had an old yellow hound. We was comin' along down the main street of Poplar with the old hound tied on behind the buggy and a cow on each side. A whole buncha' Indian dogs came and ganged the hound, and scared him to death. He made a run to get under the buggy, and ended up under one of the old cows' feet. The cow got to loping along, tryin' to get away from the dog, and every time her hind feet came forward, she'd knock the hound rolling. So here we come down the street, with the dog rolling along under that cow's feet. The old squaws was squatted Indian style along the sides of the street in their blankets, watching like it was a sideshow, covering their mouths with their hands the way Indians do, and haw-hawing at that yellow hound. I never forgot that.

"We crossed the Missouri there at Poplar. I can still find the old crossin' we used. We camped just across the river on a river bottom. That night the mosquitoes pert near ate us up, and run off our horses. The next mornin' a guy come by and told us we'd really made a mistake campin' there. If we'd a' gone on up out of the bottom, they wasn't so bad up there, but we'd camped right down among 'em.

"Guys used to hang around the homesteading country–they called them locators. When somebody come to the country looking for a homestead, the locator would help 'em find one they could file on. The old man [Gus] had bought somebody's relinquishment before they come up here, but when they got out there, somebody else had beat 'em to it, and filed ahead of them. That was legal in them days. Somebody else gave Dad a lead toward another piece that was open for filing. It was a pretty good place, but they got there in the late summer, too late to put in a crop. Louise Lindstein–she was a Farnham–later said that we stopped at Farnham's on our way into the country. Louise's mother gave Mom a bunch of fresh vegetables and potatoes to help them get by until they could get started. I didn't remember that.

"Flig Turner showed Dad that homestead. We just moved in on it, 'bout two miles northwest a' where Vida was built. None a' that land was surveyed then. Dad went over east where it'd already been surveyed, and started stepping off, with Mom driving the buggy behind. When he got to the corner of our claim, he built the rock cairn he was sposed to. He had to put his name and the land description and whatever else he was sposed to in a tobacco can and bury it in the cairn. He did purty good for not having any survey instruments or anything. When them surveyors [from the County] came around, he only had to change the boundaries of the one field out in front of the house.

"When we moved in there you could put down a rake anywhere and rake up hay. You know, dead grass that had laid over year after year. Dad raked up a big pile in kind of a L-shape and our cows and horses used it for a windbreak that winter. The cows and horses and one black sow.

Dad had that greyhound when we come up here, and one day a guy saw him and said, "I'll tradja a sow for that hound." So dad got the gilt, and the first time she came in [in heat], he took her away [to a neighbor who had a boar], and from then on we had pork to live on. The sow would have six or eight shoats, and we'd butcher the sow and save one gilt outta the new batch.

["When we first got there] Dad took the gypsy wagon off the wheels and set it down on the ground to live in that first summer–it was fall by that time–while they was buildin' the sod house. They used a shovel to cut chunks of sod about a foot wide and a foot and a half long. They didn't have anyplace to keep the potatoes [that Farnhams gave them], so they froze. They kept 'em in a snowbank froze, so they wouldn't spoil, and they'd bring 'em in and cook 'em for food that winter. We sure got to hating frozen potatoes. They get kind of sweet and they ain't good a-tall.

"Old Vida wasn't there then. Down on Wolf Creek was a little place like a town, and then somebody moved in an' started up the old tin covered hotel and they called it Terrace. There was a store there an' a'course a church and a school.

"The next summer [1913] the old man [Gus] used a plow to turn over a patch of nigger wool on the south side of a hill for sod. I don't remember what the real name of that stuff was, except that it was some kind of sedge. It had a thick curly black root that held the sod together like iron. Dad built on another room, and we used the first one as a kitchen. I think the root cellar was under the kitchen."

When Montana opened for homesteading, the government had finally realized that a self-sustaining farming operation couldn't be built on 160 acres of arid eastern Montana land. The laws had been amended to allow 320 acres per homestead claim, and a husband and wife could each file, usually on adjoining tracts. This made a total of 640 acres, a full section, which comprised the Fiskes' entire claim. Homestead filing in the area didn't begin until 1913, a year after they arrived. Gus and Lillie were recorded as the "Settlers" of the parcels in 1913, but for some reason, they didn't apply for Homestead status until 1916. Therefore, for the first four years they lived on the land, they were actually squatters, and it took until 1920 for them to prove up on the entire operation, eight years after they arrived in the area.

Gus and Lillie began to break up fields for cultivation using a team of horses and what was called a "sulky plow." It was a big improvement over the walking plows of the previous century, because although it still only turned over one fourteen-inch-wide strip of soil at a time, the operator had a seat and rode on the machine. The driver's weight helped keep the plowshare in the ground. The larger gang plows, with two or more bottoms, or blades, required more horses and more work. Gus labored with the single bottom sulky. Along with plowing unbroken sod, disking the rough clumps of sod, removing by hand all the rocks, roots and debris turned up by the plow, and producing a tillable field required weeks of hard work. The first full year, 1913, the Fiskes were able to plant only forty acres to wheat. Each year, a few more acres were broken and tilled, until by 1920, nearly 150 acres were under cultivation.

In the homestead era, farmers developed a system of barter that allowed them to farm their land without each small farmer purchasing a full line of machinery. They traded work, horsepower and machines. Lillie and Gus could contract with a neighbor to do their seeding, in return for helping with his threshing or haying when the time came. A farmer might purchase a binder, which cut and bound bundles of grain for drying, but the threshing required when the bundles were thoroughly dry was always done by a traveling crew who moved the huge threshing machines from farm to farm with horses.

Lillie worked right alongside Gus. She learned to manage a team of horses to plant grain and disk down the stubble from a harvested crop. The boys too had innumerable chores to perform while their mother was in the fields. They learned to milk the cows Gus had bought in Minot, as soon as the cows gave birth the first spring. They gathered eggs and kept track of the laying hens that would hide their nests in the weeds, only to become prey to raccoons and other predators. They had the garden to attend to, watering, weeding and hoeing. And when their parents were out of sight, they fought. They had been on the homestead a year when they started school.

"What did you learn today?" Lillie greeted her boys at the front door. Frank dropped his book and writing tools on the table, grabbed a slice of bread smeared with lard and sprinkled with sugar and cinnamon, and headed out the door to find his dad. It was the fall of 1913, and when the new school term started, she had enrolled them both. Frank had turned six in January, and Eddie would be nine in November. Each morning, the boys picked up their books, writing tablets and lunch pails, and started the two mile walk to Terrace, where the nearest school was located.

"Well, I learned four more words," Eddie replied. "See, Ma? I'll read it to you." His finger pointed out each word as he read. "'See the man! See the boy and the man! The man has a hat. Has the boy a hat? The boy can run. Can the man run? The man can see the boy run.'"

"Show me the words again, Eddie," Lillie said, pulling the book in front of her.

"Here's 'can,' Eddie said. "And this word is 'hat' and this is 'run.' And see this squiggly mark? That means a question. And this one, the line with the dot under it, means a loud voice." The boy was clearly proud of his success.

As the pair bent their heads bent over the book, a mocking voice spoke from behind them, "See the boy run! See the man and the boy run! See the boy get his ass kicked if he doesn't get that wood box filled pretty damn quick." Gus deliberately pitched his voice into a high falsetto to humiliate Lillie. "I guess pretty soon you ain't gonna need me readin' to you. Eddie can do it." He picked up the McGuffey Reader from the table. "How come you got the same reading book as Frank? Ain't you almost nine?" he said to Eddie. The boy didn't respond; he gave his father a sullen hate-filled glance. His eyes moved to his mother's face, now a bright scarlet.

"It ain't his fault he's late with his schoolin', Gus. He'll catch up. He's a smart kid."

"Well, smart ain't getting' that wood-box filled," Gus growled. He watched until he saw that Eddie was obeying, before casting a spiteful look at his wife and following his son out the door. Lillie picked up the book and sadly returned to the words Eddie had explained to her. He had made them seem magical, until Gus had spoiled it. It wasn't Eddie's fault he was just now learning to read. During all those years on the road Gus could have taught him to read–and her for that matter–but Gus just didn't have the patience. Or maybe he was just plain selfish and didn't want to share what he knew. In the early years of their marriage, Gus had read to her from newspapers and books. Maybe he didn't want to give up that power. She had always known that it made him feel superior. He hadn't exactly hidden it. So now he made fun of her for trying to learn. He had a bad idea of what was funny–always attaching sarcastic nicknames to family, neighbors and acquaintances. Some of them were just plain cruel, but he thought he was clever–like calling their neighbor, Mrs. Merriman, "Amy," after Amy Semple McPherson, that firebrand female preacher who was traveling around the country. It really wasn't funny. But it gave Gus another way to ridicule Lillie for taking the boys to those tent revival meetings. Lillie had thought that religion might be another way to assure that her boys were protected from bad influence. They didn't attend church services regularly–she was afraid of Gus's scorn–but she had started taking them to the summer tent revivals. The experience had the opposite effect from what she had hoped for. "Them bastards with all their yellin' about hellfire and brimstone scared the hell outta me," Ed said many years later. "I never had much use for preachers after that." Very soon he started refusing to go to the services. Gus reinforced his son's rebellion, in his on-going campaign of keeping Lillie off-guard and under control. So the religious training had ceased.

In the coming years, Lillie gave up trying to learn to read. She loved to listen to stories, but after Gus's display, she never again asked him to read to her. Within a short time, Eddie was able to read the "Wolf Point Herald" to her, giving him another victory in what became a life-long competition with his dad for her attention. Later on, Louise Farnham, daughter of the woman who had given Lillie the garden produce the first summer, married a neighbor named Art Lindstein, and she and Lillie became good friends. When she had time, Lillie drove the buggy down to Louise's farm, and if Louise had chores like canning beans or baking bread, Lillie took over and persuaded Louise to sit down and read to her.

As soon as the family settled on the homestead, Lillie threw herself into becoming an upstanding member of the community. She became obsessive about creating and preserving a proper image for the neighbors. Ed grew up seeing her as the true the head of the family, because of her rigid rules of propriety and her hard work and dedication to the farm. Gus, ever the salesman, preferred to find any excuse to sit and visit with anybody who listened, talking about his years of horse trading. The boys always knew that it was up to her to see to it that they had clothes and food.

In the Fiske family, violence was the solution frequently employed in all types of situations. Neighbors saw Gus as a fun-loving guy, but he hid a bad temper. He had no problem with kicking the boys in the butt, and if he got angry during a card game, he'd kick the table over and make everybody quit playing. Ed told about the many times he received what he considered bad beatings from his Dad, at least one time with a buggy whip. Fighting with his brother Frank usually brought on the whippings.

After Lillie died, and Ed married his wife, Lona, Gus made remarks to her that implied that Lillie was the one who acted out with violence. Lona said, "One time Gus was visiting us, and Ed came in yelling at me about something. When he stormed out of the house like he always did, Gus said, 'Do you know where he gets that?'

"Get's what?"

"That flyin' onto you like that. He gets that from his mother. That's the way she was. She'd just fly onto you when she got mad."

Lillie's friend Louise Lindstein strongly refuted the claim. "It was Gus that had the temper," she said. "Lillie just worked like a dog. Gus caused all those terrible headaches, and if she died of a heart attack, it was because she worked herself to death."

She went on to describe the vicious migraines that periodically immobilized Lillie in agony for up to three days. Instead of retreating to bed rest in a darkened room like most migraine sufferers, she tried to work through and around the pain. In an attempt to relieve the pressure in her head, she would tie a kerchief as tightly as she could around her head just above her eyes and brave the pain of stabbing sunlight to doggedly complete her chores or field work.

Lillie's relationship with Gus had an on-again, off-again character during the first few years on the homestead, with her slaving to make the farm a success, and him goading her because she had "made" him leave the horse trading business that he loved. She missed her family in Nebraska and Iowa, although it had been her choice to distance herself from them. Florence, still living in Lincoln, Nebraska, had become the "mother hen" who tried to keep track of all the scattered Mecum siblings and their offspring. In 1917, Lillie's mother, Etta Belle, died at the age of 54. She had been living in Colorado with her oldest son Jay, but her body was shipped back to Iowa where she had spent most of her adult life, and where most of her relatives, the Utters, still lived. Lillie made her first trip back to see her family since moving to Montana, boarding the train at Wolf Point and traveling to Davenport, Iowa, for her mother's funeral. By that time her family had dispersed–Charley and Bert still in jail in Canada, Jay in Colorado and later Washington state, and Es in California. Clifford, at age sixteen, had left the orphanage and joined the army before the start of World War I. Sophie and Elnora had disappeared.

From Iowa, Lillie made a detour to Nebraska to visit Florence, who had married Walt Sheldon and now had six children. Lillie stayed only a short time, since it was June and summer work on the farm in Montana was in full swing. She couldn't trust Gus to look after the garden, the crop and the animals, so she bought a few gifts for her sons and her friends and hurried home. Her life for the next five years was drudgery, drought and disappointment, watching crops dry up, blow away or be eaten by swarms of grasshoppers. Still, she doggedly stayed with it, unwilling to abandon the elusive dream that had brought her to Montana.

By the fall of 1922, both of her boys had left home. Ed, at age eighteen, was farming a rented place just down the road from her and Gus, mostly because he couldn't get along with his dad enough to help with the home place. The resentment and competition between them had been steadily building. Frank had disappeared again, although she knew he'd be in touch when he got into trouble or needed money. In 1921, at age fourteen, Frank had run away from home and gone "on the bum," as the family called it. In subsequent years, he got in touch with his mother time after time from places like Nevada, Texas, and at one time, Cuba. He consistently got into trouble and thrown in jail, and then wrote home to Lillie. Charges might include public drunkenness, carrying concealed weapons, or simple vagrancy. She'd send him bail money or a train ticket, and he'd come home and live off of her, until the next time. She was ashamed of him, but he was her son, and she tried to help him when she could. Lillie knew that some people, including Ed, thought Frank was a sneaky, mean, trouble maker. According to Lillie's friend Louise Lindstein, "It seemed that during the early years on the homestead Frank just loved to deliberately do things get people mad at him."

After the trip to Iowa, Lillie's loneliness for her family in the Midwest had become omnipresent. She had many friends in the Vida area, but she sorely missed her many nieces, nephews and cousins back in Iowa and Nebraska. During the summer of 1922, another humiliation was dumped on her. Gossip made its way around the Vida community that Gus had made a date with a mentally challenged neighbor girl. Of course he was only pretending, but the community thought it was serious. The "date" never came to fruition, but Gus thought the whole incident funny, and scoffed at Lillie's outrage. After harvest, she packed a trunk, got on the train and went back to Nebraska. She told Gus that she might or might not be back.

She learned that her brother Charley had been released from prison two years before and lived in Chicago. Lillie hadn't seen Charley since he was fifteen, when she had left the rented house on the alley in Davenport to marry Gus. Now he was thirty four years old. Florence told Lillie that he had completely reformed and sworn never do anything to end up in prison again. She hoped it was true.

She rented a little house in Lincoln just down the street from Florence and her family. She didn't divulge much of her situation or her plans to her relatives, but told them that she was there "to do some doctoring" for the enlarged thyroid–or goiter. In truth the condition wasn't serious and could be controlled with iodine, but it made an excuse for her to be there. She settled in for an extended visit.

What she didn't share with her sister was that her marriage and her dreams of owning a successful farm were turning to ashes. Gus's attitude towards her, and both of her boys leaving home before they were out of their teens had left her feeling hopeless, defeated and bone-weary. She was approaching forty years of age. Endless failed crops and heavy farm work had worn her down and aged her, and she had begun to believe that her plan to give the boys a better life had been in vain. She intended to do some thinking on the situation that winter.

Years later, her niece Lola recalled Lillie's winter in Lincoln when Lola was fifteen:

"She'd make fruitcakes, sit for hours and shell and cut up walnuts. She'd get a great big bowl of them done, and come down to our house. Walt [Sheldon, Jr.] would watch and as soon as she went down the street, he'd slip back to her house and eat her walnuts. She'd chase him around–coulda killed him–but she loved the kids.

"I can remember that every time she went into town she wanted to eat [in a restaurant.] When I was a girl I wanted to shop–I never ate. She'd tell us stories about Montana, and according to her, there was a big river up there that if you couldn't get across that river, you didn't get to go to town. Later on, I learned it was the same river that went past Omaha–the Missouri."

The Missouri River was a big factor in the lives of homesteaders living on the "South Side," across the river south of Wolf Point. From the time the Fiskes arrived in Montana in 1912 until 1915, a man named John Pipal had operated a ferry boat that he called the "Invincible," to ferry passengers, livestock and freight across the river. In 1915, the "Wolf Point Bridge and Development Company" spent $5,000 building a pontoon bridge, and Mr. Pipal sold his ferry. In the next three years the bridge washed out and was rebuilt at least three times, by ice in the fall and debris in the spring. Finally, in 1917, after the approaches to the newly repaired bridge were washed out, the Bridge Company hired a new ferry, called the "White City," to provide service. The pontoon bridge was never rebuilt, and the ferry served as cross-river transportation for the next thirteen years. In the summer of 1930, a concrete and steel bridge was built across the river at a taxpayer cost of more than a million dollars. Fifteen thousand people attended the grand opening of the bridge. It made "getting to town" so much easier and cheaper for Southsiders.

During Lillie's visit in Lincoln, Nebraska, the winter of 1922 – '23, Florence and Walt Sheldon planned a new house. The city had scheduled a highway to be built in their area, and several houses had to be moved to make room. Walt, a house mover by trade, saw an opportunity and arranged to acquire one of the houses in exchange for moving it and others out of the highway right-of-way. He bought a lot across the street, constructed a full concrete basement, and moved the house onto it. When Lillie arrived the Sheldons were in the process of installing electricity and indoor plumbing. She pitched in to help. Every day, she watched the dwelling emerge and dreamed longingly of such a house on her land in Montana. She knew that in a rural area, she probably couldn't have the luxuries the Sheldons looked forward to. She would still have kerosene lights and an outhouse, but a frame house would be much better than the dank, dark sod house that had been her home for the last ten years.

By spring, 1923, Lillie was again getting homesick for Montana, and–yes, she had to admit it–for Gus. As Lola told the story: "Maybe she [had been] lonesome out there in Montana, and maybe she was here just trying to find what it was she loved back there. Maybe she was trying to find a way to go back to Gus. If I'd a' knowed what was goin' on, I'd a talked it over with her. I didn't see nothin' wrong with her going back. But it was a long time later that I actually knew Gus Fiske."

Lillie started making plans to go back. She decided that she was going to insist on a decent house. The sod house was falling down, and Lillie thought that a new house would be part of their "new start." They had proved up on the homestead in 1920, so it was theirs free and clear. She started thinking about the things she'd like to have in her new house. She wanted a real bedroom, a better way to heat and cook than with wood and coal, and she'd like to be able to bake cakes again, especially with black walnuts.

The Eastern Kansas woods abounded with massive black walnut trees, and the ripened nuts were available for the taking during the months of September and October. Lillie was more than fond of the rich, smoky-sweet flavor of the black walnuts. During the years she and Gus had followed the horse trading circuit, she never missed a chance to gather the nuts for eating and baking.

Lola said, "She bought her a brand new kerosene stove, and when she took it back [to Montana] it was full of walnuts. Charley took her—that's before I knew him or was sweet on him—to Kansas and they picked sacks of black walnuts down there. They brought them home and filled that [stove] with walnuts to ship 'em back so she'd have walnuts in Montana."

Lillie went back to Montana that spring hoping for a new start. She asked Lola to write a short note to Gus, alerting him that she was coming home, and to meet her train.

May 15, 1923

Dear Gus:

Lola is writing this for me. I'll be home in three days. Please meet the morning milk train in Wolf Point. We got some things to talk about.

Lil

After being alone for six months, Gus was easier to persuade. They reached an agreement that after harvest they would start work on a better dwelling. Lillie had one warning: "If anything like that ever happens again, Gus, I'll leave you," referring to the incident with the neighbor girl. This time he knew she meant it.

A meager harvest in the fall of 1923 forced them to proceed with the new house on borrowed funds. In January, 1924, Lillie and Gus mortgaged their original homestead for $1400 and began to search for a house they could move. They found a sturdy two room house about ten miles away that some other disillusioned homesteader had built and then abandoned, a victim of the grasshopper plague of 1917 that had decimated half of the crops in McCone County. They bought the house for $200. In Wolf Point they found a house mover who had begun using a truck for power instead of horses. With an ingenious system of pulleys and skids, it took the mover only one day to move the little house. They couldn't afford the cost of concrete for a foundation, so the mover set the house on a rectangle of rocks on their chosen site, and they started making it livable. Lillie was to have her bedroom, with a real door on it, so she could have privacy when she needed it, like when those awful migraine headaches hit. The second joyful event was when the well driller arrived with his machine and the old horse that pulled it, around and around, while the bit dug deeper into the ground. They had hired a Frenchman named Gagne from down on Nickwall who was a known dowser–or water witch–to find a good spot for the well. Sure enough, when the well was only fifty feet deep, the driller hit a good vein of water that produced more than the manual pump could handle, at least five gallons a minute. They would have to delay putting up a windmill, which meant a lot of hard work hand pumping for the house and livestock, but Lillie thought she'd never been happier. The money was going awfully fast, but she thought they could probably get the house in good shape before it was gone. As soon as her new kerosene stove, brought all the way from Nebraska, was installed, she baked a black walnut cake. Sometimes, when Gus and he could keep from fighting, Ed came over and helped them work on the house.

From stories Ed told Lona, many years later, she inferred that his warped view of life had begun very early. As a child he developed a scorn and hatred for his brother Frank. In his seventies, he still told with vivid and passionate detail about the very day he discovered that his brother was a "No-good dirty sonovabitch," who was out to get him. He was six and Frank was three. They each had received one gift for Christmas which became prized possessions, Ed's a hobby horse with a wooden head, and

Frank's a small hatchet. As Ed told it, "I caught that sonovabitch out at the wood pile choppin' the head offa my horse."

From that day forward, he hated his brother, while he worshiped his mother with an attachment that was almost obsessive. A system of favoritism had developed in the family. Gus favored Frank, who had the same will-o'-the-wisp personality as his own. Ed shared his mother's serious, even grim "life is real and life is earnest," outlook. Gus entertained himself by badgering both Lillie and Ed for their earnest attitudes, and exaggerating the competition and resentment between the boys.

At school, Ed's favorite subject wasn't in textbooks. It was fighting. As he grew, he found out he was good at it. And he grew bigger than most of his opponents. Over many years, Ed told and retold his family stories of his fights with a boy named Milo Gorley, until the young man became virtual legend. According to Ed, he and Milo fought every recess, morning and afternoon, for the entire time they were in grade school, which in Ed's case was through the sixth grade. Over and over, to his attentive and awestruck family, he described with delight each blow, jumping to his feet and dancing around the table like a figure from the "Rocky" movies. He seemed to achieve almost orgiastic pleasure in hurting an opponent and watching him bleed.

From fighting in the school yard, Ed graduated to fights at community dances and other social functions. He grew to six feet two inches tall and 190 pounds before he was out of his teens. As Lona told it later, "To him violence was the solution to any problem. When he was young it worked so well. He hated Frank and could always whip him, when his dad wasn't around. He hated Milo Gorley and finally whipped him. When he went to neighborhood dances, he never took a girl. He went to see if he could find somebody to get into a fight with. To him a successful Saturday night was winning a fight. Until he was past fifty, he never lost a fight, and there were lots of 'em."

In 1921, when Frank left home, Ed was seventeen and had been hiring out for work on local ranches and farms for four or five years. He worked on threshing and haying crews on the area ranches. He was proud of his height, muscular build and his strength. He later bragged he could lift the front end of a Model T off the ground, and that he could stand in a barrel and jump out of it. Proud of his small "Indian" feet, he wore a size nine throughout his adult life. He continued to worship his mother.

At age eighteen he had saved enough to pay rent on a piece of farmland with a small one-room shack a short distance from his parents. At any given time, from one to four of his male bachelor friends moved in and stayed with him for short or extended periods of time. Those years, from 1922 to 1926, formed some of his later repertoire of stories for the dinner table–stories of making chili with horse meat, scrambling half-rotten eggs without his friends knowing, fights over card games, during Prohibition stealing a still from the local bootlegger, and countless other stories. But never did these stories include women. The Leuenberger brothers–Oscar (Oc), Warner, and Herman–Art Mossestad, and Glen McFarlane were all members of the circle of friends who "shacked up," as he put it, surviving the harsh Montana winters and enjoying youthful camaraderie. They chased "slicks" (unbranded horses), did a little trapping, shot jack rabbits for meat, and in general, stayed free of any responsibilities beyond survival.

In 1925, enticed by stories of good wages, Ed spent the winter in Butte, working in the mines. Years later he told Lona about the ten hour shifts at hard labor, saying that he could pour sweat out of his shoes after his shift in the deep mine shafts. Lona surmised that it might have been in Butte that he had his first experience with sex, and that he had found something disgusting about it. He also confided that he had tried a "reefer"–marijuana–and didn't like the effect it had on him. He told stories about hanging around the Chinese laundries, leaning on a wall smoking and pretending to wait for somebody, while he secretly watched the Chinese, the way they lived and worked, and listened to their chatter. After a time, he said, the Chinese figured out that he was watching them, and found it amusing, revealed by their sidelong glances and behind-the-hand smirks. He hadn't been outside Montana since age eight, and the Chinese seemed exotic and other-worldly. Except for his time on threshing and haying crews, and Lillie's visits back east to her relatives, the winter in Butte was the first time he had been away from his mother.

While in Butte, he continued his career of seeking out fist fights wherever he could find them. Gangs ruled–and bullied–the miners. The most notorious of these was a group of men who, in their off-work hours, dressed in bib overalls and established dominance over the other gangs. These were the Overall Gang, who became so well-known they've been mentioned in books of Montana history and rated a mention in one edition of the Encyclopedia Brittanica. The leader, as described by Ed, was "A big, smart sonovabitch," who dominated a local dance hall. One night, he and Ed got into an altercation inside the hall and took it out in the street. With his friends holding off the other gang members, Ed thoroughly trounced the leader of the Overall Gang, an accomplishment that rated telling again and again for the next thirty years to his five little girls around the dinner table. He made the beating sound so complete and decisive that he didn't need to fear retribution from the rest of the gang.

In the spring of 1925, disillusioned with the chaos in Butte and longing for the solitude of eastern Montana, Ed went back to Vida, planted a crop on his rented farm with borrowed machinery, and resumed his efforts at being a farmer. He was twenty-one. He started attending all the local functions, something he hadn't done much before–except to look for fistfights. He cultivated an image as a lady's man, careful to use proper etiquette in dealing with the ladies. He had learned to be an exceptional dancer and found plenty of partners. He later bragged that he went to a dance, found out the number of dances to be played the whole evening, and lined up a different girl for each dance. It became a source of great pride that he never forgot which girl had been asked for which dance, even four or five hours later. He practiced precise and even grandiose manners and language around females. But he didn't seem to be the least bit interested in a long term association with a woman. He never did any kind of courting beyond the local dances, and socially, he seemed to prefer the company of the young bachelors from the community.

After two years, Gus and Lillie's house was still not completed–Lillie had always had a hard time getting Gus to concentrate on a task long enough to complete it–and they were nearly out of money. Some of the $1400 that was intended for the house had been spent on seed and other expenses for the farming operation, in addition to drilling the well and installing a pump. But what they had created was much more comfortable than the sod house. It had renewed Lillie's energy and optimism, and she was again taking on some of the field work, haying and other hard labor on the farm.

Then came the day in 1928 that broke her heart, her marriage and her spirit, the day she caught Gus in his final betrayal. In his usual fashion, Gus had been gold-bricking, declaring that he had back trouble and putting off helping her with the spring work. Lillie realized that the crop simply had to be put in. They had not yet been able to afford a tractor and still farmed with horses. She hired a neighbor girl for housework and cooking, and spent several days of dirty, hard work, burning the stubble from last year's fields, an accepted practice at the time. Then she harnessed the team and began plowing the fields in preparation for a new crop of wheat. One day at noon, she came in from the field and caught Gus in bed with the hired girl. In a flat, subdued voice, she told him, "Gus, I told you if this ever happened again, I'd leave you."

She would not spend another night under the same roof. Leaving the team harnessed and hooked to the plow, she left the house and walked down the dirt road to Ed's house. He was gone. She sat down, weeping, humiliated and defeated, mentally running through her options. She could not bring herself to go back to her relatives in Nebraska again with her tales of woe about Gus's infidelity. For hours, she sat on the lone chair in Ed's one-room bachelor shack, alternately weeping, raging, and sometimes leaping to her feet and pacing, planning reprisal for all the years of hurt and humiliation, until the shadows outside were growing long and deep indigo. When finally Ed rode up to the house and entered, he was stunned to find his mother sitting in the darkened room, the stove cold. He could tell by her face and demeanor not to ask questions. She said, "I think I'll stay here awhile."

"Sure, Ma Okay." Lillie sat, with no more comment. Time went by. Still she sat, silent. Ed built a fire and started supper while she sat, staring at the floor. Wordlessly, woodenly, she ate the sparse meal he prepared, and fully clothed, climbed onto the bed. She rolled over to face the wall. Later, wide awake, she heard Ed lie down gently on the other half of the bed. She made no sound; she lay there all night awake.

For two days she kept her silence, but did some deep thinking. Nearly forty three years old, she had a hard time fighting the feeling that her life was over. As bad as she hated to leave her new house, she decided that she could accept no more humiliation from Gus. She had to start over. If she split the land with Gus she would have nearly 320 acres, enough to try doing her own farming. For years she'd been doing most of the work anyway. She was pretty sure Ed would help her get started.

On the third morning, she left the bed and started preparing breakfast. Seeing an opening, Ed asked, "What's goin' on, Ma."

"Your dad's up to his old tricks. I caught him messin' with the hired girl," she said.

Ed's fury frightened her. His face turned chalky, and his eyes, usually a slate blue, seemed to blanch nearly white. "I'll kill that sonovabitch," he declared, leaping to his feet.

"No you won't!" his mother answered. "You won't get into this at all."

His teeth clenched. "Well, what're you goin' to do about it?"

"I've decided we're splitting the place and I'll do my own farmin'," she said, "that is, if you'll help me."

Ed sat back down and stared at the floor, silent for a few moments. A glow of excitement and satisfaction started to replace the rage. If she left the old man, he'd finally have her all to himself. No more seething in silence watching his father's shoddy treatment of her–his womanizing, ridiculing her when she'd tried to learn to read. Every time over the years when Lillie had complained that she needed more help, Gus would say, "Well, you're the one who wanted to be the farmer. It was your idea to come up here in the first place." That was his excuse for being a "Manana Man," and putting all the responsibility on her shoulders. Well, now they'd see how he got along without Lillie. The sonovabitch didn't deserve her–never had.

November 23rd, 1930. Three days before Ed's twenty sixth birthday. This was Lillie's water day. She woke to a cold, miserable day–looking like snow. It might be a tough winter. She'd been responsible for watering the livestock for almost eighteen years. Up until a couple of years ago, they didn't have a well or spring–their own source of water–so she'd hauled two fifty-five gallon barrels of water every other day. She'd developed a system: harnessing the team, rolling the barrels into the back of the wagon, tying the two cows on behind, and with the team pulling the wagon, trailing the livestock seven miles down east, past the little hamlet called Vida to the spring in the creek bank. There she dipped water into the barrels with a bucket while the team and the cows were drinking. With her barrels and livestock full, she drove the wagon up to the Vida post office, to Bud Nefzger's well, where she filled up a ten gallon cream can with well water for the house–drinking and dishwater. Back at home the next day, she watered the livestock out of the barrels, so she could skip a day of hauling water. The first spring on the homestead, in 1913, Gus had built a little dam that made a water reservoir for the livestock, but it was usually dry. Sometimes in the winter, she let the animals eat snow, but other times when the snow didn't come, she had to take an axe along to the spring and break the ice to get her water. She was a small woman, and since coming to the homestead, she had become so thin she thought she looked scrawny. She weighed a little over 100 pounds, and her hair had turned completely gray in the last few years. She'd turned forty five her last birthday.

She and Gus had been married for nearly twenty seven years. She'd been spending a lot of time lately thinking about their relationship, the way it had been so stormy, before she had left him and moved in with Ed.

Apparently, Lillie coming to him for sanctuary after she left Gus was just what Ed had been wanting. After she and Gus split the homestead Ed had harvested his crop and let his rented farm go. He and Lillie moved a one-room shack onto her half of the homestead. Ed was only too eager to help her. They were starting all over again, but this time there was no money to fix up the house or dig a well. She hated being in debt, but she'd had to go to the lumber yard and buy a few things on credit—a few boards, siding and shingles—to make the shack livable. She had hoped that they would get a couple of good crops and pay it off, but the last two years' crops had been failures, and she could only make small payments.

Then, last fall, in October, 1929, the stock market crashed back east and the banks began to fail. Just a couple of weeks ago, on November 8, she had received another blow. The lumber yard filed a materials lien against her property for the things she'd bought to fix up her shack; and last year's taxes on her half of the land had only been partially paid. This was all so painful and embarrassing. She sure didn't want Gus to find out about her problems. Ed knew most of it—he'd had to read the letters to her when they came, but he didn't say much.

Since they had moved in together, Ed had been more of a help-mate to her than his dad ever had. But now that might be getting out of hand. Sometimes she really wished Ed would get a woman. As far as Lillie knew, Ed had never had a girl-friend. One of the reasons this was troubling was that Ed was way too involved in things that went on between her and his dad, Gus. That didn't seem fitting. He and his dad had always had a violent relationship, and when he was a kid Ed had been on the receiving end of severe beatings from his dad. Lillie thought that Gus was way too hard on Ed. One time when Ed was only about ten, Gus laid his finger wide open during a whipping with a buggy whip. Lillie had to soak the finger and then dig dirt out of the cut before she bandaged it, while the boy squirmed and tried not to cry. She saw the hatred in his eyes when he looked at his dad. Ed and his little brother Frank fought bitterly, and Gus had always thought it was funny to stick up for Frank just to make Ed mad. It had really caused a lot of trouble in the family.

Things had started to change for the worse as Ed got older and grew bigger and stronger than his dad. Lillie remembered a fight a few years ago when Ed, aged twenty- two, had fifty-year-old Gus down on the floor beating him senseless. Lillie had jumped into the fight and stopped him. "You just remember! That's your dad you've got down there!"

When she'd moved into the little shack on her half of the land, Lillie had to start hauling water again with the wagon and the barrels. Now, though, she went down to Gus's well for water. She only traveled half a mile from the shack where she lived with Ed. The chore became so much easier than the fourteen mile round-trip to Vida. It left her plenty of time to sit with Gus and visit. They were getting along better now than they had for years.

Things had not improved between Ed and his dad since she and Gus had split, and maybe even worse. It seemed like Ed thought that now she and Gus were separated, she shouldn't have anything to do with Gus. She could tell he stewed about it when she came back from Gus's place with her load of water every other day. Well, she wasn't going to answer to Ed or anybody else about how much time she spent with her own husband, she decided. And she wasn't going to divorce Gus, no matter what. She wasn't going to be like her mother or the rest of her family. No, the next time Ed started complaining about her "hanging around Gus," she intended to have a talk with him. It was one thing for him to live there and help her on the homestead, and something else entirely to be treating her like his own private property. How could a guy be jealous of his own dad? She had to straighten him out on that. It was high time Ed got himself a woman, and quit worrying about her and Gus. Sometimes she wished that she had never gotten into this living arrangement with Ed. Things were sure tense.

She had started the noon meal when Ed came into the house. A jar of home-canned green beans simmered in a pot on the back of the stove. She was slicing some meat left over from last night's roast.

"What took you so long, Ma?" Ed's voice was silky. "Sure seemed to take you awhile to fill them barrels."

"I was visiting with your dad."

"What you got to say to that sonovabitch?"

Lillie turned to face him. "Ed, I've had about enough of this." She said firmly. "It ain't none of your business how much time I spend with my husband, and don't you forget, he is still my husband.

She didn't see it coming. The last thing she felt on this earth was her son's big fist smashing into her jaw. She flew backward three feet, head first into the huge, cast iron wood burning range. She hit the floor like a rag doll. He sank into the kitchen chair, suddenly robbed of rage and strength, and waited. "Come on, Ma, get up," he muttered. There was no response, not even a groan. Slowly, he got to his feet and bent over her. He could see that she had wet herself. There was no movement. He had seen enough dead animals to know that she was gone.

He picked up her body and laid her gently on the bed that they had shared for the past two years. Then he began building his story, his lie. She must have died the minute she hit the stove, he mused, so there won't be much of a bruise on her head, nor where his fist met her jaw. It takes a beating heart to make a bruise.

"Okay. I'm outside. I come in for dinner. She's layin' on the floor. I put her on the bed. There's a little bruise on her temple. It's where she fell and hit the stove when she had the heart attack. That's the way it was."

Ed backed carefully away from her body and out the door, as if he might disturb her if he made noise. He saddled his horse and headed toward the Leuenbergers'. He'd leave it to them to tell the old man. In his haste to get away from the awful scene, he forgot about the green beans. By the time he got back with the neighbors, the beans were burned black in the kettle. The odor filled the entire house. For the rest of his life, that's what he remembered the most about his mother's death: the odor of the burnt beans. He never ate green beans again.

CHAPTER 15

Requiem - 1930

Lillie's death was noted in the Wolf Point Herald-News on November 28, 1930, a week after her death:

> This community was shocked and saddened when the sudden death of Mrs. Lillie Fiske was reported Friday. Her son, Ed, with whom she lived, had been out attending to chores and when he came in, found his mother lying on the floor, apparently lifeless. Later in the day, when the doctor arrived, he pronounced her dead from an acute heart attack. The funeral was held Sunday afternoon (November 30th.) The bereaved son and C.G. Fiske have the sympathy of the entire community.

Her obituary published in the Herald-News on December 5 contained additional information:

> Mrs. Fiske has a wide circle of friends who were both grieved and shocked to hear of her sudden death. Mrs. Fiske had been ailing for some time, but was apparently feeling much better at the time of her death, November 21.

Within the next two years, all of the land Lillie had sacrificed so mightily to own was gone, to the county for taxes and to the Federal Land Bank for the loan that had been taken out in 1924, which Gus allowed to go delinquent. With the object of his obsession gone, and needing to present to the community the image of a thoughtful grieving son, Ed had no reason to continue the acrimony that had defined his relationship with his dad. After her burial, he effected a reconciliation of sorts.

Gus had been waiting for seventeen years to go back to the life he loved. In September 11, 1931, ten months after Lillie's death, an article in the Circle Banner described a fire that destroyed Gus's house. Gus quickly collected on his insurance before the Federal Land Bank could interfere and claim the money, bought bedrolls and a buggy, and, with Ed, left for Miles City. That winter, through the spring of 1932, Ed and Gus squatted in an abandoned state station near Miles City, buying horses to go back into the horse trading business. During that time, Ed became acquainted with a homesteader named Charles Wintermote. He was married to a school teacher named Virginia, who soon became impressed with Ed's rugged good looks and dashing manners. She had three younger sisters living in Miles City, one of whom was seventeen years old, Lona.

The first of May, they left Miles City for Minnesota, Gus in a buggy and Ed on horseback, driving twenty head of horses. The venture had lasted only two months when the old adversarial relationship resurfaced. After a huge blow-up in early July, Ed left fifty-seven-year-old Gus on his own in Minnesota and came back to Vida, to bunk with his friends, the Leuenberger brothers. He attended a local dance and for the first time joined his notorious brother, uncles and aunts on the pages of a newspaper:

> Circle Banner
> July 22, 1932
>
> SERVING TIME FOR DISTURBING THE PEACE
>
> During a dance at Vida on the 9th of this month, Edward Fiske of Vida and Elmer McCanoha of Richey got into some misunderstanding and proceeded to fight it out outside the dance hall, and later tangled again, both times McCanoha getting the worst of it, according to reports. Fiske was arrested on a charge of 3rd degree assault, and a hearing set for the 20th before Justice Casterline at Vida. However, at the hearing the charge was dismissed by Justice C. R. Casterline and both men were charged with disturbing the peace, to which they pled guilty. Fiske was fined $25 and sentenced to thirteen days in jail, while McCanoha was fined $15

> and given a sentence of eight days in the county jail. Both have so far failed to pay their fines, but are already serving their jail sentences. County Attorney Hoover made a trip to Vida Wednesday to handle the state's side of the cases.

As Ed sat in his jail cell for the next thirteen days, eating bologna and oatmeal, he gradually developed the resolution that he would never be in jail again. He had always held himself above all the renegades in the family, and now here he was, sitting in jail just like his hated brother Frank. It was unjustified, and not his fault. That smart sonovabitch McCanoha was asking for it. That god-damn Hoover and chicken-shit Casterline throwing their weight around, giving him almost twice as much fine and time just because he got the better end of the fight.

His mother's voice and her face haunted his dreams, and he could imagine her shame and disappointment if she knew that he, her pride and joy, had been brought down. The resolve to never again get caught at anything where he could be subjected to punishment sank like iron into his psyche, and became the foundation around which all his future behavior would be patterned. He would be very careful, and from now on, no one would ever be able to put him behind bars. As he stewed with resentment, Justice Casterline and County Attorney Hoover joined the long list of people for whom he harbored a lifelong hatred.

As soon as he was released, he gathered up his belongings and headed for Miles City. He'd left a few items with his friend Charles Wintermote before the trip to Minnesota, and adding these to his meager collection of property, he set off on his saddle horse for Colorado where land had been opened for homesteading.

He was back in Miles City within three weeks. The six to ten foot sagebrush and dry lands of eastern Colorado were completely unappealing to him and he left without filing. He took up a homestead near the Wintermotes east of Miles City. The next phase of his life was about to begin, and with his mother dead, Lona Belle Vest would become the focus.

VEST

David Woodson Vest
m.
Hannah Robinson
⇓
David Edward Vest
(b. 1837)

m.

SHIRLEY

Martha Shirley
(No husband of record)
⇓
Laura Emarine Shirley
(b. 1844)

⇓

Joseph Harrison | Edward William | John Ely | Laura Belle | Martha Alice | George Arthur (Art) | Bertha Pearl | Isaac Fowler

DRIFFEL

Joseph Driffel
m.
Mary Messenger
⇓
John Henry Driffel

m.

CHURCHILL

Benjamin M. Churchill
m.
Sarah Rowland
⇓
Josephine Amelia Churchill

⇓

Gertrude Lavinna | Sarah Lona | Ina and Ila (twins) (Died at Birth)

Isaac Fowler m. Gertrude Lavinna

⇓

Lawrence Shirley (Shirley) | John Forrest (Jack) | Zetta Josephine (Teany) | Mary Virginia (Din) | Lona Belle (Lona) | Alger Rex (Rex) | Thelma Opal (Thelma) | Dorothy Mae (Dot)

Lona Belle (Lona)
m.
Edward Fiske
⇓

Kathleen
m.
Jim Cary

Frances
m.
Ernest George (1)
Murray Wright (2)

Patricia (Tris)
m.
Ron Goff

Edward
Alger
(Died at Birth)

Barbara
m.
Ray Jarsen (1)
Charles Welch (2)
Jim Richard (3)

Norma
m.
Jerry Kinkade (1)
Maurice Rowley (2)
Leon Thompson (3)
Les Lundgren (4)

Mom's Family Tree

PART V

THE VESTS

Fowler and Gertrude Vest
ca. 1925

CHAPTER 16

Illinois to Montana

In 1914 Lona was born to a father and mother who provided the training ground for the girl who was to become the perfect victim of the sociopath she would marry at age nineteen.

The story of the Vest family begins in Kentucky just before the Civil War. Six months before the attack on Fort Sumter by the Confederate navy, David Edward Vest, age twenty three, married a sixteen-year-old girl named Laura Emarine Shirley in Bowling Green, Kentucky. Records state that she was fatherless, so carried her mother's surname. Apparently, in that era, her mother could not solely give consent for her to be married, and the court appointed a guardian for her. A "Guardian's Bond" and a Marriage Bond were posted the day of the wedding. These documents were a kind of assurance–or insurance–that the parties could be legally married.

In 1861, David Vest enlisted in the local militia in Bowling Green, Kentucky. During that year, Confederate forces conducted an offensive that resulted in major battles at various locations in Kentucky. According to family lore, David was a medic–or a "male nurse"–but it is unclear whether he served Confederate or Union troops. In all census information and tax rolls before, during and after the war, he was listed as a farmer. Chances are good, however, that he was involved in war activities for the duration of the war. His and Laura's first child was not born until four years after the wedding, in 1864. By the time Laura died at the age of forty four in 1888, she would give birth to ten children, five sons and five daughters.

After the Civil War, the David Vest family left Kentucky and settled in Monmouth, Illinois. The fourth son, born in 1876, was Fowler. As an adult he was a small wiry man, five feet five inches tall and 145 pounds. He was reasonably handsome, with dark hair and hazel eyes. When he was four years old, he had a sledding accident which broke his leg at the knee. His father made the decision not to seek medical help, but to "set" the leg himself. When the bones healed, the knee was frozen in a stiff "L" so pronounced that for next thirty years, Fowler walked on the toes of that foot, lurching along with his stiff knee and crooked leg. His handicap earned him the nickname "Crip." The cruel nickname and his small stature, along with a meager education, spawned a feisty, combative nature that tended to blunt his good judgment. As a teenager he developed a fondness for alcohol which exacerbated his feelings of inadequacy. One of his methods of compensation for his perceived shortcomings was buying friends at the local saloons with round after round of drinks. "Set 'em up, Joe" became his personal mantra. At age twenty-one he went to work in a pottery, where four years later he met a diminutive, well-mannered young woman named Gertrude Driffel.

One of two surviving daughters of John Driffel and Josephine Churchill, Gertrude was pretty, with fair skin, blue eyes and dark hair, a petite woman with tiny hands and feet that needed a size two shoe. She was intelligent and capable, and had attended school through the twelfth grade. Monmouth was a college town, and many of the citizens took advantage of the opportunity for education. Gertrude fostered an ambition to attend college, and her father could have easily afforded the tuition. But he preached the doctrine of "submissive wives," and proclaimed that he didn't believe in education for women. "It makes them dissatisfied," he sermonized, dashing her hopes of being a teacher or a writer. His attitude was identical to the dogma of the southern slave owners, who passed laws against educating blacks. Gertrude resigned herself to common labor, domestic service or marriage and a family.

In 1901, Gertrude went to work at a local pottery, a job judged suitable for a woman, where she would be out of sight of the clientele. There she met Isaac Fowler Vest, twenty five years old to her twenty. Very soon, Fowler was madly in love. He peppered her daily with syrupy love notes and showered her with attention, and within a year he had convinced her to marry him.

After her marriage in 1902, Gertrude quit her job, since employment for married women was considered bad taste. Fowler also quit the pottery, and they moved to a different area of Monmouth where Fowler bought a fish wagon. Located about twenty miles from the Mississippi River, the citizens of Monmouth enjoyed fresh fish brought in by trains every day. Fowler picked up his load, packed it on ice, and made the rounds of restaurants and homes. He peddled the rest wherever he could find buyers. This was his livelihood for the next seven years. Gertrude hated the job, mainly because the practice of customers paying in cash allowed Fowler to stop in at the local taverns every day. With his pockets full of money, he impressed his drinking friends with his affluence. In those seven years, Gertrude gave birth to three children.

In 1910, homestead fever swept the country. Fowler and his brother Art began to dream of going west and becoming land barons. Gertrude welcomed the idea of starting a farm, since it would get Fowler away from the fish wagon and his favorite taverns. They chose Oklahoma as a suitable destination.

The venture was folly from the outset. Fowler's handicap rendered him unable to engage in the heavy, labor intensive work of farming. Incapable of riding a horse—his crooked leg wouldn't reach a stirrup—he had to rely on a buggy or wagon for transportation. Gertrude, with her tiny stature, was not equipped to take up any of the slack in the labor force. The homesteading venture needed the help of one or more of Fowler's many brothers. In Oklahoma, it would be Art. With animals, equipment and furniture, the two families boarded an immigrant train for the long trip. They settled in the Red River Valley in the southwestern area of the state, less than twenty miles from the Texas border. Each family filed on 160 acres of land and, living temporarily in rented housing in the little town of Olustee, set about building their homesteads.

The Oklahoma that met them was still the Wild West, only three years after Butch Cassidy and the Sundance Kid pulled their last robbery, sat for a dudish portrait in Texas and left for South America. One year later the Mecum Brothers, who would become in-laws of the Vests in the next generation, were breaking out of jail in Iowa and shooting their way into a Canadian prison. Fowler and Gertrude's little boys, Shirley and Jack, reveled in the ambience of the cowboy era. A picture taken just after the family arrived in Oklahoma shows the two boys, barefoot, hands tucked into their bib overalls, proudly lined up with a group of cowboys. The boys barely reach the waists of the lanky cowboys whose ten gallon hats are set at a jaunty angle against the western sun. The cowboys are dressed in their Sunday best, with white shirts, neckties and dress pants–rather than Levis–tucked into their knee high cowboy boots. Shirley is beaming at the camera, dazzled by the company of his rugged companions.

The disillusionment and disappointment started almost immediately. Gertrude's hopes of getting Fowler away from alcohol didn't play out, and his old habits resurfaced almost immediately.

> News Account: Olustee, Oklahoma, May 5, 1910.
>
> INTOXICATED - STOLE HORSE
>
> A horse and buggy tied to the hitching posts on the square yesterday, which belongs to Miss Edna Gettemy, was borrowed by Fowler Vest and caused considerable excitement before it was returned. The horse ran away with Mr. Vest and he was thrown to the ground with a narrow escape from serious injuries. He was severely shaken up and it was necessary to call the ambulance to take him to his home on South First Street. Vest is said to have been drunk at the time he borrowed the buggy and it is not known yet whether any action will be taken.

Another article, published in a different newspaper at about the same time, stated that "I. F. Vest of Olustee was brought to Altus Thursday charged with drunkenness and conveying whiskey." He had apparently bought liquor in Altus and took it to a baseball game in Olustee with the intent to sell it. The charges were dismissed a month later, and cost Fowler $425 in court costs, a veritable fortune to the cash-strapped family. Whether he spent that month in jail is unclear.

Fowler sent a note from Altus, Oklahoma, to Gertrude in Olustee (about twenty miles away), at about the same time:

Dear Gertie:

I am wrongfully accused of selling liquor. I will prove I am innocent of the charge and be home to you as soon as possible.

Yours as Ever, Fowler

The Vests remained in Oklahoma for five years, and according to their daughter Lona's later account, it was a disaster. Two more girls were added to the family in Oklahoma, Virginia–called Din–and Lona. Then, through letters from other family members, Fowler decided there were greener pastures in Montana. He and Art gave up their Oklahoma venture. Fowler made plans for a move north, while Art went back east.

Sixty years later, Lona shared more of her family story:

"I was five months old when they left Oklahoma. This time they went to Montana. Art went back to Illinois and a bunch of Pa's [Fowler's] other relatives came to Montana. The government had changed the rules again and they were going to get a section of free land each. To them it sounded like a lot. Uncle Jack, Uncle Joe, Uncle Tom (Bowlin), and Aunt Belle were each going to get a section, and they'd really get to be cattle barons. The thing they didn't realize was that in southern McCone County, Montana, you need about thirty acres to graze one cow and calf pair. Each of those four sections–640 acres–would only handle about twenty head of cattle–a total of eighty for the four sections they thought they could homestead. There's no way that eighty head of beef cattle would support four families, much less make them rich. That was sheep country.

"When Mom and Pa were out there on the homestead a guy named Dan LeValley saw what was going on with us–doomed to failure–and he was going to set Pa up with a band of sheep. Pa's arbitrary nature surfaced. Oh, hell, no! He wasn't raising no god-damn sheep. He was going to raise fetarita cane and corn, and feed hogs. He was like a feisty little dog. Nobody could tell him anything, like you can't raise corn or sorghum cane without irrigation. Of course Pa's idea didn't even get off the ground, and as failure followed failure, he just got more and more bitter and harder and harder to get along with, and of course, there was always the drinking."

Lona's grooming as a victim began almost as soon as she was old enough to reason. Her mother Gertrude contracted cancer, and her dependent weak-natured father displayed a need for his wife that Lona misinterpreted as love. With her quiet strength and constant deferral to her husband, who became more and more a bully as the years went by, Gertrude reinforced the notion that need was love, and a wife must submit. As Lona put it, "Mom believed that if a woman couldn't get along with her husband, there was something wrong with her, not him." His tantrums also gave Lona the idea that violence was normal. In her late sixties, Lona gave some insight into her childhood:

"My mother had eight kids. The oldest was Shirley. That was the maiden surname of Pa's mother. He was born the day before Christmas, in 1904. Then there was Jack (John), Teeney (Josephine), Din (Virginia), Lona (me), Thelma, Rex (Alger Rex) and Dot (Dorothy.) The first three were born in Illinois, Din and I in Oklahoma, and the other three in Montana. Shirley died on the Montana homestead in January of 1918 when I was three and he was thirteen. He was accidentally shot in the head with a single shot .22. I've read that a .22 slug in the head is terrible. It usually penetrates the skull, then doesn't have enough power to go on through, so it goes around and around inside the skull, just tearing up the brain. It took Shirley a week to die, and that was awful for the family. He and Jack were rabbit hunting, and their old rifle didn't have a trigger guard. They were climbing over a fence, and knocked a rock down on the trigger. He's buried out there on the old homestead. Thelma was born at the homestead, and Rex and Dot in Miles City. Dot was born when Mom was forty two years old.

"Out there on the homestead, Pa had his brothers to help him with the farm work and my folks managed to stick it out until they "proved up"–about five years. It was pretty ridiculous, them trying to be farmers. She was so tiny, he was crippled, and they were both city people. They never made any money on that farm, but they raised a cow and a pig or two, and stuff like that, and my mother taught school. At that time, it didn't require a degree to teach school, because there just wasn't anybody to teach that had one. Then Shirley got killed out there and they were sick of it. They left owing a debt on the place. It was three hundred dollars, and to them it was a disgrace. I was full grown before I knew that the place had been foreclosed on and then sold for taxes.

"They moved to Miles City a year or so after Shirley died. It was pretty rough and they were short of money until my dad got a job as a janitor for the school, Washington School I believe it was. They got along on about $150 a month. After a few years he got to be a janitor at the railroad offices, and was there until he lost his job in the Depression.

"When I was about eight or nine years old, Pa broke his leg again. He was working as a school janitor and he slipped on an icy sidewalk and broke it in the knee again. This time the doctor set it out straight, so at least he could stand up straight and walk, but his leg was still stiff.

"He was always hard to get along with, I suppose because of that crippled leg. He was a real dude, very particular about his clothes and appearance. He was hard on my mother about the way she did his clothes. When he lost his temper he would scream and yell and pound on the table, but I don't ever remember him hitting my mother. He threw a fit one time about her darning a small worn place on one of his collars instead of turning it–ripping the collar apart, turning the worn spot to the inside, and reassembling it inside out–like he told her to. She spent a lot of time crying about his temper tantrums.

"He was also insanely jealous. There was absolutely nothing to it, she was a perfect lady. They had a guy one time who took his meals with us because he worked as a janitor in the school that was just across the street. After awhile my parents decided that it was costing more than they were making because they had to have a full meal at every meal instead of just soup and sandwiches or something. But my dad, instead of telling him it cost too much, just tried to insult him bad enough that he would stop coming voluntarily. The way he did it was to start implying that there was something going on between him and my mother. Finally the guy got the message and left, but my mother was so humiliated.

"Pa would yell and pound on the table and imply that she was lazy, but I know he really loved her. He was devastated when she got sick. I know it nearly killed him, maybe because he depended on her so much.

One time she woke us up in the middle of the night, and told us, 'We're going to live in a different house now, and he's going to live in this house, so there won't be any more bawling out.' So we went to a house that Jack had rented. We even took some of the furniture. We were only gone a day or so, and he came and talked her into coming back. He always held that incident against Teeney and some of the women from the church, because they had encouraged Mom to leave him.

"My mother was very rigid about what people did or did not do. You not only did not do certain things, you didn't even talk about them. The first time your dad hit me, I just couldn't believe it had happened. It was so shameful. It put us on the level of the trashy people who lived down on the south side of town.

"Because of my mother, I grew up thinking that nothing was insurmountable. My mother had a solution or an answer for everything. Like Teeney and the velvet slippers. When they lived out on the homestead, Teeney was about fifteen and she wanted to go to a dance. She didn't have any shoes except some with holes in them. So they ordered her a new pair from Sears, Roebuck. The day of the dance Jack rode all the way to the post office to get them. It was thirteen miles. He got back about four o'clock in the afternoon with no shoes. So my mother went through her stuff and found an old black velvet dress. She got out her sewing machine, cut some soles out of cardboard, covered them with the velvet, and stitched up the nicest little pair of black velvet slippers. They were like Roman sandals. They only lasted that one night, but Teeney made it to the dance anyway.

"When we had birthdays, each kid got what my mother called a 'Birthday Budget.' Each person in the family made a birthday card by hand, and decorated it with flowers and best wishes and such. Mom fastened all the cards to a long strip of white butcher paper, rolled it up and tied it with a piece of ribbon, and that was the birthday budget. There was never any money for a present, but she would scrape up enough sugar and lard for a cake.

"We were always poor. There were seven kids, and the most Dad ever made–after they moved to Miles City–was $150 a month. Rent was $20 or $25. We didn't know we were poor. My mother wouldn't let us know it. She was really good at fixing up stuff and making it do. She had a lot of sayings, but the one she used almost as a motto was, 'Use it up, wear it out, make it do, or do without.' That's the way I grew up, so when I married Ed and went out to the farm, hardship was nothing new to me.

"My mother got cancer of the uterus, and was sick for three years. My dad was out of work. I worked at the library, and she did people's washing and mending and such. Pretty soon she got so sick she couldn't do that anymore. I came home one day–I didn't have to work mornings–and I had some plans for something I wanted to do. She said, "Oh Lona, I was counting on you to help me hang up that washing." I looked at her and her face was as pale as if she had no blood at all. So I nobly abandoned my plans and helped her. She was bedridden for fifteen months. The ladies aid society of the church bought codeine for her because we couldn't afford it.

"After I grew up, whenever I started thinking about how abused I was, I'd just tell myself to think about my mother, and feel lucky, because she had such a hard, sad life. She died so young, just fifty two, and it was just getting so things would have been a little easier for her. The kids were getting older and could have helped her. She worked all the time–it seemed like she never rested. She died the day before Dot's tenth birthday.

"In later years I didn't get along with my dad so good. He was always bullying Mom when she was lying there in the bed dying. One time he was chewing on her about letting somebody leave a bureau drawer in her room open. I said, "You leave her alone!" And he slapped me. So I packed up and went over to Teeny's. In a week or so he went back East to see Aunt Belle and I moved back in. I was the only one working, and they needed my paycheck. That's why I was always the one who was supposed to keep Pa in line, sort of take my mother's place. Thelma just hated her dad, and he and Teeney fought like cats and dogs. When Mom died–right then, that minute–Thelma wanted us to move out and get our own place. She left it up to me to tell Pa. He said, 'Mom said you wouldn't leave until Rex was through school.' I told him, 'We want to leave now. Can we have Mom's bed for Dot to sleep in?' He was really upset but he said, 'I guess you can.'

"Right after that, he and Jack and Rex gave up the house they were living in, and moved into an apartment downtown over a blacksmith shop. Then Rex quit school and went to work on the CCC. Pa got to be a terrible drunk. He would get drunk and fall down in the gutter. They finally shipped him off to Warm Springs, [the state mental hospital] and he died there after only a week."

After Fowler and Gertrude abandoned the homestead, his brothers and his sister, one by one, also left McCone County. Belle and her husband moved back east and settled in Eau Claire, Wisconsin. Soon her brother Art joined her there, without his family.

After Art left Oklahoma with his wife Amy and three children, his life seems to have fallen apart. He was born in 1879, two and a half years after Fowler. In contrast to Fowler, who was small and wiry, Art was a big, powerful man, over six feet tall, and apparently deficient when it came to conscience and values. According to his statements in prison records, he attended school only through the fourth grade and left home at age eleven. Before his short homesteading venture in Oklahoma, he married and fathered three children. At the age of forty seven, Art joined the ranks of the notorious.

Eau Claire Leader
Eau Clair, Wisconsin
Saturday, June 5, 1926

WOMAN SHOT, DANGEROUSLY WOUNDED
Mrs Bertha Mcfadden in Critical Condition after
Being Shot by Boarder at Home Yesterday

Mrs. Bertha McFadden lies dangerously wounded in Sacred Heart hospital with a bullet wound above the heart, and George A. Vest, a roomer at the McFadden home is held in the county jail without charge, pending the outcome of the woman's wound, as the result of a shooting fray at the McFadden home about 3:30 yesterday afternoon.

In 1926, eleven years after leaving Oklahoma, Art met the widow McFadden in Eau Claire, Wisconsin, while peddling magazines door to door. According to newspaper accounts in the Eau Claire Leader, he started "taking meals" at her house, and within a few weeks, moved in with her, supposedly as a boarder. Very soon he quit his job and quit paying rent. Bertha McFadden had a grown son who also lived with her, and he quickly saw through the new boarder. He put up strong resistance to the romance, but his mother would not be deterred. Art had told the Bertha that he owned a "fruit and livestock ranch in the west," and proposed marriage, even though, unbeknownst to her or her children, he was already married. There was no ranch in the west, since he'd abandoned the homestead in Oklahoma eleven years before. But Bertha believed him, sold her house, gave Art part of the money to buy a "new Ford sedan," and started planning a wedding. Then, possibly in response to her son's warnings, she started to renege. According to newspaper accounts, she "upbraided Vest for being shiftless, since the man had not worked in nine months.

At that time he threatened to kill her and her son if she failed to fulfill her promise of marriage. He had threatened death to the family even before that, but she had never mentioned it to her son. "She thought it was idle talk," said the Leader.

She was very wrong. Bertha told Art that she would not marry him until he proved he could provide for her, and he started planning a double murder-suicide. He would kill Bertha and her son, and then himself. He foolishly put his plans in writing, purchased a pistol, and "practiced shooting on a daily basis on the banks of the Eau Claire river, firing round after round at a target," according to the Leader.

According to the details that Bertha revealed after the shooting, she had given in to pressure from Art and set a date for the marriage as Thursday, June 10th, 1926. As the day approached, Bertha again began to have serious second thoughts. On the Friday afternoon prior to the wedding date, Art and his "fiancée" got into another argument about money. He demanded more of the money she had received from the sale of her house. When she refused, he pulled his revolver and pressed it to her heart. Just before he fired, she "swooned," moving the barrel of the pistol a couple inches higher, and the bullet just missed her heart. The shot woke Bertha's son from a sound sleep. He worked night shifts for Gillette Rubber in Eau Claire, and luckily was home. He rushed to his mother's room and Art fired a shot at him that went wild. The son was also a big powerful man who occasionally wrestled professionally. He tackled Art and took away the gun, and with the help of two other neighbors, hog-tied the perpetrator in the front yard.

Taken to the county jail, Art came up with a story involving Bertha's son that revealed to the authorities the kind of person they were dealing with, and his violent rage at and jealousy of the son who had interfered with his plans. According to the Leader:

> At the police station, Vest told a revolting story of alleged perversion in the McFadden family, giving this as his reason for shooting Mrs. McFadden. At the county jail, where he was later taken, he laid on a cot and moaned and spoke incoherently of being afflicted with lung trouble and wanting to talk to his sister, Mrs. Belle Bolin, East Madison street [in Eau Claire.] He called for a "Larry" at times [His oldest son was named Lawrence.] He lies on his cot in the jail and holds his sides and groans of pleurisy pains, and shakes convulsively at intervals. When questioned about the shooting, he evaded directly answering by saying that he had written a confession at the police station. Police, however, declared they had no statement from the man. The police have expressed the opinion that the man is slightly demented.

In the next few weeks, while he was incarcerated, he carried on with his drama and faked a nervous breakdown. He was examined by two local physicians, who both testified at the trial that Art was not insane.

Bertha was in critical condition in the hospital for nearly three months, but recovered enough to attend the criminal proceedings. It was at that hearing that Bertha found out that Art was still married, and how profoundly she had been duped. On September 26, George Arthur Vest pled guilty to the attempted murder of Bertha McFadden and was sentenced to "an indeterminate term of one to seven years in prison." The charges against him for the attempted murder of the son, George McFadden, were dismissed in return for his guilty plea.

According to his prison records, he arrived at the facility with gonorrhea. Assumably cured during his incarceration, he served five years and was released in 1931.

Lona said later that as a child, she could remember taking packages to the post office from her parents to "Uncle Art," who was in prison. At age sixteen she graduated from high school with her head full of poetry and Shakespeare, refined and tested by poverty to believe she could and must endure anything. Indoctrinated by her parents' influence and attitude on the role of submissive wives, she had been artfully groomed and prepared to become the lifelong victim of the man who came calling soon after her mother's death in 1932, Ed Fiske.

PART VI

EPILOGUE

CHAPTER 17

Finale

GUS FISKE

After Ed unceremoniously dumped his dad in Minnesota in 1932, Gus headed south through Iowa to Davenport, and on to Lincoln, Nebraska, stubbornly trying to revive the horse trading business he had abandoned nearly twenty years before. His gypsy wagon was long gone, and sleeping in a tent with a bedroll on the ground began to cause significant discomfort to his aging body.

During this trip, he renewed his friendship with Lillie's brother Charley. Two years into the Great Depression, Charley was well along with his "tire business, working amongst the farmers," in other words, marketing condoms. He recognized that the transient nature of Gus's horse trading would provide a perfect vehicle for selling his product, and he recruited Gus as another outlet. Charley would provide the merchandise–in volume at wholesale price–and Gus would sell at a profit. Neither of them had yet admitted that while Charley's business was on an upswing, Gus's was very near being exhausted. After the mid-1920s, power by horse was being phased out, and automobiles were taking the place of horses. Gus was able to hold on for a few more years, supplementing his horse sales with condoms. In 1935 his health began to give way. He was sixty years old and prone to various diseases of his day and age, including shingles and respiratory ailments. His doctor prescribed a special diet. In 1938 to '39, Gus spent the entire winter in and around Traer, Iowa, where Charley and his niece / common-law wife Lola, now the parents of a daughter, were wintering.

Lola related her memories of Gus's last winter in Iowa:

"We wintered up there in Traer, Iowa. That's where Gus sold his horses. That winter Charley and Gus cut a lot of the timbers out of old abandoned mines for stove wood. So we went up with a trailer and a Ford car and loaded tree limbs and mine props. Then Charley rented a buzz saw and sawed it up. Gus helped us get the wood down. Charley was driving the car up this great big steep hill and the trailer came loose and here I was setting there looking at the trailer , and Gus was standing beside me and had the presence of mind to jump and get that trailer jack and turn those wheels and run that trailer up the side of the hill. I thought how in the world could he think of that. But that's how I remember Gus–helping get that wood down. He wasn't in the best of health. My daughter Lulubelle says she can remember him, but I have a hard time believing it. She would have been only 4 years old. Gus was in poor health when he was back here, and I didn't think he would last too long. He was on such a strict diet. He couldn't have eggs, and when he was back here I cooked for him. There was the flax seed that he had to have, sprinkled on his food."

Gus sold the last of his horse herd and in the spring, 1939, he took the train back to Miles City. Later that summer, he traveled to Vida to visit Ed at the Long Branch place. By now, Ed had a wife and three little girls.

"That god-damned Charley," Gus shook his head in disgust. "You'd think that guy would learn to stay out of trouble."

"What's he done now?" Ed and Gus squatted in the shade of the old Long Branch house, waiting for the day to cool off before time to milk the cows. The scorched brown fields stretched out on all sides of them.

"It ain't somethin' a guy wants to talk about outside the family," Gus spoke cautiously. He looked around to see if Lona or the girls were near. It looked like maybe everybody was napping. He lowered his voice to a near whisper.

"He's been shackin' up with that oldest girl of Florence's–Lola. They've got a four-year-old girl."

Ed looked at the ground at his feet and didn't reply. Thoughts were racing inside his head.

"Screwing your niece is called incest," Gus said. "He could go back to prison, and this time they'll never let him out. Ol' Strawberry–you know, Myrtle, that redheaded wife of his–could cause him no end to trouble if she figures it out." Still Ed made no response.

Gus continued, "I had a feeling something wasn't quite right when I was down there in '32, after you went back to Montana and I was tradin' horses. But he told me Lola was travelin' with them to take care of Myrtle after she had that operation. I could see there was something goin' on between Charley and Lola, but I never said nothin' because he was near fifty years old. Too old to take advice from me–or anybody else for that matter."

"Maybe we oughta keep our noses out of it, Dad," Ed muttered.

"Well, you can see I've been staying out of it. You're the only person in Montana that's heard this story. And I don't 'spose you're gonna say anything."

"You sure as hell got that right."

"But I still say, it ain't right," Gus persisted.

Ed got to his feet and went into the house to get the milk pail. He filed away in his subconscious the information his dad had just given him. He would remember the details eight years later, when he began casting licentious glances at his oldest daughter. If Charley could get away with it, so could he.

Gus's precarious health held until he was able to build a little shack on wheels that resembled the gypsy wagon he had lived in with Lillie all those years ago, and he set the wagon on a small parcel of county-owned land near Miles City. His companion was a white Spitz dog he named "Whitey." In 1943 his deteriorating health forced him to enter the county-run nursing home. Frank came from Idaho to visit him, and sent a short message to Ed in Vida, "If you want to see the old man alive again, you'd better get down here. He ain't got long." Many years later, Ed told his daughter, "That was the only decent thing that sonovabitch ever did–tellin' me the old man was dying." He, too, visited his Dad, and when he went back to Vida, Whitey went with him.

Gus was miserably unhappy in the Home, which at times manifested in violence when he threw furniture and one time broke a window, seriously injuring himself. After only a few months, he died in March, 1944. When he received the message that Gus was dead, Ed made a decision. He would not be wasting time or money on a funeral. Although Gus had been gone from the Vida area for more than twelve years, he would be buried beside Lillie.

Ed bought materials and built a pine box. He recruited two of his boyhood friends, and the trio left for Miles City to bring back the body. The Vida Cemetery was a bleak, snow-covered site, the ground frozen rock-solid to a depth of two feet. All day the men worked with picks and shovels to dig a grave. Gus was interred in the frozen ground that evening, in his pine box without ceremony. He left behind his little trailer house, a few personal effects and a full case of condoms hidden under the bed.

Two years later, the money from his first good crop in the bank, Ed drove his new pickup loaded with his wife, five daughters and Whitey, to visit Frank, who had settled in Priest River, Idaho. After that visit, he never saw his brother again.

FRANK FISKE

In 1936, at age twenty nine, Frank met a woman seven years his junior from Miles City, Montana. Katy was a decent, hardworking woman with a very limited social life, who helped support her parents. Frank had inherited his father's good looks, auburn hair and lackadaisical nature, and Katy was smitten. They married, and five months later a daughter, his only child, was born. The child had handicaps that prompted the doctors to test her and the mother for sexually transmitted diseases. They discovered that the entire family was afflicted with syphilis. Frank's dissolute lifestyle had condemned him, and carried his wife and daughter along. As a last confirmation of his warped inability to take responsibility, and vindicating Ed's lifelong conviction that he was "a dirty no-good sonovabitch," Frank blamed the disease on his wife, declaring that it had been she who had infected him. He refused treatment, but his wife and daughter were treated and cured. Katy never forgave him. She stayed with him until his death, but the marriage was, for all intents and purposes, over. When he died in 1960, cause of death was listed as an advanced case of Lues (Syphilis.) It was more than fifteen years after the discovery of penicillin, a known cure that had saved his wife and daughter. Ed had not seen his brother for twenty two years, and didn't attend the funeral.

THE MECUMS

Descendants of the Mecum family are scattered across the United States, in nearly every state. The five who didn't rate star billing in this book, Clifford, Elnora, Jay, Es and Sophie, were none the less remarkable, in their tendency to display the family traits.

Probably the most tragic were Clifford and Elnora. Records from the Winfield Lutheran Home where they spent their formative years, contain poignant letters from both of them after they left the Home, trying to contact each other. Elnora's records show that she lived in the orphanage for about two years, and was "farmed out" several times to families that seemed to be looking for cheap labor. Each time she was returned to the home with lists of complaints like bed-wetting, lying and uncooperative behavior. After two years, she later claimed, she was "adopted" by a family named Bentrop. She lived with them four years, and during that time she attended school. By then she was sixteen years old. From that time until she was twenty four, her life disintegrated.

The record shows an extremely troubled child who grew into a troubled woman. Arrested for prostitution and theft, she gave authorities an outlandish story of having been born in Versailles, France, speaking only French at home, of being an exotic dancer in carnivals and Ringling Brothers Circus, of attending college for two years and of being a barber. She also confessed to "an induced miscarriage." There is virtually no way to determine what her real story was, beyond the fact that she was arrested while working as a chambermaid in a hotel, for stealing jewelry worth several hundred dollars from a guest of the hotel. She served time in a Women's Reformatory in Minnesota.

According to records and family lore, at age twenty five she married a U.S. Army veterinarian, and apparently led a happy life for at least a few years. But many years later her brother, Clifford, told his children that Elnora had died in a hotel fire. Whatever her full story is, it was unquestionably tragic and filled with misery, from the day her mother abandoned her and Clifford to the orphanage and never bothered to visit them. There is no evidence that Elnora had children.

Clifford also led an unhappy and toxic life. He left the Kansas orphanage at sixteen, joined the Army on July 4th, and served during World War I in the Mexican Expeditionary Force. After he was honorably discharged, he worked in a cotton mill in North Carolina. There he met and married a co-worker, an illiterate woman named Julia Bolick. In the 1920 census, at age twenty, he was incarcerated at a reformatory in Michigan, while his wife lived with her sister in North Carolina. At age twenty-five he served ten months for burglary in Nebraska. Back in North Carolina, he fathered five children and abandoned them. Too old and having too many children to serve in World War II, he served in the Merchant Marine as a cook from 1945 to 1949, visiting ports from Panama to Marseilles, France, Capetown, South Africa, and Scotland. After leaving the sea, Clifford generated records that are sprinkled with arrests of all kinds, from grand larceny and burglary, to assault on a female and drunkenness.

In 1961, at age sixty-one, he was arrested for fondling a seven year old girl –the indecent molestation of a child– in a city park in South Dakota. In his statement he claimed to have been drunk and couldn't remember the incident. After a psychiatric examination, he was sentenced to ten years in prison, and paroled after six. Two years later, he was killed in a car accident in Omaha, Nebraska.

Jay, the oldest Mecum, migrated to Colorado, Wyoming, Idaho and eventually to eastern Washington, working for the railroad. After at least one divorce, he married a woman with five children and became a solid family man, much revered by his step-children. He had only one natural son. He died in Yakima, Washington at the age of sixty-five.

Es–Daniel Ester–the little boy who was put on the train and sent to California at age twelve and tied on the back of a race horse at fifteen, married at seventeen and fathered eight children. He eventually returned to California, and was killed at age sixty by a horse, which reared, fell backward, and pierced Es's chest with the saddle horn. Family lore said that Es was named Ester for a "hired girl" whom Etta Belle liked. It seems unlikely that the Mecum family could have afforded the expense of hired help, so the story becomes another of the uncorroborated family legends.

Sophie disappeared from public record after her marriage to James O'Dea.

AFTERWORD

The remaining stories in my family background are extensive enough to fill several volumes. In this book I've traced only the most notorious persons and families, whose behavior generated newspaper articles and arrest records. There are still stories to be told on both sides.

In the Fiske family tree are branches that contain judges, politicians, doctors, teachers and community leaders. One member of the Fiske family, Harlan Fiske Stone, was United States Attorney General under Calvin Coolidge, and became Chief Justice of the United States Supreme Court, serving from 1941 through 1946. Another, Wilbur Fiske Sanders, served in Congress, prosecuted the Montana Vigilantes, and has a Montana county named for him. The story of their second cousin, Gus, is more humble.

It would be interesting to know if these stalwart pillars of their communities and country had secrets like the ones my family and the Mecum ancestors hid. If they did, the newspapers never caught wind of it. This is the nature of domestic abuse and violence. It's no different from other kinds of evil; it hides and flourishes in the shadows and darkness, protected by the very people it victimizes.

So what was the influence coming from these bloodlines that contributed to the person who became Ed Fiske. If genetics did indeed play a part in the formation of the sociopath that became my father, my money is on the genes he inherited from the Mecum family, which "provided the weapon" that formed the foundation of his sociopathic personality. The Mecums were also the influence that "loaded the bullets," in the weapon produced by genetics, borne out by their antisocial, lawless behavior that infected every member of the family except Lillie, to one degree or another, and played out over scores of years for at least three generations. Ed's miserable failure at human relationships, especially where his closest family members were involved, was the life experience that "pulled the trigger," when he decided that his failure was all someone else's fault, usually my mother's. At that point he began to justify his escalating violence by casting himself as the victim, a "nice guy who was turned into a mean bastard" by others.

The Fiske name carried by Gus's branch of the family died out with Ed and Frank Fiske. All of their offspring were girls.

ACKNOWLEDGMENTS

The list of people who contributed to this work will never be complete, but I will name a few. In addition to the extensive genealogy research done by my sisters, after my father died I had the opportunity to interview neighbors who personally knew the family. One of the most important interviews was with a woman from the Vida area named Louise Lindstein who considered herself one of Lillie's best friends. She gave invaluable first-hand information about Lillie's twenty-eight-year tenure on the homestead at Vida, Montana, and what she knew about Lillie's husband and sons. Another woman named Elsie Jorgenson Penner presented me with a small quilt made from silk neckties that Lillie had made as a birth present for her. She hadn't known Lillie well so couldn't give many details, but the gift was touching.

I thank Judy and Russ for again putting up with me during this final installment of the Fiske family saga. You added excellence to my undertaking.

I also thank the dozens of fans who've kept in touch by letter and e-mail, stating and re-stating their eagerness to read the final section of the Fiske story. I hope I've fulfilled your expectations.

ABOUT THE AUTHOR

Barbara Richard, the fourth of five children, grew up on a hard-scrabble farm/ranch in the Vida area of McCone County. After high school graduation, she attended beauty school, and in 1960, at age nineteen, opened her first business. In 1982, she formed a consulting firm for the purpose of helping small Montana cities and towns develop community and economic development projects. Six years ago she retired as president of the company and began the completion of "Dancing on His Grave," a memoir she started in 1982, shortly after her father's death. "Dancing" was self-published in 2006. In 2007 the sequel, "Walking Wounded" was released. The final book of the trilogy, "Chasing Ghosts," a work of historical fiction and the prequel to "Dancing," was released in 2008.

In 2006, "Dancing on His Grave" placed fourth in the Life Stories category of the Writer's Digest International Self-Published Books contest – in the top forty books from among more than 2400 entries overall. In addition, an excerpt from "Walking Wounded" called "The Blizzard of 1964" placed in the top 100 stories from over 19,000 entries in the Writer's Digest 2006 Writing Contest.

Her five children grown, Barbara has thirteen grandchildren and four great-grandchildren. She lives in White Sulphur Springs and Sequim, Washington, with her husband, Jim.

Bibliography, Resources:

Individual Research, Interviews:
Kathleen (Fiske) Cary
Frances (Fiske) Wright
Louise Lindstein
Lola Warren
Norma (Fiske) Lundgren

U.S. Census Records
City Directories
Court and Records, Birth, Death and Divorce Records, Obituaries, Criminal Records, Rap sheets in the following states: MT, SD, MN, MI, IA, NE, WI, IL, MO, OK, TX, CO, CA, WA, ID, AR
Also, Manitoba and Ontario, Canada
Personal letters
Gravestone epitaphs
Newspapers: (1879 through 1985)
Arkansas Daily Traveler, KS
Winfield Daily Courier, KS
Beatrice Express, NE
Badger State Banner, WI
Davenport Democrat and Leader, IA
Bureau County Republican, IL
Anamosa Eureka IA
Communiqué to Canadian Inspector of Prisons
From the Warden of Kingston Prison, ON
St Paul Pioneer Press, MN
Marengo Republican, IA
Cedar Rapids Republic, IA
Circle Banner, MT
Billings Gazette, MT

Wolf Point Herald-News, MT
Evening Telegram, Dixon, Illinois
Sterling Gazette, IL
Press Democrat, Santa Rosa, CA
Civil War websites
Anamosa Prison, Iowa, historian

Nothing Like It In The World; Stephen Ambrose
The Routledge Historical Atlas of American Railroads; John F. Stover
The Railroad Passenger Car; August Mencken
The Life and Times of the Steamboat Red Cloud; Annalies Corbin
Daughter of the Regiment; M.L. Laurence
Wolf Point, A City of Destiny; Marvin W. Presser
The Long Winter; Laura Ingalls Wilder
Mister, You Got Yourself a Horse: Bison Books–Edited by Roger Welsch
Tales of an Old Horsetrader–the First Hundred Years; Leroy Judson Daniels, University of Iowa Press, 1987

The Children's Blizzard; David Laskin
Almanac of American History; Miller/Thompson, National Geographic Society
An Overland Journey; Horace Greeley–Bison Books
Buffalo Country–A Northern Plains Narrative; Edward Raventon
L.A Huffman–Photographer of the American West; Larry Len Petersen
The Empire Builders; Robert Ormond Case
Vandemark's Folly; Herbert Quick
Everyday Life in the 1800s–A Guide for Writers, Students and Historians; Marc McCutcheon
1897 & 1900 Sears, Roebuck Merchandise Catalogs
Illinois, Crossroads of the Continent; National Geographic Magazine, May, 1931

The Life of Prairies and Plains–Our Living World of Nature; McGraw-Hill, 1967

My Antonia, O Pioneers; Willa Cather

Centennial; James Michener

Lonesome Dove; Larry McMurtry

Roughing It; Mark Twain

Change of Heartland–America's Great Plains; John Mitchell, Jim Richardson, National Geographic Magazine, May 2004

Time Life Books–The Old West Series; The Pioneers, The Townsmen, The Chroniclers, The Cowboys

HAVE YOU READ THE OTHER BOOKS
IN THE FISKE (FINCH) FAMILY TRILOGY?

Dancing on His Grave

The second part of the trilogy covers
the story from 1930 through 1955

An incredible true story of five sisters and their mother, in an eastern Montana ranch setting, who survived unspeakable abuse at the hands of their father. At times graphic, always heart wrenching. A must read for those seeking affirmation of the strength of the human spirit.

Walking Wounded

Sequel to Dancing on His Grave, the third part of the
trilogy continues the story, from 1955 through 1990

The continuing story of five sisters and their mother, first enduring and then escaping their father's psychopathic abuse, only to find themselves cast into the world drastically ill-equipped to cope with the demands of adulthood, marriage and motherhood. The family members find their paths mined with the untruths and denial learned in childhood, and a lack of self-esteem and faith in their own abilities. In spite of these pitfalls, the young women's innate intelligence, visceral determination and love for their children keep them striving toward normalcy.